Don't Marry the Cursed

A Dark Romantic Comedy

Political Map of Novel

(Specified for Fairy, Fantasy)

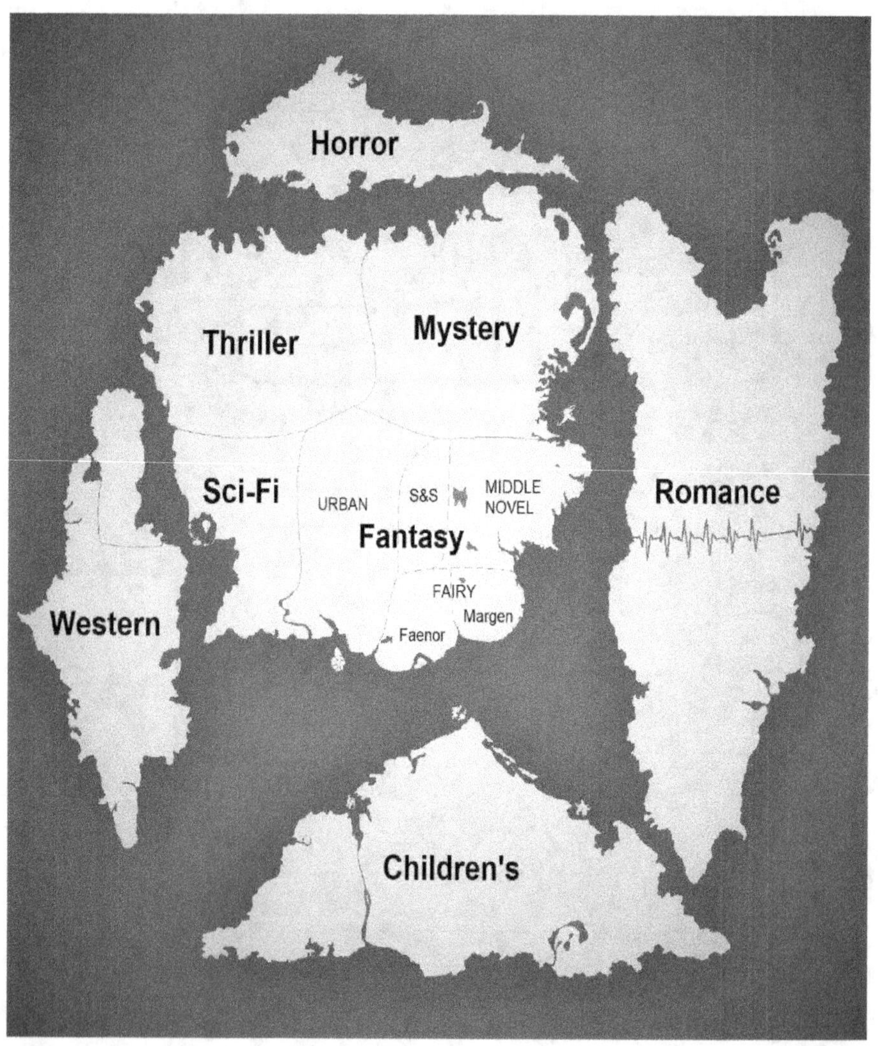

Because every great Adventure starts with a map

Don't Marry the Cursed

A Dark Romantic Comedy

HAUNTED ROMANCE BOOK TWO

C. Rae D'Arc

Cover design by: Blue Water Books

ISBN: 978-1-961733-01-5 (paperback)

Published by Bursting Box Publishing
www.craedarc.com
www.facebook.com/c.rae.darc
www.instagram.com/craedarc

To Michael
(my favorite Romance),
for all the Adventures we read
and experience together.

Note from the Author

This book and series take place in the fictional world of Novel, where "Pride and Prejudice" and "Dracula" are historical accounts of the lands of Romance and Horror. Much of this story takes place in Margen, which is the setting of English folk tales and the Brothers Grimm fairy tales and retellings. Throughout this book, several lesser-known fairy tales are mentioned and referenced, including "The Juniper Tree," "The Robber Bridegroom," and "The Yellow Dwarf." Familiarity with these tales isn't necessary to enjoy "Don't Marry the Cursed," though awareness may enhance the reading experience.

Don't Marry the Cursed

A Dark Romantic Comedy

Chapter 1

ONCE UPON A TIME

This phrase is a misconception, as history often repeats
itself.
It is usually paired with "in a kingdom far away."
That is also a misnomer, as that kingdom is often Fairy.

- *Thesis of Adventures*

THEO

My not-quite-useless ability to see blue-green auras revealed a light shade around my trembling hands. Unfortunately, my auras only revealed if I was in physical danger, not emotional. I balled my hands into fists and raised one to knock on Psi Dorm 201, located just south of Heartford University. I became increasingly familiar with this door over the past nineteen months. Behind it lived the love of my life—Pansy Finster, from Horror.

I attempted to dry my sweaty palms while smoothening my doublet. Only then did I notice my appearance.

Curses, I was a mess.

My undershirt poked free beneath my doublet. My black leather boots had scuff marks from my day's frantic activities, and my dress trousers needed more than their usual pressing. What was that white smear, and how long had it been there?

I fingered through my dark brown hair in a failed attempt to tame it. The new ring on my middle finger caught on a couple strands. Every detail of my perfect plan had been defenestrated by that ring. Bullbeggar.

My frustrated scowl disappeared as soon as the door opened. Pansy stood before me. She was a welcome distraction from the anxiety, grief, and responsibilities. Just the sight of her lifted my heavy heart.

She wore a Contemporary yellow dress that matched her wardrobe of "comfortable and easy to run in." She also wore the blue pansy-flower necklace that I gave to her after her red one broke. Her straight, raven black hair just reached her bare shoulders, dark and soft as umber. Her blue-green aura was light and safe from dangers, and its unique shortness allowed me to analyze her angular features beneath the blurring glow. She smiled at me with delightful eyes of smoky quartz. Then, she took in my grungy appearance.

"Theo?" she asked. "Is something wrong?"

"Hey," I said, releasing a heavy breath. "Will you walk with me? Plans…have changed."

Pansy would have called that the understatement of the year if she knew how much they had changed.

I had planned everything to be perfect. In a few days, we were supposed to walk as graduates from Heartford University, then take a picnic on the Regency side of Romance's Heartbeat River next to a field of pansy flowers. We would eat tea sandwiches and biscuits until the sun set over the line of majestic evergreens. Then, I would ask the most romantic question.

As if only love mattered. As if I could provide for a woman without my father's blessing. As if we could live in Romance for the rest of our days without the responsibility of 1.55 million people.

Curses, how would I convince Pansy to say yes to that? Even if she did, how would I convince Father to say yes to her? He tolerated our courtship (to put it nicely) while I was the "useless" second son. The ring on my middle finger changed my responsibilities and the scrutiny I would face.

I offered Pansy my elbow of escort as we walked out to the city streets of Heartford, Contemporary, Romance. I directed our walk away from the singular building known as the Tower. Over a year and a half had passed since the horrific masquerade that occurred within. I still remembered the fear of drowning in the trap set by Pansy's Haunting, though I drew a blank when the Supernaturals revived my life. I just remembered our auras turning black as my ability forewarned our deaths.

A diner's smells of spaghetti and breadsticks returned my thoughts to the present. Pansy and I walked past brick and marble townhouses that had been repurposed for businesses. Several showcased their products in their bay windows: wedding dresses, wedding cakes, wedding photography studios, wedding jewelry—the usual Romantic shops. This was hardly my first time passing these stores with Pansy beside me, though this was the first time my stomach churned at the sight of them.

We passed another shop that advertised tuxedos and tailcoats to buy or rent. My heart ached to recall my older brother in his ceremonial attire as Margen's Marquis. The uniform had been tailored for Greggory, and I knew it would drape loosely on me.

Pansy pursed her full lips in thought and glanced at me between steps. I failed to organize my thoughts for an entire block. When I rubbed the back of my neck, I found sweat. Disgraceful.

After the second block of silence, Pansy slid her hand down my arm until her fingers intertwined with mine. "Theo?" she asked again. "What's on your mind?"

"Hmm?" I blinked out of my anxious thoughts. Subconsciously, I had fiddled with the ring on my right hand. I clenched my fist to stop. "Just how plans never go according to plan."

Pansy smirked. "Always have a back up plan," she quoted from her brother's book about surviving Horror. As much as I wanted to join her smile, my frustrated frown remained. When I stayed silent, she prodded, "What plans went wrong?"

Just the most important part of our courtship.

We stepped into a city park. The paved pathway curved between deciduous trees in full bloom. A spring breeze smelled of sweet pollen and caused some white petals to float across our scene. Perhaps I could still provide Pansy with the perfect moment. If I could just calm my thoughts and nerves for half a minute.

I led Pansy to a metal bench along the path. We took a minute to sit, and my left arm wrapped around her shoulders as she snuggled into my side. I hoped she ignored my racing heartbeat. Then, with a deep breath, I willed myself to start from the beginning.

"I received news from Margen this morning."

"News?" she asked. "Did it explain why your dad's been quiet lately?"

"N-no," I stumbled, wondering for the hundredth time that day why my father's last letter dated two months ago. Was his silence connected to the sudden appearance of my brother's ring? Why did my weekly letters from the lords claim that all was well? Had they been fabricated? If so, why, and what were they hiding?

I rested my right hand over Pansy's, and her eyes landed on the hulking piece of metal and stone on my middle finger. The ring was massive, made of gold and fortudo gems. It was crafted from King Sayer's mines, strong as dragon scales and more reflective than mirrors. I had not seen its likeness in a year, yet there was no mistaking the gray-blue tones.

"What's that?" Pansy asked.

"This was my brother's," I explained. "Marquis Greggory Fromm, the Wind Master, of Margen. I received it this morning."

"Your brother sent it to you?" Pansy bit her lip, unsure what to say. She settled with, "It's huge."

I chuckled. "Yes, I was never meant to wear it." Her eyebrows raised and prodded for an explanation. "See," I said, "this ring signified Greggory as the eldest and heir to my father's duchy. It can only be removed by the wearer or magically transferred to the next heir upon death."

Pansy straightened and frowned. "So, that means—"

"For this ring to appear on my finger, either my elder brother visited Romance, snuck into my apartment, then deliberately removed the ring from his hand to put it on mine, or" —I swallowed— "he is dead."

She gasped. "Supernaturals! I'm so sorry, Theo. You were close, weren't you?"

"Not as close as you and Oz. While you and I both idolize our older brothers, yours actually responded in kind. Greggory is…" I paused and struggled to think of my brother in the past tense. He was…everything I failed to be. "Greggory was a champion among swordsmen and master with his ability. He was the oldest and heir to the duchy with the power to change the very winds. He also had a stubborn attitude. We disagreed on multiple accounts regarding treatment of the lower classes and cursed beings. I figured the only way to gain influence and to support the people was through political knowledge." I took a deep breath and let it out slowly to rein my emotions. "However, I am now the Marquis of Margen. His duties have fallen to me, and I must return to Fantasy."

Greggory was dead. I was marquis. Curses! As the second eldest, I elected to study poli-sci to serve as Greggory's assistant and advisor, not to be the man himself. Margen titled me as "The Trusted" because the people thought my ability was useless, and I feared to strike my opponents even in the friendliest of skirmishes. I stroked my mental bruise from the time I froze in front of the whole town in a duel against my younger sister. How could I lead a duchy of magical warriors?

Regardless of the lightness of my aura, my fingers trembled. Two hands of grief—denial and fear—gripped me by the throat.

Pansy's brown eyes met mine with turmoil and worry. "Two questions then: when do you go and how soon will you be back?"

I placed a hand on her cheek and said the cursed words. "I must leave as soon as I am capable." In full honesty, that was the reason for my disarrayed attire. After swallowing the sudden appearance of Greggory's ring, I spent the day packing and preparing for my departure. "My Masters thesis on Adventures will be postponed. Concerning my return…I may not."

She leaned away from my touch. "So, you're leaving? It's that simple?"

No, it was hardly simple. The mere thought of saying goodbye to Pansy wrenched my core. Yet the thought of abandoning Margen to collapse—my homeland and inheritance —likewise tore me apart. If I could protect Margen from my younger brothers, or just a small piece of it, I had to try.

Margen was the home of my heart, and Pansy was the keeper of it. How could I decide between the two?

I squeezed my eyes shut and whispered, "I dare not ask you to join me. I will protect Margen from my wayward younger brothers by taking the title of marquis and future duke…or I may die in my attempt."

"Not if I can help it."

"Sorry?" My eyes snapped open.

Pansy set her jaw. "Let me go with you. I can't stand aside and watch if you're in trouble. Let's see, how did you put it when you asked me to go to the ball with you? Oh! Will you let me be your sidekick?" She grinned.

My heart groaned. Was this how she felt when I asked her to go to the masquerade, and she begged me to understand how perilous it was?

"This is not the average Fairy Adventure. I know not what awaits me in Margen. This Adventure may be dangerous."

Regardless of the worry in my eyes, she laughed. "Compared to Hauntings? Seriously, Theo, no matter what we're up against, I've probably been through worse."

I opened my mouth to argue, then closed it, hoping she was right.

"Alright. You may accompany me under one condition," I said, then bolstered my courage for the audacious words about to leave my lips.

"Sure, what is it?" she asked.

"Marry me."

It was a rare moment to catch Pansy Finster off guard. As much as I enjoyed her deer-in-the-headlights expression, I mentally cursed at my delivery. I even forgot to pull out the ring! In her moment of surprise, I attempted to backtrack. "Do you remember when we first met?"

"Of course," she breathed, eyes flashing with confusion from my change of topic. "Brooke introduced us."

I smiled to remember Pansy as she walked into the gathering room with our mutual friend. Her dark and variable aura had caught my attention before my heart leapt in my chest.

"Then," she laughed, "you tried a pickup line with the most lavish bow I'd ever seen."

I ducked a little to hide my heated cheeks from the memory. "Several of my relatives asked for marriage within minutes after experiencing Love at First Sight, or Love's First Kiss. I thought it prudent to observe your Contemporary tradition to wait. Not that I had the courage to be so bold. I was nervous enough to ask you for courtship."

"What? Was I that intimidating?"

Curses, I had hoped to never reveal this. "Honestly, I thought you were a witch."

"*What?*" Her mouth dropped open around her smile.

"You wore all black" —I raised a hand in defense— "and I thought maybe the variety of your aura was a magic trick. Your spellbinding beauty was also a possible indication."

She took a turn to suppress her blush.

"Pansy," I said, taking her hand despite my trembling, "we have experienced much together, such as the masquerade, and discovering the purpose behind my ability."

"Oh! I had a new theory about why my aura's shorter now," she said. "What if the lengths are based on how much you can trust a person?"

I pondered on that, then shook my head. "There are too many variables of trust. As someone titled 'The Trusted,' I would know. I can trust Hank as a roommate and friend, though I cannot trust him to pay our electricity bill on time."

She smirked and quoted my favorite piece of advice from her brother's survival book, "It's never just a power-outage."

"Yes." I smiled, and she melted a little. "Pansy, our brothers have left us quite the legacies to carry. Please, I want to carry them together."

I lowered myself off the bench to one knee and retrieved the little ring box from my pocket. I flipped open the box to reveal a small blue-green emerald that she admired at a recent art festival. She said it was her favorite, because emeralds were known for truth-telling, healing, and protection against evil spells. Also, it reminded her of my eyes. The gem was encased by two bands of intertwining gold and silver—the two metals best known to destroy Hauntings.

"Supernaturals," she swore, half out of breath.

"Miss Pansy Finster," I began, heart beating rapidly, "will you share every Adventure with me for the rest of our lives, and marry me?"

For half a second, time slowed. My pulse raced and my focus became hyperattentive for Pansy's response. She bit her lip with nerves as her brown eyes widened.

"Yes!"

Then she jumped forward in her seat and kissed me. Recovering from my shock and relief, I pulled her close. We continued to embrace—relieved, excited, and eager for at least one piece of our future.

If only the other pieces did not involve my disapproving father and the responsibility of a million people.

Chapter 2

FAIRY'S KEYS OF HONOR:

Honesty
Obedience
Loyalty
Protect Innocence
Eliminate Wickedness

- Thesis of Adventures

PANSY

Condemnation. What did I get myself into? I was engaged. Again. I prayed to the Supernaturals that this time wouldn't end up like my first engagement.

At least it felt different. I wanted to marry Theo for so many more reasons than Sean. With Sean, I was afraid I'd be killed without him, but I couldn't imagine life at all without Theodor the Trusted. He was the only person I ever loved romantically, but that was before he became the heir to his father's duchy.

I would marry a marquis…a future duke. Crap.

After we left the park that night, Theo asked me to go over some of the previous letters he received from Margen, hoping to find clues to what happened to his older brother. We spread the rolls of parchment across my laminate kitchen table. Condemnation, Margen was old fashioned. Would I miss computers and phones the same way I missed the small towns of Horror?

Theo handed me a letter from last week, saying, "I hesitate to say how helpful these will be. I trusted Lord Freund and my family to keep me informed of Margen's happenings. However, I have received fewer letters these past months and sense that they have omitted details. Perhaps you may find what I could not?"

I skimmed the letter from Lord Freund. The formal diction seemed natural, but the topics were scattered and forced, like the writer went out of his way to say certain unrelated things. I circled a few misspelled words, then handed it back to Theo.

"Do these words mean anything to you?"

"Nights. Reed. Hour. Male." His eyes widened as he spoke the words aloud. "The knights read their mail? Which knights? Why?"

"Crap," I muttered. "Someone with influence over your mail doesn't want you to know whatever's going on in Margen. Let's see what else is coded."

We spent the next hour scanning through Lord Freund's letters to find the messages, "Ewe knead two comb hear," and "Steak you're thrown."

I stumbled over a particular code, "Sort yore farther. Bean mist?"

It didn't dawn on me until Theo read over it in his refined accent with softer "r"s. "'Sought your father. Been missed.' We need clarification, though these bid dark tidings. How soon will you be ready to depart?"

"My paramedics exam is in two days. After all this time, Sean's ghost might come back to haunt me if I don't graduate. I'd also like the time to pack and say bye to Heather."

Theo nodded. "I have some school business to settle as well. If this was anything less than a family emergency, I fear the

Dean would have me drawn and quartered for postponing my Masters Thesis."

With plans in mind, I packed the next morning between my studies. By dinner time, I was burnt out from studying, so I met with Heather. It didn't matter that she moved away last fall with her husband, Jake Kennington. We were still best friends. I kept our roommate agreement from freshman year and treated Heather with a candle-lit dinner at a Regency-styled soup restaurant to celebrate my engagement. A violinist played between the tables, and at least two proposals happened during our meal. There was also a man who brooded with an empty second plate, and another man was drenched by his date's glass of water before an angry exit.

Heather hardly noticed as she squealed like a muffled abductee—no, scratch that. Heather screamed out of excitement, not terror. As excited as we were for my engagement, we knew this meant goodbye, so we spent our limited time to its fullest. At four months pregnant, Heather ate five rolls with her salad, pink salmon soup entrée, and a plateful of chocolate-covered strawberries.

It was helpful to have another woman to talk about marriage, but our experiences were dramatically different. Romance took the top tier of the cake on wedding traditions.

"I'll admit," I said, "your wedding was really nice, but you Romantics have more traditions than Mrs. Klaus at Christmas."

"Be as it may," Heather defended, "weddings in Romance are the pinnacle of our success. Failure to respect every tradition may curse your marriage."

"Believe me, the last thing I want to do is curse my marriage. But is it too much to ask for a dress that I can run in?"

"Do you plan to run from the altar?" Heather asked.

"No," I said, "but if zombies or a murderous cousin shows up, I don't want to run away in high heels, hiking up my skirts, and no free hands to fight back. In Horror, I always planned to elope in my Sunday best with no crazy in-laws or raging exes to come after us."

"Oh, Pansy." Heather gave me a downward stare. "Are you marrying a Horror, or a Fantasy lord? Have you any idea how fortunate you are to marry well and into royalty status? I would take into advisement the wedding customs and traditions of Fairy, that you may best serve Theo and his people."

She had a point, so I let the conversation drop. I'd already accepted the fact that Theo's love was a package deal of noble pursuits and royal pains. Accepted, but not embraced. Hopefully, our discussions of politics and etiquette would help my first impressions with his family. We finished dinner, then went to her little two-bedroom cottage. I loved Heather like a sister, but then I asked about regency mannerisms and she pinned me down for "the talk."

"You were too young when your parents died," she said, blocking my escape from her family room. "I fear that any instructions your brother might have provided would have been inadequate. No disrespect to his memory, but he was a Contemporary man and most adamant about abstinence."

My faint recollection of my brother's voice whispered Horror's number one rule in my mind: *Stay away from drugs, sex, and violence.* I considered adding a footnote in the Common Sense section to never cross a pregnant woman.

"Just because Theo and I are virgins doesn't mean I don't know how it works," I argued. "I took anatomy! I bet I know more about the mechanics of sex than you do."

Heather put her hands on her hips like a mom-in-training. "That, dear Pansy, is precisely why you need my instruction. Your wedding night is not meant to be a stoic appointment with a gynecologist. It needs to be about love and passion. My parents have raised me for naught but motherhood and becoming the perfect wife. Theo's etiquette and mannerisms are similar to those of Regency, and I am sure he would appreciate it if you gave heed to my advice."

Try as I did to argue and escape, it was no use. Heather gave me all the dirty details and used her dolls as props.

And I thought those dolls couldn't get any creepier.

At least we ended on a high note as we watched a chick flick and ate Mystery dessert pastries with surprise fillings. I tried not to think about how much I'd miss some Contemporary pleasures after moving to Fairy, Fantasy.

I took my exam the next morning and answered every question with confidence. As long as I didn't fail, I earned my certification as a paramedic!

Theo brought me lunch afterwards to celebrate and help me pack. My limited possessions sprawled across the floor of my shared bedroom with Asher and Ruby. There wasn't much space between Ruby's painting easel and Asher's board game collection, but I didn't have a lot. I had no idea what to take. Even from all our conversations, I felt clueless what to expect. Theo said my Regency clothes were fine, even if they were simple trousers and loose, long-sleeve shirts. I kept my new leather emergency pack handy that strapped around my hip and shoulder for security. Theo bought it for me as a birthday gift.

He also gave me a cloak during the holidays. It was an accessory that seemed more hazardous than helpful, but he insisted. I added some requests to keep it simple, with sleeves, deep pockets for minimal pickpocketing, and a clasp at the neck rather than a draw string for choking. Theo didn't tell me how much he spent on it. Based on the thick, temperature-controlled fabric, I doubted it was cheap. Not to mention the striking, deep colors: blood red and pitch black. The cloak was reversible, though I preferred the red on the outside.

I put it beside my pack and tried to relax for my last evening in Romance. Theo and I talked about Fantasy and finished "packing" by making out. With Heather's dolls on my mind though, we kept Horror's number one rule and Fairy's Keys of Honor.

The next morning was a swing on the drama pendulum as I frantically scurried about to finish cleaning for checkout and my roommates cried the whole time about leaving. I spared myself a couple tears to say goodbye to Asher and Ruby, wishing them good favor with the Supernaturals. Then, at nine, Theo's knock on the door sent me skipping to the front room like I floated on air.

My Horror-instincts sneered; what happened to me these last nineteen months in Romance? Then I saw Theo, and my heart skipped another beat.

Such an odd sensation. Before, my pulse only stuttered with terror, not exuberance. No one else made me this happy.

Theo grinned from the doorway, handsome and perfect with his dark brown hair and blue-green eyes. He wore the same outfit as the day I first met him: knee-high leather boots, a blue-grey cloak that latched around his shoulders and draped down to his knees, with a matching embroidered doublet.

Theo first introduced himself as the son of a duke, but I forgot my initial fear that he lived in a haunted mansion as a lord. He later confirmed my suspicions. He grew up in a castle big enough to have a name. He described Ruezdad as a fortress that transitioned into a palace over the last couple decades of peace. I doubted its current state of peace after Greggory's sudden death and the vague codes from Theo's pen pal.

But, condemnation, Theo was practically a prince, and for some crazy reason, he loved me—a Horror transplant to Contemporary, Romance.

I had to remind myself that my Hauntings were over. How scary could responsibility be compared to the mass murdering and monstrous Hauntings of my past? Somehow, I believed I could face anything as long as Theo and I worked together. I loved Theo that night of the masquerade, but my love developed several times over since then.

I walked up to my royal Fantasy fiancé and took his hand in my own.

Leaving Horror had been easy in comparison. Even if it had been my home for nineteen years, I had fled from a Haunting. A year and a half later, I found myself again saying goodbye to the comfort of all things familiar with my life packed in suitcases. This time, my reason stood next to me, as Theo helped carry my bags.

"Are you ready?" Theo asked as he fingered the new ring on my left hand.

I took a deep breath. "As ready as ever."

We had a half hour drive to the west coast of Romance, where we caught a ferry across the Romantic Straight. We walked beside the railing of the top deck as the water rushed below. Most travelers enjoyed the shade and concessions below, but I preferred the ocean view and salty air. We were joined by only a few loungers with books and tanning sprays.

During the four hour boat trip, Theo went over some customs and traditions of the Fairy Kingdom. I knew of Theo's theory about Fairy's Keys of Honor. They were the topic for his Masters Thesis and were based on the prehistoric legends of Fairy. It made me smile that Theo's inspiration for his thesis came from my brother's book about surviving Hauntings.

"Okay." I rolled back my shoulders. "Quiz me about Margen."

Theo chuckled. "Alright, what can you tell me of the Fairy Kingdom of Fantasy?"

"It's ruled by your aunt, Queen Alóvera, The Phoenix. She lives in Faenor, and her sons and daughter take care of the Faenor Duchy. Your dad is Duke Konrad Fromm, the Horse, and as the younger brother of the queen, he oversees Margen, which is sometimes nicknamed as the 'grim' half of Fairy. That's what you'll inherit." I closed my eyes to map the kingdoms in my head. "You grew up in Ruezdad, which is the castle in Eimad City, which is the capital of the Margen Duchy…" I opened my eyes again. "Right?"

"Correct." He smiled. "You are prepared, my flower. You have no cause to worry."

Then I had all the worries. I asked question after question about Theo's family and life in Margen. All the while, Theo stared at the horizon, somewhere in the distance toward Fantasy. I was surprised to notice his finger tap quickly against the railing.

"Are you nervous too?" I asked.

He nodded. "I left Fantasy for Heartford University nearly six years ago. I have returned every summer since, though only for a week at a time and never as someone with influence."

"You think it'll be different?"

Theo shook his head. "Undoubtedly, though I cannot fathom how since my letters have been tampered these last few months. Regardless how we may be welcomed, I promise to do—"

"Ah!" I cut him off. "No promises. They're only broken or kept to an early grave."

Theo sighed, but locked his eyes on mine. "Just let me say this: despite the unknowns ahead, I will do my best to keep your aura light and safe from dangers."

As grateful as I was for his sincerity, it also worried me. We were deliberately walking into a danger zone with some crazy notion that we could fix it. Only my love for Theo could encourage me.

Rather than attempt to express myself with words, I kissed him. If there was one thing I knew about my future, it was that I wanted to spend it with Theo. He wrapped his arms around me like we still weren't close enough. My heart fluttered dangerously as my mind tried to grapple the fact: I would marry this man.

Some other ferry passengers called out our display of affection with hollers and cat calls. Someone even scoffed at us as "Romantics." Oh, how little they knew. Theo and I broke apart, blushing and remembering that we weren't actually alone.

The moment we stepped off the ferry onto solid land again, my head spun and legs wobbled. Except the water-to-land transition was only one cause for my symptoms.

This was Fantasy. I stood on Fantasy soil. I was born and survived to adulthood in Horror, attended university in Romance, and now I would marry a lord in Fantasy.

Two lines of people in lederhosen and kilts awaited the ferry's arrival. As soon as the first people disembarked, they began to sing and jig. Seriously.

> Welcome to Fairy, our friends!
> We greet you with open hands!
> We welcome you
> Both old and new!
> Welcome to Fairy, our friends!

I gaped. "Did they just spontaneously burst into song?"

Theo laughed. "This is a greeting tradition meant mostly for tourists. Though spontaneous singing is more common to Faenor, this is the sound I associate with coming home."

"Oh, um…Okay?" My Horror instincts wanted to suspect the dance. No, stop that. It was meant to help people feel welcomed and friendly—and not so they could catch us unaware. Friendly. Not creepy.

Still, I analyzed my surroundings to be sure there weren't any tricks.

The coastal town of Aven had the flair and atmosphere of a successful trading post from Regency, Romance. It had long wooden docks with multiple ports—some commercial, some private. A cobblestone walkway bordered the pier with massive storage bunkers and waiting bays, then a row of merchant stands and established shops. Instead of a sandy beach, the waves broke against large and jagged rocks. Seaweed and waste caught in between, which I guessed was the reason for the crappy smell.

Regardless of the stench, Theo took a deep breath and let it out slowly, a content smile on his face. "One year," he said, "and Aven reminds me of an old friend." He narrowed his eyes. "Except I do not remember it quite so crowded."

Yes, the town was crowded, and it was the people that separated this place from any I knew in Romance. I tried not to be judgmental, but honestly, the people were simply unusual. It looked like Romance bred with Hauntings as a variety of not-quite-normal humans walked by. Many had different textured skin like scales, warts, feathers, or fur. Lots of fur. A few looked completely human if not for the tail lifting the bottoms of their cloaks. Some had cat ears, pig noses, or goat legs. Others looked like complete animals walking on their hind legs. One was definitely a wolf, and I took Theo's hand for reassurance.

Oz taught me to be wary of unusual people. He explained that they were generally lonely and misunderstood, but the moment they felt mistreated, they became your next Haunting. That teaching wasn't written in his Survival Book for Hauntings, and I considered adding a footnote.

I tried not to stare, to pretend my nerves were from excitement, not paranoia.

My fiancé glanced at me and laughed. "You wore that expression the first time I met you, culture-shocked in Romance. If I may reassure you, Aven is within my father's domain. Welcome to the Margen Duchy of Fairy, Fantasy. If all goes well, we will someday care for these people as their Duke and Duchess. Gods help them."

"And Supernaturals help us," I said with a hope that Horror's angels could still hear my prayers from Fantasy.

I tried to respond with a smile while my insides panicked.

Condemnation. What did I get myself into?

Chapter 3

COMMON USES OF MAGIC:

THEO

As passengers on a transcontinental ship, Pansy and I were herded through customs check-in. There was a lot of paperwork to register our passports and foreign technology. A family of Contemporary tourists quickly became dismayed as their cameras failed to capture the beauty of Aven's streets and people. Others in jeans and t-shirts stuck out with complaints while those with cloaks and riding trousers smiled to be home. Pansy was unsurprised, though disappointed, that her flip phone and revolver failed to function in Margen.

"Do you have crossbows or longbows?" she asked.

"Of course," I said, remembering an outing we once took to a hunting lodge outside of Heartford. I had hoped to impress Pansy with my knowledge of the traditional weapons. Foolish mistake. I had knowledge, sure, even training. Skill? Pansy ended up impressing me instead. Growing up in Horror, she had learned to use all types of weapons with lethal force. She just preferred her revolver for its accuracy, size, and reload.

"We can buy you something to replace your revolver," I said. "I think you may be pleasantly surprised with the magically enhanced crossbows of Fantasy."

I picked up some immigration papers for my bride-to-be and slipped them into my side pack. Those would be easier to file at Eimad. The pig-nosed officer shuffled through our papers, then paused with wide eyes. He openly gaped as he glanced at me.

Uh oh?

"Honorable Fromm!" he exclaimed with a quick bow. "Welcome home! Do you plan to see Godiva the Priestess while in Aven, m'lord? Allow me to assign you a guard."

"My sister?" I smiled, ready to take his offer.

Pansy, however, asked, "Are we still light?"

Right, what was the possibility that this was a trap? I mentally thanked Pansy for her caution and glanced at our auras. Yes, we were light and safe from danger for now. I nodded once to Pansy before turning to the officer. "Lead the way."

Pansy's hand slipped into mine as we followed a female guard through the ferry station. She directed us around the edge of the docks, among the crowds to blend in, yet away from the bulk that we slipped between the people. I expected Pansy to be pleased by the guard's path of discretion. Instead, she narrowed her eyes and stalked the streets with the grace and caution of a hunting werecat.

Hoping to reassure her, I rested a hand on her back and gestured ahead to an ancient structure. "There is the Abbey of Aven."

The abbey was built on the outskirts of the town long ago. Now, the city thronged about it. Built of stone, its appearance crossed between a castle and a cathedral with its strong walls, stained-glass windows, and tall center. Its windows were more nautical themed than Eimad's, where I had expected Di to be stationed. I wondered when and why they had transferred her to Aven.

Pansy walked beside me. "We're meeting your sister? Remind me, what's her ability?"

"As the third child, she has none," I said. "While the mark of an ability is often a sign of nobility, magics have broader uses. Third children are born without abilities, and those with means send them to abbeys or schools to learn magic. This is a common tactic to expand a family's influence, since magic is resourceful and nigh impossible to learn with an ability."

"Sooo" —Pansy screwed her eyes in thought— "magics are different from abilities. Abilities you're born with, and magic is learned."

"Correct. Abilities do not diminish between lands and are limited to a specific trait, such as my auras, or my father's ability to transform into any type of horse. Magic fields are acquired through study and practice, and become altered or muted outside of Fantasy."

"Okay." Pansy's voice faltered as we approached the abbey's large set of wooden doors.

Our guard knocked hard, then shared a few words of introduction with the door keeper. The door shut again, and the guard turned back to us. Her chin bounced up and down as if she had a lot to say. She settled on, "Welcome back, Trusted Fromm. May your return to Margen be the return of hope."

My flicker of worry went unnoticed by the guard, though not by Pansy. I smiled all the same and accepted the guard's bow with, "Thank you."

These people expected me to save them. Save them from what? How could they have confidence in me when I had none?

The doors opened slowly to reveal the abbey's simplicity and openness. Stone pathways lined the perimeter while grass and wildflowers carpeted the court. Several priests and priestesses occupied the area, wearing brown and gray robes that draped down to their wrists and ankles. They were embellished with no more than simple cords around their waists. The priests and priestesses were all barefoot and shaved bald as they worked magic. They chanted, summoned spirits, and gracefully danced into positions of power, weaving ribbons of light, reviving an injured pigeon, and controlling elements of nature.

I removed my boots to set them by the entryway and gestured for Pansy to do the same before walking through the little meadow. The peaceful atmosphere within the bustle of the city never ceased to amaze me. I wondered if we would have time to tour the abbey. I loved to roam the hallways that echoed with mournful singing or visit the silent back courtyard for reading and meditating.

Pansy remained frozen at the doorway, gaping at the priests and priestesses. I chuckled at her amazement and joined her side again.

She snapped out of her gaze. "My mind can't get over this paradox."

"What paradox?"

"They're clergy…with witch powers."

I grinned. "Not quite. Witches are vastly different from priests. Witches hone magic through spells, potions, and animals. Contrary to your belief, most of them are not wicked."

"Yeah, that's hard to believe," she muttered.

I chuckled and gestured to the clergy around us. "Priests and Priestesses devote their education to the gods of Adventures, and are bestowed magical powers based on their skills and devotion. There are wicked clergy, yet they are rare and acquire their skills in secret sanctuaries. Rest assured, my flower, everyone here strives for righteousness."

Pansy responded by skipping her eyes between the spell casters and their spells. I continued, "I can hardly wait for you to meet Di."

"Can I say," Pansy asked, "that I think it's weird you call your sister Di?"

"Why is that weird?"

"Because," she said, "it's like…die."

I chuckled. "Only if we think of it that way. Godiva prefers the nickname just as I prefer Theo."

"Okay," she slurred, eyes zipping between the people around us until they caught on something. Her hand went to her emergency pack. "Theo! Someone's—"

I turned in time to be ambushed by a young woman. She wore a brown cloak with her hood covering her shaved head.

"By the heavens! Theo?" She twisted her neck to look under my hood. I likewise ducked to recognize my sister's eyes and smiled.

Tears gathered as Di sobbed. Were they tears for sadness or joy? A few priests turned towards her disturbance, and she ushered us to the side of the courtyard. In the separation of the corridor, my younger sister pulled me into a hug.

After a squeezing embrace, Di leaned back to pull down her hood and revealed her youthful face. She had Mother's softer nose that bubbled at the end to contrast with my straight point. The family's narrow face structure was more prominent with her baldness. She shared my thick, dark eyebrows from Father, and Mother's ready smile. We also had the same mixed blue-green eyes.

"Oh, Theo, 'may we rejoice in our trials,'" she said, quoting scripture. "Did you receive word of Greggory?"

"In a way." I rubbed my neck with my right hand, and Di's mouth dropped open.

"You have Greggory's ring! Thus it is confirmed." Every part of her drooped, including another tear. "Our brother is dead. May the gods receive his soul."

The shock, depression, and weight of Greggory's death settled again on my shoulders. I shared another comforting hug with my sister, then asked, "How did it happen?"

"Doubtless, you are unaware," she sighed. "Word says the Wind Master was on an Adventure to find Father."

"To find Father?" I repeated. "The duke is missing?" This news update was a real bundle of joy.

Di frowned. "Did you never receive my letters? Here I thought you either ignored me or I bored you with my notes on geodes. I should have known our letters were scrabble-scrambled." She waved her hand as if the problems were only expected. "Correspondents between towns have been fuzzy-muzzy for reasons unknown. I assumed the miscommunications were, in part, the reason why none has heard from, or of, Father for the past four fortnights. Greggory sought after the rumors that put Father in Divinity's Mountains. Rumors returned that the Wind Master fell off of a cliff."

That made no sense. "Greggory could fly," I said. "How could he fall off a cliff?"

"Precisely." Di nodded. "I suspect a traitor or dark magic was involved, though I cannot fathom how. Nonetheless, it gladdens my soul to see you again. You already hold yourself more surely than when I saw you last."

"Have you seen a mirror?" I teased back, happy to move on to a distracting subject. "Every year, you blossom more. Fortunately for me, as your older brother, anyone calling to court you will need to wait until after your priestess graduation. How close are you to mastering your magic?"

"I have only another year, Lord Master of Politics. Hearken, you should neglect not your duties, elder brother. I may marry after graduation, and it would be unwise of you to discount the early interests of someday suitors."

"Early interests?" I balked. "Is this an abbey or a flirting academy?"

"Verily, it is both." Di waved her hand and the air around us suddenly smelled like flowers. "Though the bishops will deny the existence of any tomfoolery, since our physical contacts are limited to 'very special handshakes.'"

Pansy snorted to the side. "Emma wouldn't have lasted a minute."

I smirked, knowing she was right, and made a mental note to meet these would-be suitors. At least I knew that Di would never settle for anything less than True Love.

"On that matter," Di said, turning to Pansy, "who is this?"

"Yes." I urged Pansy forward. "Please welcome Miss Pansy Finster, from Horror, a certified paramedic from Heartford University, and my betrothed."

"Betrothed?" Di's eyes flashed wide before narrowing on Pansy. "To a commoner?"

"You know as well as I," said I, "that the status of one's birth does not define one's honor and courage. Pansy hails from Horror and is the bravest, most loyal woman I have ever met."

Pansy blushed at my high praise. All the same, she deserved the glory. She deserved nobility even without our marriage.

"I see," Di said. "Margen could use an excuse to celebrate."

"You speak as though Father's missing status and Greggory's death are only the beginning of trials within Margen," I said.

"Yea," she said, pursing her lips and tapping her chin. "They were as the strike before the thunder. Soon after the new year, everything went topsy-turvy. I was transferred to Aven, and perhaps for the better. Eimad has since fallen under some curse."

"A curse?" Pansy asked. "What kind?"

Di leaned in to whisper, "Missing persons are reported daily. Wo unto the young maidens and mighty men, for they have become captives to the unknown thief of Eimad. Even more grievous, people have *lost* their abilities. Some of the most powerful and influential nobles have awoken to find themselves suddenly incapable to work their birth-given traits. They petitioned the abbey for help. Nevertheless, its cause and reversal is unknown."

"Only in Eimad?" I pondered. "Is that why Aven is over populated?"

Di shrugged. "In part. Citizens from Margen's capital fled to Vluz and Divinity until the latter was destroyed last week."

"Divinity was destroyed?" I balked. More problems. I rubbed my forehead in an attempt to organize the overwhelming list in my mind. Everything had fallen apart in my absence. "Let me get this straight," I said. "Eimad fell under a curse of disappearing people and abilities, Father went missing, Greggory died searching for him, and now Divinity is destroyed, with its refugees overcrowding Aven."

Di tapped her chin again. "Therein is the alpha and omega of this year."

Merlin's beard. The whole Margen Duchy had fallen apart. With the duke missing, I was the heir to piece everything back together. What a mess.

"What about our stepmother and half-brother?" I asked.

"You mean Lord Oswald the Spoiled and Duchess Abadda the Spoiler?" Di scowled. "Nay, those titles are not official, only my personal terms of endearment for the wretched tyrants. Three months ago, Oswald commemorated his sixteenth birthday with an execution of those who spoke against him.

With Father missing, Greggory's demise, you at school, me tucked away in Aven's Abbey, and Dunstan terrorizing towns from here to Sci-Fi, Oswald has already assumed the title of duke. He means to contend for the right of the duchy."

"Contend?" Pansy asked. "You mean Theo will need to fight?"

Her wide eyes worried for me. I failed to gulp down my own concerns with a heavy swallow.

Di gestured to Greggory's ring on my finger. "You have the natural right to the title of marquis, yet to keep it, you must earn the people's loyalty. If your heart was not already set on this woman" —she waved at Pansy— "I would exhort you to marry a princess with solid ancestry and the love of an army. This woman has yet to prove herself worthy. Verily, that will only come with proper education and Adventures." Di turned back to me. "Instead, you will need to meet Oswald's challenge in Eimad. Will you?"

I drew in a long breath. A fight with Oswald the Fire-breather would be to the death, and I doubted my capability to win. I would die in a duel for a title I felt unworthy to hold. Still, if Oswald was already a tyrant as a lord, I could not allow him to become duke. I was resolved, and my aura darkened. Curses, even my ability said I had a death wish. As if I had another option.

"I will go to Eimad," I said.

Unaware of my doom, Di grinned. "I offer my aid for this Adventure. Verily, I beseech you to bring me. I plead to leave this dull-null abbey."

My smile cracked. "We would be honored to have you. Plus, we probably require a chaperone to witness our reputation during our journey."

"Really?" Pansy quirked an eyebrow. "We need a chaperone?"

All the same, my sister cheered, "There shall be no tom-foolery where I stand! What an Adventure! The fastest way to Eimad is through the fallen town of Divinity. Pansy's skills as an Adventurer will likely be tested there."

"Tested?" I repeated. "What exactly destroyed Divinity?"

The priestess' mouth pinched tight and her eyes bulged with excitement. "Yea, they say it was a giant!"

Chapter 4

GODMOTHERS

Despite popular beliefs, they are not all-powerful.
They often just offer advice or help wane the effect of a
curse.
They come in all shapes and sizes, from magnificent trees
to a goldfish.

-   *Thesis of Adventures*

PANSY

A giant. I'd never faced a Haunting larger than a truck. Now, we had to travel through a town guarded by a sentient creature larger than a haunted mansion. Supernaturals.

Di ran to go pack, shouting over her shoulder to meet us at Divinity's refugee camp on the west side. Meanwhile, Theo took me shopping for a new weapon. We wandered a little, though I didn't tease Theo for getting lost in his own duchy. Apparently, businesses moved around during the last year and overcrowding. He led me to a little shop that boasted materials made from specific blacksmiths, woodworkers, tanners, and magicians.

"Is everything made locally here?" I asked.

"Not everything," Theo said, "though if we want something to replace your technological gun, it should be equally advanced with magic."

"Magic?" I asked, but Theo didn't hear me as a little bell announced our entry. Inside, every square foot of the wooden walls displayed a different weapon. A variety of blades, from greatswords to daggers, covered one wall. The sales floor showcased chainmail, plated armor, and shields. There were several weapons I'd never seen before. I gravitated toward the bows and shorter blades. Best to keep it simple with weapons I knew.

"I'll be with you in a moment," the shopkeeper said, sharpening a broadsword at the wheel. Theo stepped up to the counter, and the shopkeeper did a double take. Flustering, he set the sword aside and bowed.

"Aye, m'lord! I didn't know you were in town."

"I just arrived today. My companion needs a replacement for her revolver, and is trained with common bows. Do you have any in stock with magical enhancements?"

"Aye." The shopkeeper nodded. "Wait here, I have just the thing."

He retreated to his back storage for a minute before returning with a remarkably compact, steel crossbow with a small reloading compartment on top.

"A repeating crossbow?" I asked. "Those aren't known for their accuracy. And something that small would have a terrible draw-weight. Where's the reloading pump?"

"Aye, aye," the shopkeeper said. "I worried it would be too complicated for a non-Fantastic, but you said she was trained. This little beauty will work fine. We have a hundred-meter range out back for testing."

"Do you want to test it?" Theo asked me. "How many arrows do you want?"

Trying not to grumble, I accepted the small crossbow. A quick inspection revealed a finger trigger on the bottom handle. The machine was light enough to hold one-handed… like a toy. Did Theo think I couldn't handle a real crossbow?

I packed six arrows into the little cartridge, then prepared the load with a simple flick of my thumb. It was surprisingly easy and revolver-like. Expecting the lame range of the world's first repeating crossbows, I took aim at the nearest target of five meters. Then, I pulled the trigger on the handle. The crossbow jolted in my hand with all the power and suppression of a handgun. My arrow speared into the five-meter bullseye.

"What the horror?" I asked.

Theo grinned, and the shopkeeper laughed. "Aye, try to aim a little farther next time. Fantasy might not have all the gadgets and gizmos of Sci-Fi, but we got magic that's just as powerful."

"So, that's what you meant by magical enhancements," I said, reloading another arrow with my thumb. This time I took aim at the hundred-meter. I missed my first shot, but came closer with my second. My third arrow managed to hit the outer rim, then my fourth landed on the edge of the bullseye.

The shopkeeper nodded appreciatively. "Not bad."

Theo asked for a dozen more arrows while I made requests for gold and silver tipped arrows. The shopkeeper gave me a funny look at that. Just because Theo said most cursed people in Fantasy were civilized didn't mean I would take my chances. With everything in hand, I rummaged around with my emergency pack until all items were properly stowed.

I wanted to give Theo a truly grateful embrace when we stepped out of the shop, but the streets were even more public. Grumbling a little, I squeezed his hand and whispered a sincere, "Thanks."

He smiled back. "I hope you never need to use it."

"Me too, but I'm glad to have a ranged weapon again."

We ran into Di on our way toward the Divinity camps. For all the time we gave her to pack, she carried only a satchel and a little white dove on each shoulder.

Before I could ask, Theo called, "Mother's birds! I forgot you had them!"

Di's two birds lifted from her shoulders to flutter around Theo's head. They sang, "Welcome home, new marquis! Let us help set Margen free!"

Right. Most animals in Fairy could talk. Weird.

"Surely," Di cooed as her birds fluttered back to her shoulders. "Soprano and Alto are of Mother's soul. Never shall I part with them."

"Of course," Theo smirked. "As long as they still grant one wish a day."

Di pouted. "I have little need for wishes while abiding in the abbey. Their talents for crafting gorgeous gowns have been wasted on a priestess. However, their assistance with simple chores is most helpful. They have taught me much wisdom in the art of careful wishing. You would not believe how many times I found them flying in my chimney when I asked them to *sweep* it."

The siblings laughed while I tried to not look confused. Theo caught my expression anyway.

"Right," he said. "Di, would you explain to Pansy why you have two bird slaves?"

Di feigned offense, though proceeded to tell the story as she led us west through Aven.

Duchess Harmony Fromm, The Song Spinner, had been virtuous in every way, according to the history books. She died when giving birth to Dunstan and was buried near a tree. At two years old, Di went out every day to water the tree with her tears. Soon after, the duke remarried, and Di cried so much that the tree blossomed, then blessed her with two little doves. The birds granted her one small wish for every day that she prayed. No problem for a priestess. In Fairy, birds were particularly known for granting simple wishes like creating gowns, picking lentils and peas from ashes, and poking out the eyes of their enemies. Sweet.

"O, Brother," Di said, opening her satchel, "would you like to use my bottomless bag to carry your packs? Verily, you need not carry your luggage across Margen."

"Yes, thank you," Theo said, hefting his suitcase and slipping it through the mouth of Di's satchel. The whole case disappeared. So that was where Di kept all her things? I didn't like the idea of keeping all of our belongings together, but rolling a suitcase over cobble streets was a struggle. I shuffled a couple essentials into my emergency pack, then allowed Di's bottomless bag to swallow my luggage.

The ratio of squat bearded people increased as we reached the Divinity Refugee Camp. Wait, were those dwarves? The tents and fire pits sprawled to the forest edge. If there was any organization to the camps, I didn't see it. It was hard not to critique their problems as we passed no defenses or even guards. Kids ran around freely, men huddled in tight circles (likely gambling) while women squabbled over their rationed supplies and food. An elderly woman sat on the grass, slowly carving out a sculpture of a young family. She stared at me with wide, unblinking eyes.

"Your eyes are set towards Divinity," she rasped. "Death and evil lurk there, and they are its only residents."

"Sounds like home." I smirked back.

Theo's mouth twitched with a small smile, though his eyes remained sad as he surveyed our surroundings. His attention zeroed on a teenage girl with beautiful purple-green scales for skin. She shivered and sniffled even as she tried to knit herself a blanket. I knew that feeling: that grief too deep and painful that the only relief was distraction.

"Di," Theo said, "have you used your wish yet for today?"

"Nay," she said.

Theo nodded, then knelt before the young girl. "You need to rest or your cold will worsen. May I make a trade with you?"

The girl's eyes slowly raised to meet Theo's. Her lips trembled, but no words came.

Theo gestured for her little knitting project. "I want to trade blankets. If you give me yours, I will give you mine. Trade?"

Blinking and unsure, the girl said nothing, but didn't hold back as Theo gently took the knitting tools from her hands. "Alto? Soprano?"

Di smiled. "Harmony, I wish you to create a soft blanket that is just large enough to keep this maid warm through next winter."

The two little doves twirled in the air with a harmonious song. They dived for the little knitting project, then spun around and around until they became a blur. Yarn spun without hands into complex patterns. The birds sang a soft melody of creation and the warmth of a fire. With a cascading finish, they stopped, then flew back to Di's shoulders. Theo held a thick, fluffy blanket that was big even for him. I could have sworn there hadn't been that much yarn, and it hadn't been that fluffy. Yet, the results were undeniable. This was magic.

"Now, about that trade," Theo said, kneeling before the girl again. He handed her the magnificent creation. "You gave me your blanket, so here is mine. Maybe you can get some rest now."

The girl stared in awe at the blanket in her hands. This time, when she slowly met Theo's eyes, tears shone in her own.

I knew that feeling too—that deep gratitude for Theo, and wondering why such a man would care about someone like me.

I took his hand as we continued our walk through the depressing camp.

"Could we," I asked, "have done something with Alto and Soprano to help everyone with one wish?"

Di sadly shook her head. "Nay, they have their limits. If I make a wish too complicated, they tilt their little heads at me and do nothing. They are flighty birds, after all."

"It is a pity we cannot do more," Theo said. "These people are unaccustomed to living in the open. All their lives, they had the mountains protecting them from all sides. Not only did they lose their homes, they lost their way of life. They mined rocks and lived off the trade between Fairy and Middle Novel. They lost all of that."

"Thus it is," Di cooed at one of her birds, "until some brave Adventurer vanquishes the giant. To the stables we go. Eimad is a two-day journey by horse. We should reach Divinity by sundown." Di turned to me to ask, "Do you know how to ride, or shall we share a steed?"

"A horse?" I'd never ridden a creature, Fantastic or not. I preferred to trust my own two feet over four of another's.

"No matter," Di said. "You may ride behind me. Short Fuse should be agreeable."

"Your horse's name is Short Fuse?" I panicked.

"I adopted her," Di said. "She has never been terse with me since Father spoke to her."

She led me down the stalls to a horse that jumped and kicked its front hooves forward while neighing and tossing its mane back and forth. Di's doves flew in circles around the horse's head, adding to the mayhem.

"I know," Di said. "It pleases me to see you!"

I hung back, pinning myself against the far wall.

Short Fuse whinnied, "Will weee go runniiing?"

I pressed even harder against the wall. "Your horse talks too?!"

"Of course Short Fuse can talk," Di giggled, stepping up to the crazed animal and stroking its neck. The horse stopped jumping, but its head continued to bounce up and down. "So long as she runs in Fantasy or Childrens, she has the power of speech with other sentient animals."

"Whhho's your friend?" the horse asked with a whuff.

"This is my brother's betrothed, Ms. Pansy Finster." Di gestured to me. "Behold, she is new to Fantasy."

"I'd saaay," the horse neighed in a sort of laugh.

"She shall join us on an Adventure to reclaim Eimad," Di explained as she opened the stall to enter and began loading equipment.

I never considered the preparation needed for an Adventure. Since Hauntings usually came by surprise, my emergency pack was a necessary accessory. But what did Adventures require? My confusion increased as Di took up her cloak and grabbed a small prayer book.

She squealed, and my eyes searched for the Haunting. Nothing. Like a kid at Christmas, Di almost sparkled with excitement. So it was a Heather squeal?

She said, "What better way to become reacquainted with my older brother and his betrothed than an Adventure?"

I'd never seen someone so eager to face death. Was she an adrenaline junky? As a priestess, that seemed a strange contradiction. This loon was going to be my sister-in-law. Condemnation.

With the help of a leprechaun-ish stable boy, packing was short work. Actually, the longest part of the process was helping me to mount the horse. Di had the fanciest saddle in the stable, but it was rough on my ischial tuberosity. It was even worse when the horse moved. I held tightly to my soon-to-be sister-in-law as Short Fuse trotted through the gate. Our pathway was immediately surrounded by a dense forest.

Di's birds chirped above us, "Turn back! Turn back! There's blood down this path!"

My arms tensed around Di's waist.

"Peace unto you," she said as her birds landed on her arm. "The journey is at times half of the Adventure. Nevertheless, our travels may be a walk in the woods."

By the tone of her voice, I knew she meant to be comforting. She didn't understand that when a Horror walked through the woods, disaster always struck. She didn't know that the last time I traveled through the woods with my fiancé, Sean was abducted and merged with a poltergeist spirit who later tried to kill Theo and me. I pled to the Supernaturals that this would end differently. Happily, to be specific. Was that too much to ask?

If there was one place I hated more than abandoned grave-yards in the woods, it was the woods themselves. Every tree was a hiding place. Every direction was dangerous. What bandits or crazed animals could swoop down from the canopy? What traps and snares waited beneath the uneven ground? The rustling leaves behind were the footsteps of a stalker. The wind up ahead was the bated breath of an ambush. What if we took a wrong path? What if we got lost? What if the bugs bit me and gave me diseases or infections? What if the plants we brushed against were poisonous?

Riding on the back of the horse behind Di helped me feel one step farther from most of the dangers, but my eyes darted with every snap of a twig. The eight horse legs made a lot of snapping.

We rode straight into what Di and Theo called Notting Forest. It was probably named for its knotted trees and twisting branches. Theo told stories about playing in these woods and camping throughout the night. I think he meant the stories to be comforting. Instead, I considered my fiancé lucky to be alive.

I hunkered down as the path plunged into the foliage. Ten minutes in the woods was ten minutes too long for my liking. If I was skittish before, now I was spastic. We rustled bushes, rubbed against trees, and left footprints in the soft and untamed ground. Forget the fact that we had a nature priestess and ruler of the land with us. We couldn't own the trees. We had no say over a shrub. We were trespassers.

Supernaturals, this place was going to kill me.

Chapter 5

ANIMALS IN FAIRY

They have equal or greater intelligence to humans.
Beware what you say in their presence, or you may wish
they were mute.

- *Thesis of Adventures*

THEO

A half hour into our journey, Notting Forest engulfed us, and Pansy slumped over Di's back, asleep. Despite my assurances of our light auras, she had been more nervous than a jackrabbit in a werebear's den until Di "accidentally" slipped a sleeping spell into Pansy's water pouch.

"You drugged my betrothed?" I shouted. I had forgotten how it felt to argue with my sister, though suddenly our hours of childhood debates and bickering flooded back.

"Yea, would you rather that my birds pluck out her eyes and sit in her ears to dull her senses? Her fidgeting made Short Fuse skittish."

"Short Fuse is always skittish! Hence her name!"

"Hey!" the horse whined.

Di patted her horse in comfort. "Your intended wife and my horse do share an amusing amount of qualities."

"Are you comparing—"

"O, consider our heritage, Theo. Father's title is 'The Horse.' If she marries into this family, the horse jests have only begun."

"Regardless, would you drug your horse? No! We need Pansy awake for our journey through Divinity. How can she be tested as an Adventurer while she slumps over, unconscious?"

"Doubt me not, I am not dense," my sister scowled at me. "I used a diluted spell. She shall be awake and alert before we reach the mountain."

I grumbled to myself and faced forward, knowing there was nothing I could do, only accept the current situation. Di pulled Short Fuse next to my horse, Miles, to shove her big sorry eyes in my face. Her expression was so pathetic, I had to laugh.

"You are still the same silly little sister," I said, reaching to flip off her hood. She tried to dodge and slap my hand away, though her movement was limited with Pansy slumped against her. Her hood flipped back to reveal her shaved scalp.

"Hah! Serves you right, baldy." I grinned.

Di's smile played at the corners of her scowl as she replaced her hood. The rest of her scowl transformed into a pixyish smirk as she asked, "Supposing that Father allows your marriage, how soon may I expect nieces and nephews?"

My brain took an extra second to comprehend her question. My face took the next second to flush.

"You have discussed this with your betrothed, have you not?"

"We have," I muttered, and rubbed my neck. Though Pansy's paranoia had lessened since the masquerade, her fears were deeply rooted in innocent things, such as dolls, fluffy animals, and... children. She grew up with a dysfunctional family and few role models, though she assured me that she would love any child of ours with all her heart. That was before we knew that child would someday be a duke or duchess. "However," I said, "I had no intentions of sharing our family planning with my little sister."

"Family…planning?" Di asked, as if the phrase was a foreign concept. It technically was. In Fairy, people had as many kids as possible since there was a higher mortality rate until the age of twelve. Those who survived their first Adventures were expected to help with their family's businesses. "Does your betrothed not understand your need to produce heirs?"

I ground my teeth. Heirs to what? Before Greggory's death, I hoped to settle with Pansy at a small estate in Aven or Vluz. Now, I had all of Margen to inherit. Yet, considering the state of it, could I scrape away with anything to my name?

Desperate to change the subject, I asked, "How about that giant of Divinity?"

Di rolled her eyes, though took the bait. "Yea, suppose we cannot avoid a bumble and tumble with the giant. How would we defeat it?"

"Good question," I said, doubting we could accomplish such a feat. "That would depend on its size, intelligence, weight, and number of heads."

My sister nodded. "Yea, the best way to vanquish a foe is to understand him."

"Pansy would probably have some ideas if she was coherent," I muttered with a pointed look. Di replied with a cheesy grin of exaggerated innocence. "We should take inventory of our assets. You know divine magic, Pansy is fast and a great combat fighter, and I…can see auras that warn me of danger."

Curses, I was still useless.

"Let us not forget our tools," Di said. "I have my birds, a book of healing prayers, and a connection with the god of soil. I am fairly talented at creating dirt walls."

"Impressive," I said. "It seems you excelled in the abbeys. Pansy will have her survival book and emergency bag with several small weapons, while I have…a horse."

Still useless. Miles snorted in agreement.

"The stable boy included a sword and shield on your saddle," Di pointed to the items looped behind me. "He asked that we deliver them to Professor Vieseth—remember her?—when we reach the Western camp of refugees."

Yes, I remembered Professor Vieseth as Divinity's leading Lady. I spent a summer in her palace while studying their hierarchy based on education levels. However— "I thought the sword and shield were decorations."

"Allow me to analyze them." She guided her horse beside mine to unsheathe the blade. Heaving the sword, my sister grunted, "Nay, these are very much real." She balanced the blade and tested its sharpness. "A fine blade at that. Steel, double-sided, and sharpened with a magical enhancement. It is a hand and a half sword, but weighted well. Its name is Videliz, meaning 'faithful,' and 'loyal,' in the language of magic; a worthy sword to slay a giant."

She sheathed the sword as I inspected the shield. I learned the basics of many skills as part of my noble education. I knew just enough about blacksmithing to recognize both items were masterfully crafted. The shield was an elongated shape and bold design. I spun it to brace against my arm. Two straps on the back allowed arm support and a firm grasp.

"The angle," Di said, "is to deflect arrows and is meant to cover your whole upper body."

"Yes, I am familiar with the uses of a shield," I said, putting it back.

"Indeed," Di teased. "I recall your skills with a shield and its forms. It is the sword in your hands that worries me."

I glowered at my sister, though was unable to argue.

What was I doing on this Adventure? How would I fight a giant or Oswald? I was a politician, not a warrior.

Hours passed as I played catch-up with Di. Despite our intermittent letters, a year was a lot to process between siblings. I told her of my education at Heartford, my roommates, and the pranks we played on each other. Then, how I met Pansy, how she helped me discover the use for my ability, and the haunted Adventures we shared.

"You fought a devil spirit?" Di gaped.

I shrugged. "Pansy was the real Heroine. I mostly helped by seeing its aura when it was invisible and forewarning others of danger. My ability was helpful again last summer, when I helped Pansy save her roommate from a perverted stalker."

My sister hummed in thought. "The lightness and darkness of the auras reveal when people are in danger, even when the dangers are not known?"

"Correct."

"Behold, you have a gift of foresight! Your ability is valuable indeed, and you have yet to discover the meaning of the lengths!"

I sighed. "Yes. That is still unknown to me. All I know is Pansy's is particularly short. I have no idea why."

"Hmmm…When a single ability has multiple components, it is common for the factors to share a focus. You may assume the lengths are related to the cause for the shades."

I considered that. "How? The shades for possible dangers shift as easily as a person walks into a room. The lengths are generally constant."

Di shrugged. "I only say what other abilities have shown."

We continued to discuss various meanings for my auras, though I already had most of these conversations with Pansy. I felt no closer to discovering the meaning of my auras' lengths by the time the sun was well hidden by Divinity's mountain and my betrothed stirred.

"Good evening, Pansy," Di said.

"It's evening already?" She stretched her eyes and every joint in her body. I imagined it was an uncomfortable nap. "How was I asleep for so long? I didn't think I'd sleep at all on this trip. Did anything happen?"

"Theo found a sword," Di said. "Ye be warned."

I hid my heated cheeks by busying myself with my horse's reins. Pansy smiled at me, her eyes crinkling. Her mirth melted at the sight of the mountains.

The Divining Mountain Range was particularly known for its great heights and magnificence. Snow-capped peaks built the horizon before us and stretched to both sides as far as the eye could see. I considered it ironic how the residents of Divinity rarely saw the beauty of their own mountain, since they spent so much time inside it. Their pointed caps remained under snow all year. Now, in the late spring, their feet flourished with green trees. The tallest peak was Divinity, and inside it was the great and abandoned city.

At least, what used to be great. The fifty foot stone door built from the mountain itself was broken. Half of the gate was ripped away, creating a new and jagged entrance into the mountain.

For all the foliage, I expected to see and hear more wildlife. Instead, the only rustling was from the brisk wind.

"Turn back! Turn back!" Di's birds called again. "There's blood down this path!"

Di hushed her birds and urged Short Fuse ahead, unaware of her dimmed aura. Both of our horses whinnied and stepped to the sides instead of forward.

"Come now, Miles," I patted my horse. "Your aura fares better than ours at present."

Pansy cringed as our horses clomped loudly on the stone pavement. "We can't hide from a giant with this racket."

I considered a quick idea, then asked, "Short Fuse and Miles, will you be able to outrun the giant, should it give chase?"

Miles quivered a little at the thought. "Maaaybe without your burden."

Short Fuse snorted, "I could outruuun a lump of meat even whhhith you on my back."

"We will continue on foot," I said, dismounting. Our auras each lightened. Confirmation. Whatever the reason, it was safer for us to continue on foot. "Di, send Soprano and Alto to fly ahead. Scout our route, and send word to the camp ahead of our coming. Miles and Short Fuse, rest here for an hour as we pass on foot. Then charge through, making all the racket you wish, so long as you can flee the giant."

Di dismounted and smiled fondly at her birds and horse. "Gods be with you till we meet again on the other side of Divinity."

We removed ourselves and our equipment. I grimaced as I took hold of the magically-sharpened sword and shield. I had been nervous to return to Aven because I knew not how the city had changed. Now, I feared returning to Divinity, knowing exactly how it had changed.

Climbing through Divinity's broken East Gate, we entered the dark cavern. The temperature cooled significantly, and Di created a ball of light with one hand to reveal the magnificent city remains with blue shadows. We delved deeper into the cavern, farther from the safety and light of the entrance. I knew all too well how the darkness could play tricks on the mind.

"Di," I asked, "do you know a spell to increase our night vision?"

"Yea, if you desire it." My sister placed her thumbs to Pansy's eyelids and curled her fingers around her temples.

"*Deum de Lumine; benedizide zibi,*" she whispered. She removed her hands and Pansy blinked.

"Supernaturals," she gasped and looked around. "It's not like noonday, but this is much better. And you speak Latin?"

Di shrugged. "In a manner of speaking. The language of magic is similar to that of the dead. Verily, I am surprised that the spell worked as well as it did. The God of Light must be in a good mood today. Theo, may I bless you?"

I bent forward for my sister to perform a similar prayer over my eyes.

Pansy was right. The spell made a magnificent improvement. My vision adjusted, and I could see the crumbled streets as if the sun dawned behind the city.

As if I walked into a dream, I recognized the place, though it was completely different. I had visited the town of Divinity many times, including a summer of studying their trading economics and political system. I somehow knew where I was, even though the scene was contorted.

Columns and archways stretched several floors high to support the mountain above. A few of them were knocked out from the destruction. Divinity had been a stronghold and thriving town, built from within the blue-grey mountain stones. Buildings that once stretched to the cavern ceiling had been smashed to rubble across the streets. The streets themselves were crumbled by massive footprints. Fountains and beautifully carved columns lay in pieces, hardly recognizable for their original depictions. The stony face of a child lay cracked at my feet, while the outstretched wings of a bird were torn off. We wandered through the city, passing crumpled businesses and collapsed homes. Even if the monster was vanquished, returning and rebuilding would be a long process.

Pansy grabbed my arm. Her intense brown eyes met mine, then darted to the nearest building.

"You don't," she asked, "sense we're in danger?"

Her aura was less intense than usual, though the darkness of our auras was only dampened by the darkness of the cave… as far as I knew.

"Death is always ten seconds away, remember?" I tried for a smile. "I appreciate your concern, though this town holds no immediate dangers for us."

Pansy let out a breath. "I don't like this. Sneaking around a massive Haunting sounds like a disaster waiting to happen."

I nodded and put a hand on her shoulder, turning us forward again.

We passed debris and crumbled stone, taking the cleanest route down the main street. The guard posts and roads were abandoned, but a whisper in the wind said we were watched.

"The thing about ghost towns," Pansy whispered from behind, "is they only appear empty because we can't see the dead who now reside there."

"Whooh," Di shivered from behind. "Do all Horrors have such morbid mentalities?"

"Don't blame me for stating the obvious," she said.

A hoarse roar whispered in the wind, sending a shiver up my spine. Pansy and Di paused as they heard it too.

"That would be the giant," I said. The echoes of the cavern made it nearly impossible to pinpoint the giant's location. "Tread lightly."

Pansy breathed with a measured calm, and her eyes sharpened. The destruction made it difficult to remember which path led through the mountain. I needed a familiar landmark to point us in the right direction. That took us to Divinity's palace, Nomine Domum.

The palace's massive doors could house a giant. It was more of a mansion for luxury and comfort than a fortress such as Ruezdad. Nomine Domum had been built with the stones mined from its own mountain and the riches of trade between Fairy and Middle Novel. The stones sparkled with a mixture of basalt rock and crushed crystals. Marbled statues of legendary Heroes lined the arches and saddled the buttresses.

Their stone faces were not enough to protect the palace. Many of the sculptures were smashed. Ripped curtains fluttered through broken windows. A footprint as long as my two meters crushed the front stairs. The North Wing had been replaced with a singular boulder.

"What's that sound?" Pansy started. "How long ago did we leave the horses?"

I turned my face to her and my ears back towards Divinity's East Gate. A clatter of hooves on stone crashed into the cavern. They steadily grew into a cacophony of thunder. Had an hour already passed? Either we or the horses lost track of time as their unseen figures charged through the mountain.

Pansy hissed as an angry roar exploded within the city.

The ground rumbled and the mountain shook around us. The mighty roar boomed into the great cavern and bounced around like a bowl. From the sound and gust of wind it created, this giant had to have a pair of lungs the size of whales.

I widened my stance for balance as the ground shook with thundering footsteps. Where was it? How could something so massive remain hidden? Pansy put her back against mine, and Di watched a side angle.

A crunch of stone sounded from a tall structure to my right. My eyes followed the trail of falling rocks to find fingers wrapped around the top of a bell tower. They were the size of tree trunks with nails as large as my shield. They were filthy with dirt and grime, chipped without shape. A bulbous face emerged from behind the tower and came into view. His aura grew longer when his eyes landed on us—not that I knew what that meant. The humanoid creature stepped *over* the houses. I amended my earlier thought that the palace was large enough to house the giant. Its courtyards were mere playpens. I realized that the giant probably destroyed Divinity because only the cavern of Divinity could house this monstrosity.

It hunched over with a thick body, enormous eyes, nostrils, and gaping mouth. The monster stared directly at us and straightened to its full height of twenty meters. There was no running from this monster. He would catch us faster than we could say Gingerbread Man.

"It's as tall as the mountain." Pansy gaped, stepping back.

"Close, but you have missed the mark," Di said, her voice shaky. "Behold, a Mountain Giant."

I quivered. They became nearly extinct after Jack the Giant Killer, and usually stayed in the northern mountains. I had only seen them in pictures, and never heard of one this large.

"Run?" Pansy begged.

"I fear that would be unwise," I said. "Running would only spur a chase." Which we would quickly lose. Assuming I could run at all. My legs weighed as heavy as lead, and my arms refused to do more than quiver.

I racked my brain for a plan. I fought with words, not swords. What could words do against a cursed giant? There was no reasoning with this monstrosity. Mountain giants were particularly known for their primitive brutality. Our only options were kill or be killed.

Chapter 6

DESTINY

It is unavoidable, though frequently not what we expect.
Victory is often achieved only after a show of courage
and the acceptance of one's destiny.

- *Thesis of Adventures*

THEO

The ground shook with thunderous booms for every step and syllable of the giant's rhyme. "Fee, fi, foe, fum—"

"I hear a giant, slow and dumb!" Di chanted.

"Shhh!" I swung my hand to clamp over Di's mouth. She dodged, grinning as the Cheshire cat.

"Who goes there?" the giant boomed. "Who disturbs my song?"

Di ignored him and continued with her own version of the giant's chant, "Now he lives, but soon is dead! Thrust a sword into his head!"

The giant turned around until his bulbous eyes landed directly on us. "There you are!"

"Hold on," Di muttered, "that was supposed to work."

"Run!" Pansy yelled, grabbing my hand. This was not how I planned to become a cowardly Hero, though I saw no alternative that kept us alive. We needed a plan. To plan, we needed a place to hide. We ducked through the palace doors as the giant's fist smashed what remained of the porch stairs.

The stone palace quaked as the giant punched at the front door. I scrambled on my feet and among my memories for a good hiding place. Somewhere close to the entrance, somewhere too small for the giant to reach us, somewhere strong enough to withstand any blows…

The basement storage!

I directed our dash down another hallway, hoping my memory served me right. I threw open a door that led to a lounge hall. Not that one. Another door. Nope. Curses! It had to be around here somewhere!

"Theo?" Pansy's voice shook with the same vibrations as the palace from the heavy footsteps.

One more door opened to a dark stairway. There!

"Quick!" I waved for Pansy and Di to go first.

Pansy held back and moaned, "Basements." She went down, squeezing her eyes tight as if to will away the situation. I followed at her heels. Just in time. A cacophony of noise erupted behind us as the giant smashed into the main entryway. A massive arm snaked through the wreckage, wiggling fingers for us.

We ducked and held onto each other in the darkness of the stairwell.

"Do you think we can wait out its anger?" I asked.

"Verily, it is a giant in Margen, not a troll in Middle Novel," Di puffed, a little short of breath. "You cannot simply pull a Bilbo and talk it to death. Giants are not monsters that turn to stone in the sunlight."

"I know," I flustered. "Do you know a spell to drop a club on its head or something?"

"I tried a spell," she said, "to 'thrust a sword into his head.' Verily, it was ineffective. What makes you think I could knock it unconscious?"

"I read it somewhere in a history."

Di gave me a side look. "I am a priestess, not a wizard. I perform magic by communicating with the gods, not waving a stick and levitating a massive tree."

"What *can* we do?" Pansy asked, exasperated. She dug through her emergency pack, grunting with dissatisfaction over her tools. She gave her six-inch utility knife a glance before pulling out her new crossbow and a couple arrows. "The best I can hope to do with this is shoot its eyes. Anything else I have will feel like a pinch."

"Consider the histories," I said. "Jack the Giant Killer. Our grandfather, the Valiant Tailor. Even Tom Thumb, in perspective. Giants are brutish and tricked by goading their pride."

The palace stones cracked as the giant attacked again. Dust shifted, loosening pebbles around us. Maybe Pansy was right about the dangers of basements.

"Hearken," Di said, "we have no time to dig a hole deep enough to pike off its head from ground level, or challenge it to an eating contest where we falsely slit our bellies to release porridge and make room for more food."

Pansy raised an incredulous eyebrow. "Those worked in the past? I don't see any of those as plausible, or remotely possible."

"What if we dance in its stomach, or chop it down from the knees?"

My sister gave me a pointed look. "Do I hear you say 'here am I, send me' to be swallowed as Jonah? Besides, stomach dancing only resulted in vomiting, not death."

I grimaced, admitting that was a less desirable choice. "How do you kill a mountain?"

"Deforestation?" Di offered.

"I prefer to avoid them altogether," Pansy griped.

"You break it down," I said, "bit by bit at a time. Wear it down with water, or with bigger rocks."

"Again, we have not the time, nor the resources," Di said as the palace rumbled around us.

"No. However, the mountain does," I said, an idea sprouting. "Di, exactly how strong is your connection with the soil god? Can you bury the giant?"

Di caught on. "My connection is strong enough, however the spell requires some preparation."

Pansy loaded an arrow in her crossbow, happy to have a plan. I was happy that she was not included. Then she asked, "Can you camouflage me? I'll run out and lure it away."

"What—no!" I started. "We will not use you as bait."

"There's no time for anything else," she said.

As if on cue, the palace shifted and a half-meter hole opened above us. The giant's face leered down on us.

Pansy nearly cut me off with a dash away. First, I pulled her back into my arms for a heart-pounding kiss. Right in front of my celibate little sister. She coughed lightly, and the giant made a cat-call from above.

When we parted, I kept her close to whisper, "Be careful."

"I'm always careful," she said, "but I don't make promises during Hauntings. They're only broken or kept to the grave."

I recognized the quote from her brother's survival book. Merlin's beard, I loved her. I prayed the gods would protect her.

The giant's face disappeared from above, though a horrendous roar erupted nearby. The roar demanded flesh. The hole became blocked again as the giant's eyeball bent low overhead and stared right at us. He smacked the ground and it rumbled like an earthquake. If I had the gumption, I would have poked its eye then and there. Jack the Giant Killer would have been so bold.

Instead, I stood frozen in fear.

Thwick!

The giant flinched back with a mighty roar. A small arrow protruded from its left eye. Pansy aimed her crossbow at the hole again, but the giant was already gone.

"Crap," she muttered. "My arrow didn't even bury in. I can distract it, but I'm counting on you to work your magic."

Di cast the spell to make us seemingly disappear. I could still see our auras, which lightened with our disguise. Pansy's short aura slipped out of the hole, quiet as a mouse, and the giant growled in frustration.

"Mondez, god of the mountain," Di murmured invisibly beside me, "this beast will tear you down. We, your humble servants, wish this not to be so."

"You cannot hide!" the giant roared with a deep voice.

"You wanna bet?" Pansy shouted from behind the giant. "I bet you can't find me!" she called. "Come get me, you inflamed appendix!"

"What you say?" the giant roared. He stood and lumbered away from our hideaway hole.

"That's right! I called you an inflamed appendix!" Pansy bullied. "You know how the appendix is *useless*? Even when it's good and calm, no one cares if it's there or not! Did some *turd* get in your way that you decided to get all explosive? When it inflames, it's a hazard to be removed! And that's what you are! Waste that no one, not even your *mom*, wanted to keep around!"

There might have been a snicker from Di.

Pansy's aura darkened with each moment she ran around the giant. Her invisibility kept him from seeing her, though his feet trampled around wildly. Pansy lost her footing amid the trembling rocks, and she fell to the ground with a small yelp.

Her aura darkened.

"Pansy!" I shouted. Her aura lightened only slightly as the giant turned his attention on me. Oops. "Di?" I panicked. "How goes that spell?"

"These things take time, Theo," she mumbled.

The giant followed the sounds of our bickering and took a lumbering step forward. Curses, I doomed Di and myself to save Pansy. Where was she?

"Hey!" a shout echoed back to us. "Lumbering, fumbling, soon to be tumbling—Supernaturals, I don't know how you guys talk like this—come get me!"

I stepped away from our little shelter to find Pansy. Even with my ability to see her aura, hers was so dark and thin, I almost lost her. My heart clenched in my chest as she dashed between his feet. It was a dangerous move, bold and daring. Merlin's beard, would she ever cease to amaze me?

Behind me, Di murmured to the ground, pleading to the rocks around us, as Pansy risked her very life to keep the giant distracted. And what was I doing? Clenching a sword and shield while standing there, useless. I wanted to reach out to Pansy, to help her somehow. Could I cut at the giant's legs? Could we back him into a corner or find a rope to trip him? Frozen as I was in fear, I also burst with the need to do something, anything to help these women I loved.

Di slammed her palms to the ground, and clawed at the dirt. She built a relationship with the rocks that surrounded us. Then she commanded them.

"Mondez, monzdro zebelire!"

The mountain shifted, digging out a trench and replacing itself around the giant. As the beast struggled to step away, the rocks enclosed around it, solidifying around its ankles, building up its legs, surrounding its waist and torso. They continued to climb up its body until the rocks rolled over its head. Pebbles and dust filled in the cracks, entrapping the giant in a bulbous, yet smooth, mound of stone. With the sound of dust settling, the cavern became deathly quiet.

Di collapsed to the ground, breathing in heaves. Our camouflage weakened and faded until we were fully visible again. I had no idea magic would take so much out of her. My two favorite women in the world were exhausted from the battle. Yet, I stood completely unwinded.

Useless.

"Di, are you alright?" I asked.

"Define: 'alright,'" she said, smacking dirt off of her cloak.

"We're alive," Pansy said, panting. "I think that's as much as we could ask for."

Pansy slowly walked back towards the great mound.

"Is it dead?" she asked.

"Nay. Nevertheless, it is suppressed," Di said. "Our goal is to pass by Divinity, not redeem it."

"Yes," I sighed. I was more than happy to leave the giant to more capable Adventurers. "How long will your spell hold?"

"One can only assume," Di said with a finger to her chin. "Never before have I tested my rock security blankets for longterm holding."

"Rock security blanket?" Pansy smirked. "That doesn't sound like the prison tomb I expected."

My sister put a hand on her hip and stared at Pansy with a hint of sass. There was the little sister I once knew.

Before she could say anything, a small snap whispered through the rocks. It was the only warning we had before a ground-breaking crack thundered through the cavern. A dark line raced across the giant's mound. Our auras darkened.

"Get back!" I shouted.

The crack stretched and branched into a dozen more. The mound burst open with a roar.

I raised my shield and ducked as a large chunk of rock flew for me. It crashed into my shield and broke off a bolt. The giant's thunderous boom threatened to collapse the mountains. Debris scattered everywhere; dust fell and clouded our vision. A horrendous roar followed the boom, shaking the ground as an earthquake would. The roar grew louder, closer, and more demanding. The scraping sound of massive flesh against stone was our only warning before a boulder smashed through the air towards us.

"Run!"

Whether it was shouted from my own mouth or another's, I knew not, as the word repeated over and over in my head.

The boulder crashed into the pavement where we previously stood. It broke into bullets of pebbles, and lifted a plume of dirt into the air.

Run. Hide. Find safety. Protect Pansy and Di. Where were they?

The cloud of dirt and dust swirled as the giant rose to its feet. Somewhere in the dusty haze, the love of my life and my sister struggled.

Curse stealthiness, I needed to find them. I needed to hear them and know they were alive.

"Pansy! Di! Where are you?"

"Here," a quiet moan came from my sister.

Pansy replied with a "Shh. If we can't see you, then neither can the giant."

I followed the sound of her voice to pick out a thin aura several feet away. She crouched in a defensive position.

Momentary relief lifted my heart until something in her words demanded attention. Giants never sang about *seeing* Adventurers.

"I smell your blood!" the giant roared. A rush of wind announced the coming of the giant's hand.

Pansy's aura became ebony.

My mind stopped and my body worked on its own.

Pansy.

I ran.

I ran as fast as I could—faster than I knew I could. The giant's massive aura and hand continued to swing for Pansy. She shouted my name, her voice a mere echo in my determination. Di flung a dog-sized boulder through the air to crash into the giant's side. The giant was hardly fazed as he reached for Pansy. For both of us.

I had a moment of panic as I realized where my body had taken me. I was next to Pansy, right in front of her! And the giant's hand was directly on top of us.

I almost froze again. What was I doing here?

Pansy.

I was helping Pansy.

The leash that tethered my muscles snapped. I was incapable to fight as a child because I had nothing to protect—no pride for myself, for my ability, or for people I loved. I was the useless Fromm.

No more.

I shoved my shield at Pansy and gripped the magically-enhanced sword with both hands. Pansy fell away as the giant's hand dropped down like a cage. With a mighty yell, I stabbed upward and through the giant's palm. A normal hand-and-a-half sword might have caught in the bones and muscles. Videliz sliced straight through. The giant's fingers twitched with a spasm of pain. Then they closed on me. Fingers the size of tree trunks pinched my arms and legs to my body. I struggled in vain to free myself.

The giant looked down at me and lifted me from the ground. He grinned, bulging eyes and breathing death between decayed teeth.

"Got you."

Pansy erupted with a desperate scream. "Theo!"

The more I struggled in his grip, the more he tightened. Di and Pansy screamed for me from below. I prayed to the gods they would be safe. I prayed that Pansy would forgive me for bringing her into this. I prayed—Great Merlin, could I escape this?

The giant raised me to his face. He truly was massive, and his extra long aura extended him another ten centimeters out. My entire body only measured the length of his nose. His mouth opened and became a tunnel of saliva and teeth. The muscles of his tongue rolled eagerly.

Bullbeggar! He planned to eat me! No meal preparation to stall, or tricks to make him kill himself. I would go down, boots and all, unseasoned and whole.

Time seemed to slow down as the mouth grew wider and wider—or was I just getting closer and closer?

Whenever I thought of a future death, it was by illness or cruelties of the mind and mankind. Never like this. I wanted to hold my beloved and slowly pass into the night. Not face digestion with my body pinned between massive fingers, staring down a slimy path of rotten teeth and a rolling tongue. I never predicted my death this way. This was a warrior's death, and I was no warrior.

The giant's hand loosened to throw me into its mouth. All the better, I figured. If this was my death, I was determined to make it my own. I wouldn't let the giant's teeth clamp down on me. I braced myself against its hand and gripped the sword. Then I jumped straight down its slippery throat.

Chapter 7

VIRTUES OF HEROES:

Charity
Humility
Courage
It is a fairly simple list.

- *Thesis of Adventures*

PANSY

"THEO!" I couldn't believe it. I refused to. Theo didn't appear around the giant's neck. He didn't escape and reach the giant's vital spots.

The giant gulped, and something large rolled down its esophagus.

"No-NO! THEO!"

He didn't respond. How could he? My mind replayed the image of that Theo-sized lump slipping down the giant's throat. The only man I'd ever truly loved, my fiancé, my Theo. He couldn't be gone just like that!

A dark part of my mind whispered, "Why not?" Everyone else I loved, or who loved me, was dead. Sean. Oz. My parents. Even Emma. It was only a matter of time before Theo was taken by the monsters of this world.

"Theo?" Di whimpered beside me. The horrible reality of our situation finally seemed to hit her. She'd likely regret this day for the rest of her life, wishing she could have done more to save her brother. Like how I wished I'd done more for Oz.

Theo.

My chest clenched and every muscle in my body sagged. I might have given up fighting if the instinct wasn't ingrained into me. Determined as a fool, I gripped my crossbow. My muscle memory wouldn't let me give up. If Theo sacrificed himself to save me, I couldn't let his final act go to waste.

The giant grinned with satisfaction.

I ran back to the mouth of the palace, where Di knelt in a daze.

"Theo?"

Mental shock. Her limbs were heavy with exhaustion. I doubted she would help to beat the giant. In that case, I needed her safe and out of the way. "Get up, Di. We need a better position. Do you know the palace layout, or somewhere we can climb to reach its level?"

"Theo does," she said in a daze. "He lived here for a summer."

"Theo's—" No, I couldn't say it. Even the thought made my mouth dry. A small part of me believed he was still alive. Denial: the first stage of grief. No! Fight first. Despair later. Fear and survival were excellent distractions.

"I could shoot its other eye, but my crossbow can't punch a hole through its skull. We need to reach the giant's vitals. That means climbing up to its level or bringing it down. We can go for its neck or lower chest. Taller people have a longer thorax, positioning their hearts lower."

"Yea," she said, unfocused.

"Supernaturals," I muttered, and stashed my crossbow to grab her by the arm and pull her toward the remains of a bell tower across the street.

Somehow the giant snuck up on us. It was a condemned giant, for crying out loud.

A fist smashed into the ground beside us, breaking the street and rocking us off our feet. I considered the possibility of stabbing my little knife into its veins. Such a task would slow me down and put me dangerously close. But it was the only way to reach its vitals.

I flipped out my knife, grit my teeth, then threw myself onto the arm that was chest-high. I began to climb up toward the elbow when the arm quivered and lifted from the ground. That was when I realized the stupidity of my decision.

Why did I leap to my death to ride on a limb as big as a minotaur?

I started to slip off as the arm rose higher. I grabbed onto his arm hairs with one hand, and stabbed my knife into his skin to anchor my other. The giant yelped like I'd pinched him. Crap, my best weapon was only a stinger against this thing.

Wind rushed past me as the giant waved its arms to fling me off. My body rose and smashed back down, lurched and twisted as I held on for dear life. He slowed down and I gasped for air, hoping for a break. Sitting on its knees, the giant held me at least fifteen feet off the ground. Then the shadow of its other hand lowered over me.

I had two options: jump and break my legs, or stay and die like Theo.

Gritting my teeth, I yanked out my knife and pushed myself off the edge. I've had more graceful falls in my life. My mind screamed like a little girl pushed off the high dive. Fortunately, I tumbled onto the giant's thighs before I hit the ground. Rolling with a knife in my hands seemed like a safety hazard, so I threw it in the middle of my rolling. I tumbled down the hairy slide that came to a sheer drop to the cobblestone street. I landed on my left knee, crashing on my hip and shoulder.

I sucked in air between clenched teeth to keep myself from crying. Condemnation! At least my legs weren't broken.

I counted my blessings and struggled to roll under the giant's knee so he couldn't see me. The giant grunted above in confusion. I allowed myself three seconds to breathe and wallow in pain.

Rest & Relaxation over, I sat up to plan my next move.

"Pansy! Are you alright?"

I jumped to find Di running at me.

Crap, what was she doing? She revealed my hiding spot and endangered her own life as she ran toward the giant. The giant's leg shifted from above me.

"There you are!" He smiled like a cat to a mouse. More like a lion, for size comparison.

Di reached my side. Rather than help me to stand, she fell to her knees beside me.

"Di! Get out of here!" I pushed myself to my feet and searched for my knife. It was nowhere to be found. Crap, now I was in the middle of the danger zone without my weapon.

Arms slammed around us, blocking our path.

"Caught you!" the giant roared with glee.

Di screamed. She stood there, paralyzed with shivers, staring up at the giant's uncomfortably close face. Well, its mere existence in the world made it uncomfortably close, but I could see our reflection in its bulbous, dark irises. The crazy priestess had wide eyes of fascination even as she gaped in fright. I didn't look nearly as terrified as I felt.

The giant grinned like a sadist about to deliver its punishment. The ground rumbled as the giant tightened his arms. His elbows slid together, grinding the rocks and narrowing our space.

Standing inside the circle of the giant's arms was like standing inside a compressor. The arms closed in. I could see my pathetic obituary: Death by hug.

No! I did not survive nineteen years in Horror to die like this! We would escape this!

I grabbed Di's hand as the giant opened his mouth wide and breathed a stench worse than zombie breath. Leaning over, its mouth caved above us. It umbrellaed our heads, then stopped. Moaning and wiggling its tongue out like a Cthulhu tentacle, I ducked and pulled Di down with me.

"Gaaaargh!"

The giant wiggled its head, unable to reach us on the ground with its elbows blocking its forehead from lowering.

"Run!" I pulled Di with me toward the light from beneath the giant's armpits. I prayed the giant wouldn't swing its arms out to collapse its body on top of us. Little did I know that was the least of my worries. Right as we broke free of the giant's arms, its hand swept in to catch us. Death by handshake gone wrong.

Di and I were squished together in the giant's grasp. I tried to wiggle out, but its grip tightened. Di and I screamed together as it pinched our legs and ribs. Air whooshed around us as the giant sat up and brought us up to its face.

"Now I eat you!"

I screamed without shame. The giant opened wide and drew us to its mouth. That rancid breath! Could I die from its stench? Or would I bleed to death from its bites? Would I go down whole and burn in its stomach acid? I hated to imagine any of those happening to Theo even as a ridiculous thought imagined him still alive and fighting for his life.

I was close enough to compare its teeth to the size of my head when the giant's eyes bulged and mouth quivered. With its face so close, each phase of its discomfort was clear. Its complexion paled, eyes squinted with unease, lips raised into a snarl of disgust. Its chest heaved. A bulge squeezed *up* its esophagus.

The giant threw us to the ground to clutch his stomach. Our callous landing didn't give us time to escape the acidic juices that spewed from the giant's mouth.

Our efforts to cover our heads with our arms were in vain. Hot and chunky soup of half-digested animal parts pummeled onto us like a fifty foot waterfall. It was a hundred times worse than the bath of leeches I took to prove to my middle school "friends" that I wasn't a pansy. The smell alone inspired death wishes. A human jawbone washed past, and the worst of my fears imagined it was Theo's. He couldn't have dissolved that fast, right?

Thunderous coughing overhead brought my attention back up to the giant. He shook with violent efforts to cough something else out. Metal gleamed from the giant's neck. I stared at it, confused, until it grew with a small slice through the skin.

The sword! It must have caught the wrong angle when coming back up!

The sword cut to the side of the giant's neck, and he roared. I clapped my hands over my ears, regretting the motion as it splattered puke to places it hadn't dripped.

With a juicy rip, the sword sliced halfway through the neck. The giant quivered, then collapsed dead to the ground. Its head toppled sideways to reveal Theo—half-singed and soaked with giant innards.

He fell to the ground, completely uncaring that he landed in the steaming pool of puke. I worried he fainted but heard a sound I never thought to hear again.

Theo laughed his head off.

Wait—I amended my word choice with the half-decapitated giant beside us. Theo laughed like a maniac.

Di and I ran to his side.

"Bullbeggar!" he heaved.

Di snapped back. "Theo! Language!"

"Sorry, I—" He paused to catch his breath. "He almost *ate* me! I cannot believe that worked!"

Di's smile cracked and she joined him with the hysteria. I continued to stare wide-eyed at my fiancé, shocked and beyond grateful he was alive. Alive, though maybe on the touch of crazy, considering his uncontrolled laughter.

"That was" —he grabbed his stomach and breathed heavily— "the craziest thing I have ever done!"

"It was brilliant!" Di said.

"Never do it again!" I said at the same time. "Supernaturals, Theo! I thought I lost you!"

His eyes found mine, and his laughter faltered.

"Forgive me, my flower." He sat up and reached for me with a sticky hand. He paused and thought better of it, but I dropped down and pulled him into a hug. I was already covered in barf. A slimy hug was worth it. He chuckled in my ear and held me close, squishing the juices between us. "Killing monsters is not a laughing matter. I am just overjoyed to be alive. I meant not to worry you. It is the fate of Adventures. They may be messy at times."

"'Messy' doesn't even scratch the surface," I said, pulling my nose away from Theo's stench. "This is vomitous."

Di grinned. "Would you say it is wretched?"

Theo squeezed his eyes as if her pun hurt him physically. "That was awful, Di." The siblings laughed like this was simply another day in Fantasy. Supernaturals, I hoped not.

In the true manner of Horror, we ensured the giant's death by fully decapitating it. Theo began the work with his sword, but threw up. With my background in Horror and as a paramedic, cutting through flesh and muscle was all in a day's work. Still, I'd never used a magically-enhanced sword before to cut so much flesh. Di braided the giant's hair into rope and casted a levitating spell so she could carry the massive head as proof of our victory.

Theo, Di, and I trudged through the mountain in silence. I took most of Theo's weight as he leaned between us for support. We were a mess of a trio. Our desire to escape that mountain's cave of death overpowered our need to rest.

We stepped out of the darkness of the caves to be welcomed by the darkness of the night. Campfires flickered in the distance, lighting our destination. I never thought the chaos of a refugee camp would be a welcoming sight.

Our horses waited at the mouth of the cave. They wouldn't let us touch them, sticky as we were.

"Then make yourselves useful," I moaned, "and grab us some help from the camp ahead."

Short Fuse wuffed, "Sopraaano and Alto flew ahead. Weee will bring them back wwwith help."

Our horses ran off. Di lit our path with another of her balls of light as stars twinkled in a clear sky. We walked for another ten minutes before Di's birds returned with aid.

A small woman in scholarly robes rushed to us with a haphazard collection of knights. Their torches and mix of weapons made them look like a mob. I hung back with Theo as Di stepped forward with her ball of light.

"Professor Vieseth," Di said as an introduction. Her bow looked more like a drunken lean.

"Priestess Godiva! Lord Theodor!" Professor Vieseth called. "Your birds said you met with the giant, Magnanim?"

"'Met,'" I scoffed, "is an understatement."

The professor's eyes went wide as they shifted between our worn group and the massive head behind us. "You're still alive? How did you kill it?"

"Marquis Fromm," Di explained, "had himself swallowed, performed a jig, then used Videliz to slice its neck from the inside."

Theo struggled to stand straight and present the giant slaying sword. "Your people in the east camps greatly desire to return to their homes. When we reach Eimad, I will ensure reconstruction—" He cut off in a coughing fit.

"Theo?" I asked.

I reached to steady him while Professor Vieseth called for a stretcher. "These Heroes vanquished the giant, Magnanim, and redeemed Divinity! Give them our best medical attention! Our people will return to Divinity and feast like kings!"

The knights bustled about as one transformed three bandanas into stretchers. Theo was probably the only one who needed the service. Di and I were more tired than injured, but the stretcher was as good as a palanquin for my exhaustion.

We each rolled on, splattering whatever puke hadn't crusted over.

"Sorry for the mess," I groaned like a polite zombie. Some of the knights coughed or pulled scarves over their noses to filter the smell.

Sweet relief. I relaxed and rested my eyes as the knights whisked us away. They slowed when they reached the camps, crowded and chaotic as they were. One look or scent of us, and any bystanders hurried out of the way. The knights took us to the medical tent, where we spooked some servants. They tumbled outside, spreading hysterics about a trio of people who smelled like they'd come back from the dead.

Not far off.

The tent was divided into two so we could undress and bathe. They dumped hot water over Di and me, then gave us bathrobes to warm up. Supernaturals, the fabric was soft.

Finally clean and smelling like poppies, two healers bustled about our wounds.

Di drank tea that magically revived her strength and had bandages wrapped around her hands.

As for me: "I fractured my patella, pulled my gluteus minimus, and probably have a contusion on my shoulder. My anterior talofibular ligament might be twisted, but I don't think it's torn. Otherwise, I'm fine."

The two healers blinked at me with wide eyes. "Are you a healer? We could use some help with Lord Fromm."

"I'm a certified paramedic. How can I help?"

"Paramedic?" one healer asked. "Is that a class?"

"Yes," I muttered. "It was two years worth of classes."

"Do you know magic?"

I grimaced. "No." This was exactly what frustrated me about coming to Fantasy. What good was my medical education when Fantastics simply waved their hands and—poof—all was fine?

"Oh. Then please sit here, and we'll ask if we need you. Priestess" —she bowed to Di— "do you know healing magic?"

"Yea, I know some. Verily, my talents lie with the God of Rocks."

The healer waved Di over anyway. "Your immediate assistance will taper his burns." Without another word, she turned Di to Theo's side of the tent. I sat back and grumbled.

"Pansy?"

I looked up, surprised to hear Theo's strained plea. The healer poked her head around the divider with a small sigh.

"The lord requests your assistance."

Every ounce of my humility shoved down my desire to shout back, "That's right, he does!"

I hurried around the divider, then nearly stumbled.

Theo lay on a gurney in nothing but a towel around his hips. His bathrobe was strewn aside to reveal his bare chest.

Supernaturals, I got to marry this man?

Theo wasn't a fighter, but he still worked out. He kept up with me during our morning runs with weights in his hands. We hugged enough that I knew he was muscular, but not over-whelming. All the same, I ogled like the virgin I was. The only imperfections with his physique were the discoloration of burns—

Right. Burns. I should help with that. I joined Theo's side with Di while the other two healers attended us for supplies. Working together, we started with my paramedical know-ledge, cleaning, disinfecting, and bandaging his wounds. Then, Di stepped in with her magic to speed the healing process.

The priestess bowed her head with exhaustion and swayed as she prayed. At one point, her prayers blurred into a low moan. I reached over to shake her awake.

"Don't." A healer paused me. She stared at Di with anticipation.

Suddenly, Di sat straight and her eyes snapped open to mine.

"*You*," she said with a voice that echoed with age and wisdom beyond her own. Her skin glowed, and all of her cuts and scratches disappeared.

"Yeah?" I answered.

"*You share a bond with this man*," she said with that echoing voice.

"Yeah, we're engaged," I said.

"A spiritual bond," she clarified. "Your hearts and minds are linked by power only known to the gods. Who did this?"

"Supernaturals," I cursed, then realized that was the correct answer.

"Angels of Horror. Intriguing. You are healed enough now. My work here is done. Farewell."

The glow faded from Di's skin, but her scratches didn't return. Di's eyes rolled back, and she flopped to the floor.

"Godiva!" I shouted.

"Wha—Forgive me, did I fall asleep?" Di blinked.

A healer helped her back to her chair. "You were used as a conduit for the Goddess of Healing."

"I—" She wavered. "By the heavens. Thus explains my depleted strength. Did I prophesy?"

"You said Theo and I are linked through our hearts and minds." I sat back, dazed. "So that's what Sean did. During our Haunting, when Theo was drowned, Sean saved him by bonding us."

The bond saved Theo's life in Romance. What else could it do if it was still in effect?

Chapter 8

COMMON REWARDS TO VICTORIOUS HEROES:

Fortune
Improved living conditions
The ideal spouse
Similar priorities

-   Thesis of Adventures

THEO

I woke up the next morning with my aura light and safe. My skin was tight in some places from the healing, though I felt as fresh as rain. A new set of clothes in my father's blue-grey hue waited for me with a note from Di. I smiled at my sister's thoughtfulness, though was unsure how to react to the fancy new belt and scabbard for Videliz. Dressed and shaved, I stepped from my partitioned section of the medical tent. I was immediately greeted by Pansy, Di, and Professor Vieseth.

"How do you feel?" Pansy asked. "Professor Vieseth wanted to know our plans."

"Fantastic. Are you ready for another Adventure?"

"Another one?" She paled.

I rubbed the back of my neck. "We still have the journey to reclaim Eimad." Curses, did we have a death wish? As if near digestion was not enough? I was a fool for putting Pansy in danger. "If you desire to stay here until Eimad is—"

"What? No." She reached for my hand. "I thought I lost you once already. I don't care how messy it gets; I want to stay with you."

I took a deep breath and nodded. She was more than I deserved. "Very well. Perhaps we will recruit some help."

Di skipped to my side and straightened Videliz at my hip. "Shall we assemble a team akin to the Ring Fellowship?"

"Hopefully not that drastic." I chuckled nervously.

The professor stood from her seat and approached. "The Charger Prince was scheduled to arrive on the morrow as Queen Alóvera's aid from Faenor."

"Prince Alun is coming?" I asked. Of my three cousins, I was most eager to introduce Pansy to the youngest son of Queen Alóvera. I hoped he brought our mutual friend as a surprise for Pansy.

Professor Vieseth nodded. "He may prove useful for your journey to Eimad. In the meantime, I suggest we celebrate our victories. Consider it Divinity's wedding gift to you as we announce your betrothal. Many citizens have already returned to the mountain to clean and restore the city. Please join me for the return to Divinity, as I would like to reward you for your heroism."

My sister squealed with delight, causing Pansy to spasm. "Ooh! Treasure? And a wedding announcement feast! Do not forsake me from these days of glory."

I smirked. "Di, what need does a priestess have for treasure?"

"A wedding reception?" Pansy squirmed. "How long will that take? We still don't know where the duke is, or what's going on in Eimad, or how to protect it from your brothers."

Di laughed. "Peace unto you. Fairy is well known for our spontaneous celebrations."

Professor Vieseth nodded. "We'll have you ready to leave when the prince arrives next dawn."

True to the professor's words, the rumors of our wedding spread as quickly as a wildfire. Several curious citizens spied on us as we led the refugees returning to Divinity. Di and Professor Vieseth bombarded Pansy with questions regarding our reception, though my betrothed had few opinions to share.

"In Horror," she explained, "we mostly elope or have small ceremonies with only the closest of family and friends."

Each time Pansy gave a dissatisfying answer, Di prodded her with options. Indeed, my sister had an entire portfolio that organized and planned a wedding based on various themes.

"Um, Di?" Pansy pondered aloud while glancing over a scroll on flower varieties. "Why do you have all this? I thought priestesses weren't allowed to marry until after graduation?"

My sister waved a hand in dismissal. "Is a woman forbidden to dream before her time?"

As her older brother, my insides squirmed to think of my little sister falling to the whims of some stranger. She would always be fourteen in my eyes. I knew she would settle for nothing less than true love, though I was glad that she still had another year in the abbey.

"I have all the research you need," Di continued. "Imagine an evening feast with musicians, theater, and clowns—"

"Ew!" Pansy cut her off. "Who invites creepy clowns to a wedding?"

"O, they are mere fools," my sister said with another casual wave.

Pansy panicked, "No-no-no, there will be no clowns."

"I agree," I said. "I always found clowns more annoying than comical."

My sister sighed with disappointment. "So be it."

After Di and Pansy pondered over themes and styles of celebrations, the professor arranged a group of magicians and designers among the citizens. There was a surprising number of Eimad refugees in our procession who fled in fear of losing their abilities. With the Eastern Refugee Camps flooding into Divinity at the same time, the only place large enough to host everyone was the undestroyed half of the palace.

Regardless of the destruction and ruins, the citizens of Divinity celebrated to be home. Lights and magic filled the broken streets, quickly returning Divinity to its lively splendor. The Great Hall of Nomine Domum was transformed into a crystal wonderland. Colors across the spectrum decorated the walls against the black stone. Gems on the ceiling twinkled as stars. Specks of fairy dust floated above our heads to add light and joyful currents.

Even still, the most inspiring addition to the scene was Pansy. I openly gaped when a servant asked to take our traveling cloaks, and Pansy's attire was revealed. Di had convinced her to wear a loose gown for the event. The silver drapery tied around her waist and cut below her knees in the front. That was probably from Pansy's request to make the dress more suitable for running. Her little blue pansy necklace shined under the fairy lights. With a laurel of white flowers, she was as beautiful as a goddess.

My own doublet of Fromm-blue was as sharp and formal as Videliz on my hip, though I still felt underdressed beside Pansy's beauty.

Professor Vieseth had Pansy, Di, and me wait in a lounge until the Great Hall was full of guests. She brought us out to stand at the raised podium as everyone cheered. With a simple raised hand, she quieted the throng.

"These Heroes deserve our eternal gratitude," her tiny figure bellowed over the crowd. "Marquis Theodor Fromm, the Trusted, of Margen, and his intended wife, Miss Pansy Finster from Horror, and his sister, Priestess Godiva Fromm, of Aven. These are slayers of the great giant, Magnanim! We will sing praises of your victorious Adventure. May you ever feel welcomed to Divinity, which we will rebuild, thanks to you."

The crowd cheered, and a corner burst into song:

> Divinity has been saved!
> The Fromm fam'ly name be praised!
> The Trusted Lord
> Our town restored
> Divinity has been saved!

By the end of the first verse, the song spread, and the whole crowd sang along for the second verse.

> The city of Eimad sings!
> Of union with bells and rings!
> The lord will be wed
> To Horror, it's said!
> The city of Eimad sings!

Pansy raised an incredulous eyebrow at me. "They wrote a song about us? We've only been here for two days!"

"Yes..." I slurred, unsure which side to take on the issue. "They like to do that."

My betrothed snorted a sort of laugh and shook her head as if to say "whatever" to her bewilderment.

I took her hand and led her down to mingle with the citizens. Although I met some of these people a decade ago, all was forgotten now. If I was to become their duke, I figured it wise to become reacquainted.

Professor Vieseth introduced us to Lord Bachmann, who oversaw the wells and water supply within the mountains. His family had a minor ability for coaxing water currents. Lord Kaufman was in charge of the markets with Lord and Lady Fischer. Then there was Lady Hoover with a minor rock ability, Lord Feld from the outside forests with some sort of plant ability, and Lord Weiss did…something…

The names and occupations jumbled in my mind, yet Professor Vieseth seemed eager to introduce us to even more lords and ladies.

The amount of Eimad refugees worried me. Almost every half-human or sentient creature in the room had fled from Eimad's persecutions. I wept to hear of their unjust trials, unwarranted discrimination, and public beatings. The name of Oswald the Firebreather became synonymous with the Oppressor of Margen, spoken with venom on their tongues. Whether or not I could defeat my younger half-brother, I was convinced to stop him somehow.

Other citizens left the capital city after the renowned Lady Lehrer lost her ability for potion making. Sir Schermer and his knightly friends had fled to protect their fighting abilities. I wondered who remained to protect and fight for Eimad.

A familiar face approached me, and I sighed with relief. Lord Anthony Freund and I exchanged greetings with friendly slaps on the shoulders.

"Took you long enough," my pen pal joked. "Apparently, my coded letters were either too easy to spot and erase, or too complicated that you missed the hidden messages of our impending doom. Another month longer, and I would have come for you myself."

"Your letters claimed all was well," I said. "It was only after my brother's death that I thought to assume otherwise."

Lord Anthony growled, "Better late than never, I suppose. You are here now, saving Divinity, and" —his eyes landed on Pansy— "marrying an exotic beauty. Charmed." His pale green eyes remained on hers as he bowed to kiss her hand. Pansy blushed.

I cleared my throat. "Pansy, this is my friend from Faenor Preparatory Academy, Lord Anthony Freund of Eimad's Seers. He has an ability to see others' abilities."

My friend straightened, and his attention reluctantly returned to me. "No longer. My ability is lost. Parents of newborns must explore by old fashioned methods to discern if their infant has an ability and what it might be."

My jaw dropped a little. "Anthony, forgive me, I did not know."

"I figured as much," he said with a smirk, "due to your lack of response when I wrote of it. I had theories that either Romance had turned you into a man with no love for his kingdom, or our letters had been tampered. Considering your persistence to receive news of my family, affairs in Margen, and the abilities I perceived, I safely assumed the latter."

"I am so sorry," I said. "Perhaps you may join us to Eimad as we seek to right the wrongs."

He took all of two seconds to consider it. "No," he said. "I appreciate the invitation, however, I fear that I am a bit useless without my ability."

"Antho—"

"This is not pity," he said, cutting me off before I could lecture about how great he was with or without his ability. I knew the lecture by heart after a lifetime of believing my own ability to be useless. "No," he continued, "I relied too much on my ability. While Divinity's scholars desire to study my predicament, perhaps now I may learn magic and become an official Seer. On one hand, it is simpler to see people without their abilities. On the other, I grieve the lost opportunity to see your enchanting betrothed through your auras."

I cleared my throat again and consciously unclenched my teeth. "Yes, perhaps it is better if you remain in Divinity for the time being."

His eyebrows went high with a bemused smirk. "Very well. Good evening, Lord Theo, Miss Pansy."

He left with another bow and a wanting glance at Pansy. She coughed in a failed attempt to hide a curious smile.

"What?" I asked.

"Were you jealous?"

I sputtered in my response. Of course I was. Lord Anthony was a handsome young man with Contemporary experience from Urban cities. Even without his ability, he was ambitious and clever enough to become someone of great influence. He was a loyal friend, and one whom I deemed worthy of Pansy's interest. He was probably safer than my hazardous Adventures.

My intended wife blushed and shook her head with incredulity. Before I could ask what she meant by it, another grateful guest commanded our attention.

Pansy said little during the interactions. She spoke when asked a direct question and slowly sipped from her apple cider. She refrained, as always, from any alcoholic consumption, and I accepted only the lightest of wines. A few hours into the evening, however, the laughter and songs grew louder and lewder.

Graced with a break between introductions, I fingered Pansy's hand for her attention. Onlookers cooed at our affection as I leaned down to whisper in her ear, "I know the attention and crowds discomfort you. You are brave indeed for enduring the courtesies of nobility."

"Yeah," she said, shuffling uneasily. "Can I leave early or is that rude?"

"Not at all. A future marchioness may come and go from her own betrothal celebration as she pleases. Professor Vieseth insisted we spend the night in her guest chambers upstairs. Do you want me to escort you?"

She shrugged. "I'll need someone to direct me through these hallway mazes."

I smiled. "Exactly. Also, I would appreciate the pardon from the festivities to serve as your escort."

I asked her to wait for me at the main door while I retrieved our cloaks. I could have drafted a servant to fetch them, though it was a small task to accomplish myself. At least, I thought it would be.

The coat closet was large enough to walk through and filled with outerwear from the hundreds of attendants. Thankfully, the cloaks of my Fromm blue and Pansy's red were easily recognizable.

"I heard congratulations are in order."

I froze. There were some voices I said goodbye to long ago, bidding them a good life and secretly wishing to never hear them again. I put on my best politician's smile and turned around.

"Lady Greenwood! What a pleasant surprise." Curses, I was never good at lying.

My first love—and heartbreak—stood in the doorway, casually and obviously blocking my exit. With the cloaks folded over my elbow, I walked towards her, hoping she would see my desire to exit and make way. Instead, she straightened and smiled, taking my approach as a greeting.

Lady Greenwood could have been a direct descendant of the princess who was ensnared by the Yellow Dwarf. She was just as vain, undisciplined, and also beautiful in a way that drove several good knights and lords mad—including myself. Her long blonde hair that many women envied was piled on top of her head with jeweled pins. Her pointed face had hardened since our youth, and her posture lost its delicate vulnerability. She no longer feigned innocence.

"You once called me your Cinderbella," she teased, a smiling twinkle in her eye. "Did you forget my given name, or did you forget how intimate we once were, Theodor?"

"How fares your family?" I asked, hoping her question was rhetorical. I was determined to finish the game of pleasantries and not to play hers.

"Which one?" she huffed. "My drunken ex-husband or my squandering parents? Whichever you say, I left them back in Eimad. I needed a fresh start in Divinity. Their absence is all the better not to embarrass your celebrations. Then again, I hear every party needs a good gossip."

"I am sorry to hear that, Lady Greenwood," I said.

"Cinderbella," she insisted.

I responded with a gesture back to the main room, towards crowded and pleasant company. She ignored the gesture and shuffled in her dress to bring more attention to it. How did she afford the dress if her family was truly as destitute as she claimed? It was twice as shiny as most gowns, and the corset squeezed so tightly that her bosom looked ready to burst free. It was difficult not to stare when it was so ridiculous. Curses, she smiled from my uncomfortable glance.

She sighed and leaned against the doorframe, as if to make her arched back and stretched neck look casual as she blocked my passage. "I hear you will challenge your brothers for the duchy. Seems quite the endeavor. Then again, you always have been more ambitious than your abilities."

"You came to mock me then?"

"Oh no-no-no. I applaud your ambition, dear Theodor. You have proven much of yourself since your return to Margen. I do not mean to dwell on the past, but…I never stopped thinking about you…and what we could have been together—a team to topple the terror of Divinity." She smiled. Gentle and perfect, her smile was an expression that was too practiced and without honesty.

To think I once fell for that. I highly doubted she would have fared as well against Magnanim as Pansy had. I counted the seconds, hoping to return to Pansy in the main room.

Lady Greenwood laughed, again an expression so perfect it must have required days before a mirror. "Did you catch that alliteration at the end? I did not even think about it! It—ah— 'simply slipped' from me!" She laughed again, then her eyes turned dreamy. "Oh, Theodor, remember the words we shared? One would have thought you were in love with me."

She smiled knowingly. Yes, I had loved her. Once. I had told her as much, yet she pretended to discredit my words so she could flounce herself to other men. I figured silence was the best answer and hoped she would drop the subject. Either she ignored my disinterest or was too duncical to notice.

"A team to topple the terrors," she mused. "I never imagined you would return from Romance with such Adventures! How does the song go? 'The lord will be wed, to a *Horror*, it's said'? Is she truly horrifying?"

"Then you mock my betrothed?" I narrowed my eyes at her. She batted hers in return.

"Theodor, dear, if she is a Horror, she is a *Contemporary* with neither land nor title. She may treat you like a man, but you are much more than that. You are a gentleman in need of a *lady*. You would be better served by a wife who understands the hardships of court life."

"You pretend to know someone better suited to me than the love of my life?" As if that would be herself? Lady Greenwood was the same as always, except now she disgusted me.

She gave me a pointed look. "You are still naïve, Theodor. I married for love when I should have married for status. Little did I know that love can fade with time." Then she smiled and batted her eyelashes again.

I sighed and took her by the elbow to turn her aside. Still, I needed to walk into her extravagant dress to push through the door. She swung around to throw herself at me as if she were some helpless damsel. She clung to me and I raised my hands to my side, hoping that if anyone happened to pass by, they would see my unwilling participation in the embrace.

"Please, Theodor. Lord Greenwood's ability for hunting and gathering rare herbs was compatible with mine for earth cultivation. He had great dreams to grow in influence until he lost his ability. Never did I imagine you would be so ambitious for the duchy!"

As I expected, she was only after my ability and title. "After Greggory's death, I am the eldest. Why would I not take my rightful place to save Margen from the terror of my younger brothers?"

She bit her lip and turned sad eyes up to me as if she could make herself small and innocent. "I cannot say it was a surprise when they scared you away all those years ago."

I mindfully took a breath to steady my emotions. This conversation had a distasteful start, and it became less pleasant with each exchange. Pansy would not merely show unwillingness to a strumpet. She would defend herself. Fight back.

I pried Lady Greenwood's fingers from my arms, then pushed away. She grabbed onto the arm I raised to ward against her.

"Theodor, dear, if I knew then what I know now, I would not have chosen as I had."

I jerked my arm from her yearning fingers. "If I knew then what I know now, I would have spared my tears for you."

"You cried over me?" She managed to moisten her own eyes with the thought. Curses, she was beautiful behind the mask of charades. Regrettably, she wore the mask so often that she became it. She was the embodiment of everything I detested about noble life.

"Please," I said, "you said every party needs a good gossip. You seem to fill the need for embarrassment well enough without your family. Now, if you will excuse me, I desire to return to my betrothed. Good night, Lady Greenwood."

"Cinderbella," she offered, one last attempt for intimacy. I turned away without acknowledging her.

Finally in the bustling room of celebrations and camaraderie, I hurried to the entrance. Pansy stood near the doors, thronged about by vying men, including Lord Freund. Her smile was beyond genuine when she saw me. Her eyes filled with relief and tenderness.

Merlin's beard, I loved her. She was an imperfect woman who was perfect for me. Heart still pounding with anxiety from Lady Greenwood, I pulled Pansy aside and into my arms, then smashed a kiss to her lips. Never before had I been so bold to publicly claim a woman, though the sight of those men surrounding her boiled my blood. The essence of apple cider on her lips was more than desirable. I forced myself to break away before the onlookers could hoot and holler over our passion.

"Forgive me," I whispered. "I am most eager to escape these crowds. Shall we?"

A shy smile lifted her rosy cheeks. She rested her hand in the crook of my elbow, and we exited the Great Hall together.

Chapter 9

MIDNIGHT

The clock's strike of a new day is a time of magic.
Spells are broken or enforced.
It is wisest to spend the hour at home.

- *Thesis of Adventures*

PANSY

Theo led me through the stone hallways of the half-destroyed palace. The main stairway was wide and grand enough that we could use it even with a boulder settled into its right side.

We had to turn around a couple times as the easiest path was collapsed, or Theo simply forgot which turn to take. I'd normally be terrified to be lost in such a grand and ruined structure, but I felt comfortable at Theo's side. He laughed, gambling kisses for each wrong turn and joking that, "Even the act of searching for sleep is an Adventure."

Eventually, we came to a hallway of open doors to bedrooms. One had my limited belongings stacked to the side and a small reservation card with my name on it.

"Ah, here we are," Theo said, straightening with confidence and relief. He raised my hand to his lips and kissed each of my knuckles, lingering on my ring finger. "I bid you a good night, my flower."

"Where are you staying?" I asked.

"I believe we passed my chambers across from Di's," he said between kisses around my wrist, guiding my hand up his cheek. "I will be near if you need me."

"You seem," I said, "extra Romantic tonight. Did the celebrations make our wedding feel more real?"

He smiled and sighed, raising my hand around his neck, then leaned in to touch his forehead to mine. "Forgive me. I was ambushed by Lady Greenwood while retrieving our cloaks."

"Lady Greenwood?" I repeated. I never met her, but I despised her for treating Theo's heart like a plaything.

"Remembering her despicable behavior just increased my wonderment and appreciation for you," he said. He slid his hand from mine, across my arm and to my neck, weaving his fingers through my hair.

What were we talking about again?

Rather than attempt to continue the conversation, I stepped into his embrace. My mind was a fog between the sensation of holding him and my growing desire to hold him closer.

His nose caressed down and around mine, bringing our lips near as he whispered, "I love you, Pansy."

I loved him too, more than my own life. Actions spoke louder than words, so instead of telling him, I kissed him. For the first time in a while, I didn't need to stop at a peck. I could kiss him passionately without anyone coughing or interrupting. So I did.

Still, I felt exposed in the hallway. I grabbed Theo by his doublet and pulled him to my room. His arm snapped out to brace himself against the doorframe.

"Pansy, what—"

"You're not a vampire," I said between kisses. "You can cross thresholds."

"No, it is inappro—"

"Not if you marry me."

"I will."

"I mean tonight," I said, and he drew back. I nodded to the celebrations somewhere below. "We already had a reception. I've always thought that the smaller the better for weddings. All these traditions and ceremonies leave me clueless. I worry I'll mess up everything and curse us. Can't we elope?"

His wide-eyed unease spoke for him. Royalty didn't elope; royalty was meant to be in the spotlight. The mere thought of a crowded wedding made me squirm. I wanted Theo to love me enough to break with tradition. I wanted to love him with all that I had and to be loved in return.

I didn't give him a chance to reply as I smashed his lips with mine again. Theo hesitated before he kissed me back. His arm relaxed from the doorframe and dropped to wrap around my waist. Something inside of Theo broke. He stepped into my room, then closed the door with his foot, kissing me, gripping me all the more.

I allowed myself to become lost in the moment. For the first time in too long, I stopped worrying about the fact that I was thousands of miles away from familiar land, that we nearly faced death yesterday, or that we were marching into battle against powerful tyrants. I focused on Theo and wanted to memorize the feel of him. Even with my fingers knotted in his hair and roaming over his back, I couldn't get enough of him. Theo must have agreed as he expanded our kiss into un-explored areas. While the motions tensed my nerves, I also relented to them. We weren't in Horror, and we would marry soon, after all.

My heart pounded harder and the desire to push the boundaries grew stronger. My Horror brain and Romantic heart argued.

*Keep the number one rule…*but we'd marry soon anyway.

*Don't let your guard down…*but I was still in control…right?

*Don't disappoint those you respect…*but would I disappoint Theo if I stopped now?

It was difficult to think as I sank in the depth of Theo's embrace. Even as Oz's words echoed through my mind, I didn't think of my brother until an image of his face slammed into my consciousness. He wore his classic stern expression of a reprimand.

This isn't only about you. Theo has people he can't disappoint: Professor Vieseth, the citizens of Divinity and all of Margen, and Di.

Her innocent face hit me next, and I unvelcroed myself from Theo.

"Horror, you're right," I stuttered on my own breath.

"My flower?"

"I'm sorry, Theo, we need to stop. For Di's sake."

"Stop…for Di?" Theo wondered, dazed, like he was waking up. "Pansy, you tease me in, now push me away? Did I do something wrong?"

"No-no. I know." I winced. "I was being selfish. But as much as I'd love a small wedding, I love you more. I love you enough to have a big Fantastical celebration. I love you enough that I can wait to be your wife, even if it's days, weeks, or months away."

Theo groaned. I could sense his inner battle as he closed his eyes and measured his breaths. Trembling, he stepped back. "If that is your wish, my flower. Please forgive me."

"Right, because it's all your fault." I grinned and stepped away to rest against the wall. "Supernaturals, I've never been so tempted in my life."

"You speak for both of us." His lips went thin as he pinched back a guilty smile. "Please open your door before I say curses to Horror's number one rule."

"And condemnation to Fairy's Keys of Honor." I smirked and opened my door. Like an addict escaping a drug factory, Theo hesitated, then dashed out to the hallway. I rounded the door frame, entertained by the sight of him dazed and winded. He flustered with his fancy new doublet, tightened the laces and straightened it properly.

"How about a raincheck?" I asked. "We can pick up again after our grand and Fantastic ceremony."

"Yes," he sighed, the sense of duty weighing his shoulders down. "The best way to prove ourselves worthy of Margen is to act responsibly." Then a smug smile released from his guilty clench. "May I request we seal that promise with a gentle kiss?"

"Yeah." I smiled back and restrained myself as Theo slowly approached me again at my threshold. Still breathing heavily, he softly stroked my hair back, then rested his hand against the doorframe, barring my way into my room. With that movement, I became fully aware of Theo's position to me. With my back against the wall, he had caged me and was closing in. If he was anyone else, I would have felt trapped, possibly terrified for my life. Instead, my heart pounded heavily with anticipation as he leaned closer.

Condemnation, he was too alluring for his own good.

He kissed me again, lightly touching my lips without any added pressure. Slow and begging for release, this kiss made me crave him even more than our previous passion. He left me hanging with only a sample, delicious with the perfect mix of sweet and savory. He deepened the kiss with a brief motion before breaking. I gasped for air, unaware that I'd held my breath.

"That was…cruel," I said. "Are your kisses caffeinated? I feel like you cut me off too soon to crash."

Theo grinned mischievously. "You were the one to pull me into your room. I had to teach you a lesson."

"Lesson learned. If I'm going to have a cup of Theo, I need free refills."

"I meant about seducing me." He stared me down with a smile.

I smiled back to let my tease show. When I considered saying goodnight, however, my stomach churned. "I don't like the idea of splitting up, even for sleep. The last time I slept without a roommate was…" Actually, I couldn't remember if I'd ever slept alone in a room. The idea sounded dangerous.

"I cannot stay," Theo said.

"Please?" I asked. "I'll draft a maid to chaperone us, and I'll sleep on the couch—"

Theo stopped me with a finger to my lips. "First of all, no. The word of a servant is not enough to secure our reputations. Second, I would take the couch. If I had to wrestle you into the bed, I would."

I let his words sink in, then snickered.

Theo blushed. "Do not linger on that thought."

"Too late."

He combed his fingers through his hair and groaned, "What am I to do with you?"

"I'm pretty sure you're going to marry me," I teased.

He leaned close again and spoke with a low growl between a devilish smirk. "I meant until then, you Contemporary temptress."

I wanted to retort that he was the tempting one, when a voice blared through the hallway.

"Divinity has been saved! The Fromm fam'ly name be praised!" Di stumbled around the corner and grumbled, "Who wrote those lyrics? Verily, I could do better. Oh, Theo, Pansy? Has sleep not taken you? Alas, for good fortune! They separated us, yet I require a bunkmate to prevent my sleepwalking."

"Pansy needs a roommate," Theo said, much too eager.

I sent him a playful scowl as Di grabbed my arm. "Come now, sleep awaits before our journey tomorrow."

Theo responded with a smile that made my heart lurch. He winked and whispered, "Raincheck."

Chapter 10

NUMBER ONE RULE OF FAIRY:

Be careful for what you wish.

-   Thesis of Adventures

PANSY

The next morning, I gave myself a sponge bath from the sink. Di said that in Fairy, cloaks were required while baths were optional. At least Margen had indoor plumbing, even if the only temperatures were between cold and freezing. I dressed into my dark traveler's trousers and a loose, long-sleeve white shirt under my miraculously cleaned red and black cloak.

Professor Vieseth summoned us to her office before breakfast, and I felt like I'd been called to the principal's office. Floor to ceiling bookshelves lined every wall, and the middle space was occupied with a desk and table. Both were stacked high with parchment scrolls, feathered pens, and ribbons. Colorful strings bookmarked every piece of literature in the room, and the professor pressed a purple ribbon to her current scroll of study before standing to greet us. She excused everyone from the room except Theo, Di, and me, and a single servant.

That put me on alert. Why didn't she want witnesses?

The servant held a bundle of thick cloth in her arms. Glancing around secretively, the professor removed a ten-inch wooden stick from the bundle. With more reverence than I thought a stick deserved, she offered it to Theo with a low bow.

"Divinity is ever in your debt," she said. "Please accept our gifts of gratitude. To Lord Theodor Fromm, the Trusted, and rightful heir of Margen, we bestow the Wand of Gandiduz. We would trust none other with our most powerful relic. May he use it to continually bless our land and people."

I didn't know anything about magical objects, but based on his wide eyes and awe, I figured it was special.

"I cannot possibly accept—"

"You must," she said. "We are in no position to protect and guard our greatest treasures. We cannot allow this to fall into the wrong hands. We trust those of the Trusted Marquis, Slayer of the giant, Magnanim."

Theo steeled himself and accepted the wand. "I understand. May Divinity stand stronger than its mountains."

She smiled and took another object from the bundle. The blade of a dagger glistened in her hands as she turned to me.

"To Miss Pansy Finster from Horror, we bestow the Knife of Vulgur, that her resources may be as sharp as she."

I was both grateful and concerned. First, a magical cross-bow to replace my trusted revolver. Now, a special knife to replace my old switch-blade? Was Fantasy going to take away everything familiar and replace it with its own magical version?

I'd received enough unwanted gifts to know how to feign gratitude. My pretense, however, was overwhelmed by curiosity as Di gaped openly at my gift. She practically drooled.

If the Fantastical Priestess found it fascinating, I guessed it couldn't be too bad.

Not knowing how to flower my words of questionable gratitude, I said a simple, "Thanks. Let the Supernaturals keep you in good terms."

Professor Vieseth blinked, then smiled. In turn, Di was given a rare book of ancient divine prayers. There was still a bulk in the bundle of fabric. With another motion from the professor, the servant slowly lifted the layers away.

My insides tensed on high alert. What was in there? Why didn't they touch it? Was it cursed?

The last fold slipped off to reveal...a rock. Theo and Di gasped. Okay?

"Is that—"

"The wishing stone?" Di finished for Theo.

The professor smiled. "If you had not redeemed Divinity, I was going to wish for our next mission to succeed. As you granted my wish, I see it only fair that I gifted you the opportunity."

The royal siblings glanced between themselves in eager astonishment. They looked to me, but the only expression I could give was confusion.

Theo coughed to school his expression and turned back to the professor. "May we have a few minutes to consider this opportunity?"

Professor Vieseth smiled. "That would be wise."

Theo took my hand and stepped aside. "Do you remember the number one rule for Fantasy?"

"Always be careful what you wish for," I said.

"Yes." He nodded and gestured toward the professor's rock. "In some rare Adventures the Heroes are given rewards for their success. It may be a magical artifact or enchantment."

"Yeah. I got a knife and you got a...wand?"

Theo held the stick carefully in both hands. "Yes, the Wand of Gandiduz is the only one of its kind. It grants its master—regardless of her or her magical capacity—the power to cast spells."

"Verily," Di said, "a master wizard would have no use for it. Nevertheless, the Wand of Gandiduz is a treasure to anyone else, especially the common folk and nobles with abilities."

Theo nodded. "Your Vulgur Knife is also rare and infused with magic to replicate a unique weapon from Sci-Fi. It can shoot electricity from its blade."

"Oh." I looked down at my new weapon with fresh curiosity and respect. These were definitely dangerous items to use and keep. I glanced around our secretive room, grateful the professor bestowed these gifts in private.

"Now" —Theo sighed with wide eyes, like he couldn't take it all in— "she offers us an opportunity with the Wishing Stone. It grants one wish every three years."

"Okay. So, right now we can choose a wish? Whatever we want?" I asked, putting it all together.

"Yes, and remember, we need to be careful for what we wish." Theo leaned back. The professor stayed in the center of the room and watched us. She wore an expression of amusement, like our internal struggle pleased her. These people were crazy.

Considering our options, I said, "Professor Vieseth was going to wish for the restoration of Divinity. Can we wish for the restoration of Margen?"

The siblings pondered, but eventually shook their heads.

"To what end?" Di asked. "Without knowing the cause of Margen's issues, we cannot specify how it should be resolved."

Theo nodded. "There are too many loopholes and unknowns. Recall the incident of the Monkey's Paw."

I grimaced. "The Monkey's Paw" was a well-known historical account of a Margen family that immigrated to Horror. The young family needed money, and the dad found a monkey's paw with three wishes. They wished for money. Simple...but vague. Their little boy was killed in an accident, and the family received insurance money. The mom was so torn with grief that she wished for her son to be alive again. The dad knew that their boy would be undead and cursed, so he spent the final wish to make his son rest in peace.

"Okay, then," I said. "We wish for something that can help us restore Margen. I don't like the idea of asking for another powerful weapon or item. They easily backfire when they're lost, broken, or stolen. What about an ability?"

"Abilities can be powerful," Theo agreed, "and transfer between nations, though they are more specific than magics. You also bring up a good point regarding our new tools. We should find a way to use them in secret."

Di and I nodded.

"Good," Theo continued. "Concerning an ability, however, I am finally satisfied with my aura ability. To ask for another one, more useful…I would feel ungrateful for the ability given to me at birth. How would you feel about gaining an ability?"

"Me?" I rocked back. "I don't know anything about magic."

Di said, "Therein is a valid reason why you should learn."

"Why don't you ask for something?" I asked her.

She waved her hand like she couldn't care less. "Pish posh, my lack of an ability has allowed me to learn magic. I have all my needs met save for a loving husband, which is forbidden to me for another year anyway."

"Politically speaking," Theo added, "an ability would be a powerful tool to earn the people's respect." He took my hands and met my eyes. "I trust you to use an ability to benefit others, not to be caught up in its power as my brothers were. It is highly unlikely we will have this chance again. Magic often causes more problems than it solves, though if we consider the circumstances, it may be beneficial."

I squirmed a little under his intense analysis. "Then we should ask to enhance a skill we already have."

"Yes, and you already have many skills," he said, redirecting my open target back to me. "The wisest choice would be something that could assist everyday challenges, and not just this Adventure. What do you desire for yourself?"

"Oh, um…" I pondered. What would have been helpful during our fight against the giant? What would continue to be helpful against Theo's brothers? "Maybe speed?"

Theo blinked like he was surprised I came up with that on my own. I figured speed would enhance my fighting skills and my capability to run away.

"I guess I need to be specific," I said, "so…to have super speed, or is that too Sci-Fian?"

"The Shoes of Swiftness then," Di nodded. "You want the ability of the Shoes of Swiftness."

"Shoes of Swiftness?" I asked. "What are those?"

"Verily," Di said, "they are one of the great magical items bestowed upon Heroes of old. The Sword of Sharpness, Cap of Knowledge, and Cloak of Invisibility are others."

"The shoes," Theo added, "give the wearer the capability to climb any mountain or run as the wind. I am unsure exactly how they work, though legends say you just think of the place and you are instantly there. If you want not an object, then wish for just the ability."

I considered that. If no one was exactly sure what they did, then who was to say what its ability would be? I amended my request. I wanted speed not only in my feet, but also for my thoughts and attacks. Would two times faster be enough? No, doubling my speed wouldn't have changed much against a giant. What if I was five times faster? That would make me as fast as a horse. Miles and Short Fuse had been fast enough to escape the giant.

Di turned back to Professor Vieseth. "We have decided."

"We have?" I asked, suddenly nervous, like I was about to retake my medical certification exams.

"Yes," Theo agreed. "Be sure to word it very carefully."

Di added, "No wishy-washiness, or you might end up with the literal feet of the last wearer of the shoes."

I stared at them with wide and unsure eyes. Theo encouraged me forward with a small dip of his chin. I faced Professor Vieseth, swallowing hard and praying to the Supernaturals that I wouldn't mess up. "I wish for the ability to become five times faster."

"I knew you would choose wisely," Professor Vieseth said with a light chortle. "Many fools jump to wish for the first desire on their mind, like a sausage on their wife's nose. Long live the Fromms, but I imagine your brothers would have asked right away with a power enhancement. Your strategizing pleases me." She stepped forward, then held out the stone to me. "Are you ready?"

I squared my shoulders. "I'm ready."

I wondered when and how I learned to be so good at faking courage. Maybe it came from years of fighting for my life and bluffing against Hauntings so they wouldn't bother me.

With a shaking hand, I reached out to touch the stone, repeating my wish in my mind. I wished for the ability to instantly become five times faster. A cold sensation rushed through my body, starting at my fingertips on the stone and surging up my arm. It raced to my heart then burst up and down. My toes tingled and my scalp shivered. I gasped. Then it was over.

Did it work?

I looked back to Theo and Di. Their faces remained frozen in anticipation. They didn't move. I turned back to the professor, but she was also still.

Supernaturals. What did I do?

I placed two fingers on Theo's neck, feeling for a pulse. His throb was far too slow. What was going on? Did I accidentally place everyone under a curse?

Kisses broke curses, so I tried one on Theo. No change.

My heart rate quickened as I admitted this was beyond my knowledge. I ran outside for help, but found none. Everyone was still. No, not quite. The campfire waved slowly upward, and the racing dog leapt in slow motion. Five times slower.

Condemnation, was I stuck like this?

I ran back to the stone.

"Hold on," I said. "I wished for the *ability* to *become* faster. Not to *be* faster. I was clear on that, so that means I should have an on-off switch, right?"

No response. Horror, I was talking to a rock.

I raked my fingers through my hair, frustrated. I paced around the tent and was torn between the desire to scream or to meditate.

"Wishes require sacrifice."

"Who's there?" I jerked toward the voice of an elderly man, but saw no one. Everyone was still in slow motion.

"Yours in particular," the voice said, "is powerful indeed."

"Who are you?" I demanded.

"I am the soul of the Wishing Stone."

Condemnation, the rock talked back!

I approached it like a vampire hunter as it continued to speak. "You did not leave many loopholes for me to ensnare you. Except you did not specify how you wanted to become five times faster. Five times faster than what? Than time itself? Of course, then you may age five times faster."

I gulped. Even if I lived for another eighty years, that would only be sixteen for Theo. Waiting for everyone to slowly catch up would quickly become frustrating.

The stone continued, "You have the scent of a foreigner, yet the blood of a giant on your hands. Few Fantastics would wish as carefully as you have. Who taught you such caution?"

"My brother," I said. Theo helped, but I didn't want to put any blame on someone in the room.

"Yes," it hissed. "It is all in his book then?"

My hand snapped to my emergency pack around my leg. "How do you know about that?"

"I am a stone as old as time itself, with powers to grant abilities, and you wonder how I know what is in your pockets?"

I grunted. Fair point.

"Will you let me see it?" the stone hissed.

"What do you want with it?"

The stone laughed. "Hah! More of that caution. Yes, I must see these instructions he left you."

"And if you don't?"

"Then remain in five times speed until the end of your days."

I gulped. This definitely wasn't how I wanted to spend the rest of my life. "What do you want with my brother's book?" I asked again.

"To read it."

I blinked. His request seemed simple enough. I wasn't sure how a stone would read a book, but it was a small price to release me from this time dimension.

I unlatched my pack and pulled out *Oz's Haunting Survival Book*. I opened the front cover and turned it around for the stone to "see." However that was supposed to work.

"Yesss," it hissed happily. "Such a personal treasure—studied, revered, and loved. A fair trade."

"Trade?"

Oz's book fizzled in my hands. Ash rose from the pages and floated to the stone.

"Wait!"

A third of the little book was already disintegrated and absorbed by the stone. I let go with one hand to grab the dustings, but more of the book fell away.

"No!"

The stone chuckled like a dungeon keeper locking away its prisoner forever in the dark. The last of the ashes melted into the stone, and sound returned from the world around me.

I sank to my knees. Sobs broke from my heart and escaped from my mouth.

"Pansy?" Theo asked, surprised. "Hold on, what happened?"

"Oh, dear," Professor Vieseth murmured. "The wish was too great. The stone demanded payment."

"Payment?" Di asked.

Theo's hand slid across my back until his arm wrapped around me. "Pansy, what happened?"

I struggled to breathe between the heaving in my chest. "It…ate…Oz's book."

"It—" His arm stiffened around me. "Your brother's book is gone?"

I refused to reply. I wouldn't confirm the loss.

"A book?" Di asked. "Is that all? By the heavens, what a simple trade."

Theo stood and marched up to the professor. "Can we trade them back?"

"You know wishes are non-returnable," the professor muttered.

Di scoffed. "Can you not buy a new book? Or make another?"

"That book was the only copy written by her brother," Theo growled. "He was the only family she had, and that book was all he left her when he died three years ago."

"Oh." Di softened. "That is unfortunate."

"Unfortunate?" Theo snapped. "She staked her life on that book! It saved her from Horror and made her the woman she is today!"

"Then why did she never make a copy?" Di argued, defensive from Theo's shouts. "If it was her bible and a possible savior to others, then verily, why keep it to herself? We lose that which we save, and gain that which we give away!"

I squeezed my eyes shut, pressing my tears out and down my cheeks. Some deeper consciousness urged me to push away—push away the sorrow, the pain, the fighting. Push everything off until it all slowed down. I reached into that desire like fishing down a well. I leaned over on my tippy-toes until I feared falling over and tumbling down into that abyss. Then I grabbed something. I wrenched it upward and *pushed* it away.

Sounds faded to slow echoes. I was in that stillness again, going five times faster than time itself. It was an odd relief to silence the shouting. It freed my mind to think—about the loss of my brother's book, about my switchblade, my revolver…

They were such little things that added up to the fact that everything had changed since I left Horror. Even Theo had changed by becoming Marquis. The unknown future gripped me with fear. Terrifying as Horror was, I missed the familiar roads and simple life of never worrying about tomorrow, because—who knew?—I could be dead before dawn.

Loneliness accompanied me in my slowed time. I could run away like this. Run away from everything. But where would I go? Back to Romance? No. Romance had been as temporary as the foster homes of my childhood. Besides, Romantics always said that home was where the heart was.

The guardian of my heart stood beside me, arguing for the sake of my brother's book. No, Theo hadn't changed. Only his responsibilities. I couldn't abandon him when he needed me more than ever. No matter where I was in the world, Theo was my home. If he made his bed in Fantasy, then so be it. I would become a Fantastic.

As if gearing up to fight a Haunting, I braced myself and embraced my fate of unknown Adventures.

I stood and managed a wan smile at my fiancé's heated debate with his sister. Theo was a fighter after all. But I didn't want him to ruin his bond with his sister because I lost mine with my brother.

With a slow breath, I pulled myself back into regular time. In doing so, a small weight of exhaustion settled on me. Maybe it was the crying or the fighting, or maybe it was the effect of aging five times faster than everyone else while in that unique time frame.

"It's okay, Theo," I said.

He did a double take toward me, surprised by my words and seemingly sudden calmness.

"Pansy? How is it—"

"It's okay," I said again. "I have it memorized. I'll make another one. And maybe this time, I don't know, I'll get it published."

Theo blinked, then wrapped his arms around me again. His simple embrace soothed away even my worst emotions. He held me close and whispered, "Pansy, I am so sorry. Are you sure?"

I forced myself to breathe slowly. "There's nothing we can do now, right? What's done is done."

"Unfortunately, yes." He leaned back and rubbed my tear-stained cheek with his thumb. "Forgive me for asking you to take that wish. I understand if you hate me for it."

I shook my head. "You didn't know. If anyone, the professor should be apologizing for not warning us."

Professor Vieseth hiccupped, nervous to be brought into the accusation. Theo's eyes narrowed his aim of fire on the professor. I palmed his cheek to turn him back to me. "I chose this ability. I won't refuse it now. Oz's legacy depends on it."

A corner of Theo's mouth twitched with a smile. "We have time to experiment. We have another day of travels before we reach Eimad."

Chapter 11

OVERPOWERED ITEMS:

Iron Cauldron
Cloak of Invisibility
Shoes of Swiftness
Sword of Sharpness
Cap of Knowledge
(This list is incomplete)

- *Thesis of Adventures*

PANSY

I went downstairs to join half the town for a late breakfast. Theo wanted to ask Di's birds for a favor, leaving me alone in the room full of strangers. I was like a child among witches. The dwarves of Divinity shoved my mouth full of exotic foods and asked me a million questions.

"How did you kill Magnanim?"

"What was your part in the Adventure?"

"Are you going to save Eimad and Margen?"

I was pretty sure they already heard Theo's accounts, but wanted to hear it from my lips for some crazy reason.

Unfortunately, their most common questions were: "When and where will you wed?"

"When will you return to Divinity?"

"What goals do you have as Margen's Marchioness?"

Ummm…

Only an hour had passed since I made peace with becoming a Fantastic. I needed more time to swallow the idea of becoming royalty. How could I make goals for a duchy when I barely understood the goals I made for myself? My future decisions now impacted thousands of people with families and foreign lifestyles.

Theo stepped into the room, tugging on his right sleeve and resituating the giant-slaying sword at his hip. As much as I wanted to test my new speed ability to rush to his side as fast as possible, I excused myself properly and approached him like a noble. Supernaturals, being a lady was hard.

Theo offered greetings and accepted food for our trip. He escorted me away from the fire-hazardous crowd with hopes of glory for their town. I released a long exhale as we stepped out of the room and I reached for Theo's hand. A thicker material covered his forearm under his sleeve.

"What's this?" I asked, picking at the cuffs of his undershirt.

Theo tugged me to the side of the hallway before rolling back his sleeve. Underneath, he wore a metal brace that was too clean and tight to be chainmail.

"I asked Di's birds to make this arm brace," Theo said, sliding his hand over the shiny material. "I designed it that I may wear the wand inside, along my forearm."

I raised my eyebrows. "To protect it?"

"Yes, and to hide it," he clarified.

I grinned like a proud parent. "Sounds like something I would have done. I don't need to read all your histories to know that a powerful magical artifact comes with an ugly bloodline. People would kill for such an item."

Theo shrugged. "Professor Vieseth excused everyone from the tent before she revealed the wand. If people ask, we may say the magic was bestowed to me by a wish when we defeated Magnanim."

"Alright." I bit my lip. "I don't like lying to people, but it's safer if no one knows you have it."

Theo nodded. "Are you ready to go? Di awaits us in the stables with my cousin."

All I knew about Theo's cousins was that they were the children of Queen Alóvera, of Fairy. As if meeting the extended family wasn't intimidating enough, Theo's cousins were princes and princesses. No pressure.

Walking down the stables, we passed pens of the usual animals, like pigs and goats, and then animals I didn't recognize. The unknown creatures scattered in a flutter of feathers or lazily rolled around in balls of scales. Di stopped to talk *with* her crazy horse. Rather than panic over my impending doom via a talking horse named Short Fuse, I followed Theo's focus down the stables.

At the end of the aisle, a man held open a great map, blocking his face and chest.

All of my instincts screamed not to approach anyone if I couldn't see his/her face. I allowed Theo to approach first, knowing he would see any danger from our auras.

My fiancé grinned without precaution. "Did you bring me a souvenir from Sci-Fi?"

"Depends," a deep voice replied without lowering the map. "Did you bring me a bullbeggar from Romance?"

Theo's eyebrows went high. "I would discourage you from saying that around Di."

"Bullbeggar is just another wibbly-wobbly word in Sci-Fi." The man behind the map chuckled.

Theo smirked. "Do you miss space already, or are you just tired of how Faenor fawns over its prince? Is that why you came to Margen?"

"I came to collect my bullbegging souvenir from you. Did you forget my request?"

"Your request for a perfect wife was a little more than I would call a 'souvenir.'"

"Though you had no trouble finding one for yourself," the deep voice slyly remarked, finally dropping half the map to fold into itself and revealing a man about the same age as Theo. The half-dwarf was a couple inches shorter than my five foot five, but I guessed no one dared to tease him. He was a stocky man with bulky muscles and a bulbous nose. He shared Theo's dark and groomed hair, though he maintained a trimmed beard.

"Prince Alun, the Charger," Theo said, "since you insist, allow me to introduce you to my betrothed, Miss Pansy Finster, from Horror."

"So the rumors are true," the prince said, appraising me like a house.

I squirmed a bit, wondering. "What rumors?"

"That you are hauntingly beautiful."

I stumbled on my own feet, embarrassed, surprised, and embarrassed to be caught by surprise. The prince let out a low rumble of a laugh and Theo joined him.

"Those rumors came from me." Theo winked at me before he turned back to his cousin. "Regardless, I pitched you a good match so you have no need to take mine."

"Careful how you answer that, Alun," someone said from behind me. My breath caught as I recognized the female voice, and I spun around.

"Brooke!" My surprise and her tease turned into joy. Brooke Steamings, a Sci-Fian of the Steampunk district, had been one of my roommates and first friends in Romance. She spoke with an interesting nasal accent and wore clothes that mixed between futuristic and vintage. We stayed in touch after she graduated in International Politics and started an internship on the starship *Celeste*. "What are you doing here?"

"Pretty much the same thing you are," she said, wrapping me in a hug. She smelled like oils and flowers. "Taking a break from school to hang out with my super royal boyfriend."

"Wait." I put the pieces together. "This is *Alun*?" Brooke's long-distance boyfriend was Theo's cousin—the youngest son of Queen Alóvera? "I thought Alun was a Sci-Fian?"

"Alas, if only the gods made it so," Prince Alun said, slipping into a melodramatic Regency tone. He walked over and hung a lazy arm across Brooke's shoulders, but spoke to me. "I attended Caladan University to major in Interplanetary Poli-Sci, then met Ms. Steamings on the *Celeste*. Theo thought she and I would strike a match, but little did he know how far it would burn. Even as Brooke was born in Sci-Fi, so was my heart. How typical."

"You," I accused Brooke, "didn't say anything about him being a prince."

My friend simply shrugged. "Royalty doesn't mean as much as your station when you're on a starship like the *Celeste*. I totally forgot that Theo was royalty when he introduced his cousin. I thought Alun was impressive enough as the Chief Engineer of Weapons."

"So," I said, reconfiguring my first impression, "*Prince Alun, the Charger*? Did you charge into battle or something?"

He laughed. "No, but I like to let people think that."

Brooke grinned like a kid with a secret. "Can I tell her?"

"Sure." The prince shrugged. "She ought to know my ability if she becomes family."

Their whole conversation baffled me as I waited for an explanation.

"'The Charger' is about his ability," Brooke said. "He can totally use Sci-Fian technology *outside* of Sci-Fian territories."

"What? How?" I asked. "The land of Fantasy breaks all technology from other places, like my phone, taser, and revolver. And crazy Sci-Fian crap can't work anywhere outside their zones. Okay, except for that one corner in Western, right? Isn't that the whole reason for their war over there?"

"That," Theo said, "is the fascination of his ability. He is a charger, such as a battery. He alone can utilize Sci-Fian machinery whether he be in Fantasy, Romance, Western, wherever."

"Because unlike magic," I realized, "your abilities can transfer between continents. That's incredible!"

"I admit," the prince beamed, "it is bullbegging awesome. Mother almost sent another in my stead to aid Divinity's camps. She considers my ability too valuable regarding the current Sci-Fi and Western conflicts, and worries about Eimad's ability disappearances. I argued that if she could leave the boring safety of Faenor and go to the cursed Eimad to inquire after the duke, then I could come to the destroyed Divinity. For all the good I did. I hear you vanquished Magnanim?"

Theo grinned. "A messy affair, that one, and a tale meant for the road. If Queen Alóvera is at Eimad, we should meet her with swiftness."

I opened my mouth to ask more, but Di cut in from behind, "There shall be time to become better acquainted as we journey. Harken, Prince Alun, a wise man doth expand his vocabulary beyond expletives."

The prince muttered, "Whatever," but his red face and ducked chin were apologetic.

We saddled our horses, then—true to Di's word—spent the next several hours sharing our recent experiences. Theo updated Alun about our struggles against the giant while I chatted with Brooke. To everyone's entertainment, we shared stories from our time as roommates, and she updated me on her internship as an external affairs counselor on a starship.

"Alun convinced me," she said, "to take the summer off so he could introduce me to his family. Talk about super intimidating."

I grinned back. "At least they're not labeled 'terrorists' and 'tyrants.' How do you think I feel about meeting Theo's brothers?"

"Behold," Di chided in front of me, "forget me not."

"Sorry, Di," I said, "you're not bad."

"Yea!" my future sister-in-law cheered.

Still, my insides writhed as I thought about meeting the queen. "Theo, can you quiz me about your extended family?"

"Alright," he said. "Why is Queen Alóvera titled The Phoenix?"

"Uh," I slurred, "something about a tree, a bird, and coming back to life…"

Theo laughed. "My grandfather was King Fromm, The Valiant. My aunt and father had a wicked stepmother when they were yet children, and they had an Adventure similar to the prehistoric event of 'The Juniper Tree.'"

"Right." I remembered. "When Queen Alóvera and Duke Konrad were kids, their wicked stepmom 'accidentally' beheaded Alóvera as she leaned into a chest. She put Alóvera back together so when your dad slapped her for not listening, he thought *he* beheaded her."

Prince Alun laughed. "You can bet Uncle Konrad has never hit a woman since."

That fact offered a small relief to my nerves about meeting Theo's dad. I continued the history, "The stepmom cooked Alóvera into a soup and fed it to her dad, the king. Feeling terrible about 'killing' his sister, Konrad buried her bones under a tree, and the bundle of bones turned into a bird. The bird sang around the town and was given gifts for its song, such as a wand, a wishing stone, and a cauldron. The bird gave the wand to the king, the stone to her brother, and dropped the cauldron on the stepmom, killing her. After that, the bird transformed back into Alóvera, who has abilities like a phoenix…Wait a second," I paused as details locked into place. "Was that the same wishing stone we saw this morning?"

To my astonishment, Theo nodded. "The wand is also a treasure you may know."

Prince Alun did a double take. "You saw the wishing stone?"

Di opened her mouth like she was ready to spill beans, but I interrupted, "Theo wished for wizardry magic, Di wished for a spell book, and I wished for a speed ability."

The prince frowned. "I thought—"

"You got an ability?" Brooke gaped at me. "That's super cool! And Theo learned magic? What's it like? Can we experiment when we set camp?"

I agreed and pointedly ignored Di's grumble. As much as I wanted to speak openly in front of Brooke, I didn't know Prince Alun enough to trust him. Also, I didn't want to burden Brooke with such a dangerous secret.

Theo said, "You may have heard of the cauldron and its Adventure with Prince Gwydion and Little Dallben. The iron cauldron has dark powers connected to death and restoration of life."

"Wow," I said. "I found your aunt's story hard to believe, but there's proof of it."

Theo shrugged. "Adventures tend to swing on the line of incredibility." I didn't argue since all my Romantic friends thought Horror's histories were unbelievable.

A couple hours before sunset, Theo directed his horse off the path.

"We will stop here for the night," he said. Prince Alun and Di agreed readily, but my stomach squeezed with unease.

"Here?" I asked. We stood in a small clearing of wild grass beside the dirt road. "We're out in the open."

"The gods created the land and trees," Di said as she dismounted to twirl in the long grass. "They are open to all creatures, and invite all to come and worship them."

I bit my lip nervously. "Couldn't you, I don't know, magic up a small mud hut so we at least have shelter?"

Theo gave me a bewildered look. "You want to create a strange dwelling in the middle of the woods? Does that not break rules of Horror?"

"When you put it that way…" I muttered.

Theo smiled and my worries ebbed. "It is a rule in Fairy also, my flower. Witches, giants, and ogres most frequently make their abodes in strange cabins within the woods. If Adventurers pass by, it is better to appear open than to hide and leave suspicions to their imaginations."

"Right." I couldn't disagree, but I also couldn't feel comfortable about sleeping outside. It didn't help when Di suggested we split up for duties.

"It is a disagreeable prospect," she said, pointing to Alun and Brooke, then Theo and me, "to allow couples to pair. Thus, Brooke and Pansy shall prepare the tent and the bedding, while I arrange the campsite. Alun and Theo, have you the skills to hunt for our dinner?"

The Charger Prince grinned as he retrieved a peculiar battle axe from his pack. It hummed and glowed to life in his hands.

"I can fish," Theo said, "though I have no rod nor string."

Di gave him a downward stare. "Hearken, you are now a mumbling-bumbling wizard. Transfigure a stick and long blade of grass, then obtain our dinner."

Theo blinked. "Right." He stared at his arm brace like an instruction manual written in another language. "How?"

Di sighed, and the evening was spent in a subject that terrified most Horrors: magic. To my surprise, Di asked me to translate some words from Latin for similar translations to the language of magic. I watched from the shore as the siblings lured fish into their hands with no more than words.

Di tried to teach Theo how to grow his own wood for perfect fires, though her instructions were vague and complicated. How much wood would a wizard wack if a wizard would wack wood? Enough to burn a witch?

When it came to starting a fire, I considered myself a cheater with the matches in my emergency pack. Apparently, those were too mundane for Fantastics.

"Pansy, what is the Latin translation for 'fire?'" Di asked.

"*Ignis*," I said, feeling like a virtual assistant. At least they wouldn't ask me for tomorrow's weather. They could probably change that with magic anyway.

Theo pondered, then looked to Di for confirmation. "That becomes *igniz?*"

"Prove yourself," Di said, gesturing to the pile of wood that she previously cultivated and chopped with only words.

I struggled with my new reality. Theo could do magic. Theo, my adorably humble, yet confident, fiancé could do magic. He grew up thinking he was useless because he didn't understand his ability. First he found a purpose for his auras, then he earned his Masters in Political Science, and now…

"*Igniz!*" Theo pointed his wand arm at the logs. They burst into fireballs more than twice their size.

With my mind on high alert, the next second appeared to slow down. Instincts warned me of the possible dangers, and my eyes analyzed where and how. Without another thought, I ran at Di and pushed her away before the fire reached her. I caught her a moment before she hit the ground. Her muscles were loose and unprepared for the impact.

Time seemed to return to normal as Di blinked at me in surprise. Theo struggled to douse the fire.

"*Ajua! Ajua!*"

He drenched our little campfire with the firehose stream that shot from his wrist. All of us were in the splash zone, but I pulled Di away before it sprayed us.

Theo laughed, wet like he came in from a storm. His eyes flickered with confusion as he looked around. His eyes crinkled with a youthful grin when he found us.

"Oops."

Di joined his laughter. "That was fantastic! Theo, you must harness your strength to control your power. Pansy, by the heavens! You are as the wind!"

"What?"

"Verily, you moved beyond my sight. One moment I was before Theo, and the next I fell. Then you rescued me from my fall to return my feet. I had not the time to react."

"I used my new speed ability?" I asked.

Theo frowned. "You can already use your ability subconsciously?"

I squirmed and hoped I hadn't used it too much to age myself days beyond everyone else.

Alun returned with a small boar that Brooke helped set over the fire. They watched and snuggled as Di helped Theo and I practice our abilities and magics. Dinner was delightful, but I hardly remembered eating between the practices that extended into the night.

I learned that my ability only had one speed. As soon as I tapped into it, I moved on another plane of time that interacted with the world at five times speed. Though I worried about aging faster than everyone else, simple math reassured me that twelve minutes of real time gave me a full hour with my speed. If I spent a total of one hour in my speed every day for a full year, that would only make me fifteen days older than every-one else. I could handle that.

Theo and I quickly became target practice for Prince Alun's stun gun and Di's spells. I dodged with my speed while Theo blocked with a magicked shield. Brooke sang a chime like a video game, then announced, "You've learned a new skill."

I also learned that my rate of exhaustion was the same, as I tired five times faster than everyone else. Theo's spells also took a toll of energy that, try as he did to explain, I didn't under-stand.

Theo and the prince bid us goodnight as we prepared for bed in the tent. I didn't want to leave the boys to sleep under the stars but saw the wisdom in separating. Brooke laid down and was out like a light bulb. Di whispered a spell and became as conscious as a rock.

As for me, well, I hated the woods. I couldn't stop thinking about the last time I spent a night in the woods with my fiancé. Sean had been taken and turned into a Haunting.

After everything Theo and I survived, I did not want to die in my sleep because of one night in the woods.

Chapter 12

TRAVELING

Do not travel alone.
Leave some evidence of your passing (such as bread
crumbs or lentils) in case you become lost.
Never venture from the path.

- Thesis of Adventures

THEO

At dawn, I knelt beside my sleeping princess and stroked her hair back from her cheek. Pansy winced, then the unexpected happened. Her normally short aura blasted outward ten centimeters. Far too fascinated by her aura, I was blind to the palm that came at my face. To say that she slapped me would be an understatement. Pansy smacked me back with the force to ward off a monster.

"Curses, Pansy!"

I rubbed my jaw. Her aura shrank back to normal as her eyes opened and widened with recognition.

"Oh! I'm sorry!"

"This is one sleeping princess who will *not* be woken with a kiss." I laughed. "What just happened?"

"I'm so sorry, I didn't know it was you!" She sat up and fingered the place she recently smacked.

"I hesitate to ask, yet for the sake of experimentation, will you do it again?"

"What?"

"Whatever it was that you just did," I urged, "do it again."

Confused, she tapped my face with her hand—a half-hearted slap. Her aura remained as short as ever.

I frowned. "No, it was different."

"Of course, the first time I planned to behead you."

"Is that how it works?" I gasped. Di said that abilities with multiple components would share a focus. Was danger its focus?

"What are you talking about?" Pansy rubbed her eyes.

Right, Pansy could only help me sort out my thoughts if I shared them with her. "Your aura spiked when I caught you off guard. Yes, I recall your aura spiked other times when I surprised you, and you nearly attacked me."

"I'm sorry," she groaned. "You should know better than to surprise me. It makes me go on alert and ready to fight back."

I grinned. "Indeed, that explains your short aura. You truly are marvelous, my flower. I need more examples to prove the theory, though it makes sense."

"I'm sorry, what?" she asked.

"I know you just woke up, yet will you theorize with me?" I glanced around the tent to Di. Yes, her aura was only a couple centimeters. Most people measured along the shorter side, except Magnanim's was longer. "The darkness of the auras shows when a person is in danger, correct? I think the length of the auras shows when a person *is* dangerous."

Pansy squished her tired eyebrows together. "How am I less dangerous now than I was five seconds ago? I could still behead you if I wanted."

"Allegedly, yes, you have all the same skills and opportunities to hurt me." That unhinged my theory, unless— "The lengths must be based on intentions, similar to the shades. An aura is darker when another person intends to hurt them, and in that way I have a bit of foresight. Likewise, if a person intends to hurt me, their aura becomes longer. How did I not see this before? It all makes sense now! Pansy, you wonderful woman—"

I smashed a kiss to her forehead rather than to list every insufficient compliment in Novel. All the while, Pansy sat dumbfounded.

"Supernaturals, Theo, you can see who's dangerous? You could spot assassins and traitors! That's really useful!"

I could pick out dangerous monsters with long auras, and collect confidants of those with short auras. Who would have guessed that The Trusted could know who to trust?

Then I remembered Pansy's aura when we first met.

"No," I muttered, "how can that be? Your aura previously fluctuated more than anyone I ever knew."

"Oh, yeah," she said, eyes shifting through memories that made her blush. "Maybe because I couldn't figure out if you were my next Haunting and I'd have to kill you."

"You had the capabilities to do so." I nodded, then frowned. "Hold on, you fluctuated a *lot*. You truly considered hurting me that often?"

She replied with a non-repentant shrug. "You paid a lot of attention to me, and that freaked me out."

"Then I finally convinced you of my love, and you became my shortest aura." I grinned.

"Yeah, that would explain it," she said with a stretch. "I'll take that kiss now."

My betrothed smiled, and Di made a gagging noise. Ignoring my sister, I wrapped my hand around Pansy's neck and pulled her close. I kept our kiss simple, a mere thought to the kiss we shared in Pansy's guest room.

All the same, Di complained, "Shall every morning require a gag-bag? Betrothed people are the embarrassment of society."

I laughed as we separated. "Are you jealous, priestess?"

Di grumbled something unintelligible and ushered me out of the tent. The only reason I was allowed inside was because I told Brooke of my desire to kiss Pansy awake. While Di gagged, Brooke had quietly beamed over our affection.

Now that Pansy was awake, however, I was removed that she could dress appropriately for our travels. As we planned to ride into Eimad this day, we would best enter with the pride of a Marquis and Marchioness. With that in mind, I joined Prince Alun at a small stream to wash myself. I shaved, shined my leather boots, and changed into my Fromm-blue doublet and cloak. Prince Alun wore his full uniform as a prince of Fairy.

We returned to the camp to finish packing our gear. The women took their dear sweet time to prepare for the day. I had my sleeping gear strapped to my horse and they still babbled inside the tent.

"We have only the tent now—" I turned, then did a double take to gape.

Pansy stood at the mouth of the tent, wearing a dress worthy of a princess. She bit her bottom lip and blushed adorably from my slack jaw.

The only other time I had seen Pansy in such a dress was during the masquerade. At that time, she had also worn running shoes and a feathered mask. To compare the two dresses was to compare glass to diamonds. This dress matched my grey-blue hue with gradients to darker shades at the ground and wrists. The bottom part poofed out to emphasize her thin waist, and her top was presented nicely with a wide dip. She wore the blue pansy necklace I gave her. Someone had also lent her a diamond bracelet and silver boots. Her hair was up in a bun with even more jewels.

I remained frozen in place as she approached me. Forget the forest and uneven ground, she moved as gracefully as a swan. She smiled at me, with her beautiful brown eyes enhanced with makeup.

"Merlin's beard," I breathed, "what did I do to deserve you?"

"Probably something awful," she teased.

"Indeed, I am full of awe."

She looked down in shyness and swished her dress back and forth. "It's surprisingly breathable. Di's birds made it flexible for running, but I feel like walking on eggshells. I don't want to touch the fabric and soil it with dirty hands."

Di cheered happily from the tent's entrance, "Something borrowed, something blue. Eimad's first impression of their Marchioness will be marvelous."

Pansy chewed on the inside of her cheek and muttered, "What would Oz think if he saw me now?"

I fingered her chin to turn her up to me. "I think he would be proud."

"Or concerned." She smirked. "Sure as Horror, he'd be surprised."

"As you never cease to surprise me," I said, and placed a light kiss to her lips.

Di walked by and gagged. "Who let Cupid out? O, it was I with that dress of Mother's creation. 'Thank you' would be an acceptable response."

"Thank you," I called to my sister without removing my eyes from Pansy's.

We cleared our campsite, and Di whispered some words to the ground to return life to the trampled plants. Pansy squirmed at first, though agreed to "Leave no evidence of your presence."

I listened to Di's words and watched her hand movements. With the magics of a wizard, my powers were less nature-based than those of the priests. Instead of concentrating on a connection with the god of whichever element I wanted to affect, my magic required knowledge of the words and hand motions, then precise and controlled execution of the spell. I was a novice, to say the least, though I felt secure with my shield projections from last night. I could remember the magic translations for "soil," "water," and "fire." "Air" was the easiest: *aura*. Di also said that *lugz*, meaning "light," was a word she frequently used.

We had a quick breakfast before setting off towards Eimad. Pansy was as squeamish as ever until Di plucked out a tune on her lyre. Her voice was young and sweet, singing words of springtime innocence, summer bliss, autumn Adventures, and winter wonder. Her birds added their voices of harmony after the first round. The sun shone above the horizon, and the forest chittered around us. It was a beautiful day.

Many of the trees were still in bloom and smelled fresh. I pulled on a wild tree-flower and passed it to Pansy. She twirled it between her fingers and smiled.

"Condemnation," she said, "I didn't think it was possible to enjoy a walk through the woods."

Indeed. We rode towards Eimad—my home. Unfortunately, Father and Greggory would not be waiting at Ruezdad to welcome us. Instead, my tyrannical half-brother would challenge me for the right to the duchy. Who knew what the duchess would do to aid him? Also, we had stolen abilities to find. Then, when this was all over, there was the daunting lifetime duty of taking care of Margen as its future duke.

I refilled my water canteen with a mere flick of my wrist and analyzed the short auras of those around me. I understood my ability. I had magic. I was surrounded by beloved supporters. Regardless of what lay ahead, for the first time, I thought that maybe I could challenge Oswald. Impossible things happened every day.

We crested a hill and stepped to an edge of the forest for a breathtaking viewpoint. The great Divining Mountain peaks built the northern horizon while the valley air glimmered with magic.

Near the edge of the Thornwood Forest, the trees broke way for a calm lake and a sprawling city. Lake Eimad shimmered blue. Ahead was the grand city. The buildings expanded from the capacity of the Outer Wall, overflowing with businesses and homes to the forest line. The city was slightly elevated on a gradual mound that peaked with a stone structure, large enough that its proud glory could be seen even from this distance: Ruezdad Castle.

The scene would have been picturesque if not for the dark, swirling clouds above Eimad. The eye of the storm glared down on Ruezdad.

Di gasped. "Verily, is that storm not akin to Greggory's ability?"

The storm had all the signs of the Wind Master. How? He was dead. How else would I have his ring?

"Come on." Prince Alun urged us down the hill. "We did not come all this way to be turned around by a little wind. My mother said we could find her in The Rook."

I frowned. The visiting queen should have been enjoying the safety and luxuries of Ruezdad's castle walls. Why was the queen in prison?

Chapter 13

HEROES

They are commonly youthful and orphaned.
If they are not orphaned, they are often disowned or abandoned.
They care for others despite their own cursed situations.

-   Thesis of Adventures

PANSY

We entered the city of Eimad and dismounted our horses to walk along cobblestone streets and buildings of wood and stone. Thank the Supernaturals. My gluteus maximus was sore. The city was built like a Regency town decorated with magic. We passed a saddle maker's shop that showed off leathers, and another stall advertising magic carpets and bottomless bags. Nearby, a blacksmith and buckle maker chatted over swords. Tools clanked and sparked by invisible hands. On Drury Lane, I smelled the sweetness of a muffin shop and the hay of a stable, which was loud with horse whinnying conversations. We walked by buildings and stalls of markets and craftsmen. It was similar enough to towns in Regency, Romance, that it almost felt familiar. Almost.

Unlike the limited Regency towns I knew, there was a layer of grunginess over Eimad. Buildings were damaged and vandalized. Paint peeled, wood splintered, stones chipped, then moss and mold grew in the cracks. Bits of trash and waste lined the streets, like it was too bothersome to remove the rubbish, so they simply pushed it aside.

There was a surprising amount of people sitting in the streets. Many of them wore handkerchiefs around their faces, as if to cover some disfigurement. One man's face was almost entirely covered, but the fur around his eyes was still visible. A woman had a large bow over her head as if to hide her cat ears. I recognized many of the same animal traits that diversified Aven, though people here tried to look as human as possible.

These weren't Hauntings trying to disguise their monstrosity. These were simply people trying to live normal lives. It made me sick to think how they might have been discriminated against and persecuted for no fault of their own.

This was a town in need of a Hero. Maybe a few.

Theo's eyes glistened as he surveyed his hometown. "What happened here?" he whispered. "How could so much change in one year? Over there was Lady Schuler's shop for curiosities. Around the corner should be Mrs. Kaufman's bookstore. What is that vandalism on Master Bahr's dueling arena? Di, do you know the meaning of that symbol?"

I followed Theo's gesture toward a particular two story, cylindrical building. Half of it was charred from an old fire. The other half was covered in red painted rows of "M"s and "W"s, like teeth. The symbol marked several other ransacked businesses and homes.

"We heard word of it in Aven," Di said. "It is the mark of the beast. Citizens with animalistic traits or features have been forced to wear it in Eimad."

"For others to harass them?" Theo guffawed. "That will be the first order to be subtracted. Whoever did this to Margen will—"

A kid darted in front of his horse. Miles reared on his hind legs as the kid scampered across the street. Di and Short Fuse went to calm Miles, allowing my fiancé to catch the boy by his arm before he slipped into an alley. The kid wore rags and bandages over furry, starved limbs.

"That was a foolish thing to do," Theo said to the boy. "Scaring Miles in that way was dangerous." The kid shrank back, guarded and scared. "I do not wish to hurt you. You look hungry. Would you like some food?" That got the kid's attention. Theo turned around to shuffle through his pack. He pulled out a chunk of wrapped boar from last night's dinner, then approached the kid again.

"Here," he said. "Please, eat. Share it with your family."

The boy shied farther into the alley.

"Or," Theo tried, "you can share it with a foe to make sure it is not poisoned. Then, perhaps, your foe will become your friend. Merlin knows, this city could use some kindness."

He left the meat outside of the alley, then returned to us. He didn't even look back to see that his offering was swiftly accepted. Instead, he searched his pack for more food to share with an old woman who hobbled out of a home.

Supernaturals, I loved that man. Sometimes, the world didn't deserve good men like him. But good men like him helped the world anyway.

We let our horses run to a nearby stable, then made our way to The Rook near the outskirts of Eimad. It looked every bit like a fifty foot version of the chess piece. Theo called the building a prison, but I didn't see any outside security other than two ogre-like soldiers standing outside the small and singular entrance. To my surprise, the small door required both ogre soldiers to pull it open. I asked Theo for our aura lightness every couple seconds, but he continued to assure our safety. Did this broken city somehow break his ability?

We stepped into The Rook's small stone lobby with a desk manned by a heavily armed minotaur. Architecturally, the room wasn't complicated—a wooden door on the opposite side, and a stone stairwell spiraled up and down on our left. The furnishings were also simple; the half man-beast sat at a desk and chair, and hundreds of crossbows lined the walls. They magically shifted their points according to our positions.

Condemnation, I knew this was a trap.

Prince Alun stepped forward, and a fifth of the crossbow arrows followed. "We were informed that Queen Alóvera is in residence."

"Of course." The minotaur bowed. The mild mannered beast boggled my mind. "We have been expecting you, Prince of Faenor, Marquis of Margen, and Priestess of Aven. You may all see her up the stairs in the maps room."

The royals barely acknowledged the direction before heading up the stairs. The minotaur jutted his hand forward to stop me. "All of you, except the common Horror."

"Pansy?" Di asked.

Theo frowned at the minotaur. "Excuse me? If she is refused, then I refuse to go."

The minotaur growled back, "*Queen Alóvera* is *waiting* for you."

Theo didn't budge.

"Theo," I whispered, "what's my shade?"

He forfeited his glaring contest to check my aura's shade. "It is light."

"Then you shouldn't make your aunt wait." I hated to separate, but I didn't think that keeping Theo would put me in the queen's good graces.

Theo still didn't budge as he contemplated his next move. "Very well," he said, taking my hand and pressing a quick kiss to the back of it. "I shall return at the earliest convenience."

I tried to smile and put on a brave face as the royals and Brooke turned away and disappeared up the stairwell. When their steps faded into silence, I folded my arms and tried my own staring contest with the half-man half-bull.

"So, I sit here and wait?" I asked.

"Not exactly," he said. "You have your own meeting to attend."

Before I could ask what he meant, he let out a great huff of air and blew out all the torches in the room. Two thick hands grabbed my arms and lifted me off my feet. Judging by the shifting weight of my handler, he carried me as I failed to struggle free. I screamed, though more from strategy than terror. Could Theo hear me?

I paused for breath and listened to the click-clomp of hooves against wood. We followed the click-clomps into another room only a few feet away. My friends didn't seem to hear my screams. Then, a thick door slammed shut, sealing my fate. The sound of hooves muffled with a whoosh of fabric. The thick hands set my feet down, and my last kick attempt made me stumble.

Fire flickered as a torch was lit, then another. I winced from the sudden light, dim as the fires were. Blinking hard, I struggled to focus on the man who stood with his back to me.

For a brief second, I thought it was Theo. That thought was quickly dismissed. This man was bigger, a couple inches taller than Theo's six feet, and his heavy muscles built him wider. His long, dark hair was combed neatly back into a low ponytail. He wore a blue cloak over his shoulders with gold embroidery along the seams. Squinting, I recognized the emblem of a horse face within the folds.

A horse. Was this Theo's dad, the Duke of Margen, and my future father-in-law? I thought he was missing. Could he be Oswald or Dunstan?

My insides squirmed. Everything about the man's posture screamed "brooding monster." I was sure he would turn around and spring at me before I could escape. If the duke turned out to be a vampire, would Theo forgive me if I decapitated him?

I tried to tap into my speed ability. Nothing happened. What the horror?

The man turned around, and I found myself staring at an older version of Theo. His age confirmed that this was Duke Konrad Fromm and not one of Theo's younger brothers. Theo and his dad shared the same narrow face and sharp jawline, the same low eyebrows and straight nose. I realized Theo's easy smile did wonders to his face compared to the sternness of the man before me. The duke's forehead and mouth were bulbous like Di's, and his slightly receding hair was striped with grey above his ears. His eyes were probably the biggest difference. Compared to Theo's blue-green, Duke Fromm's were solid sapphire blue.

Was this how Theo would look in twenty-five years? Not bad.

Unsure how to greet a duke, I said a simple, "Duke Fromm?" and bent over in a bow without breaking eye contact. "We heard you were missing."

Someone snickered from the shadows. "Don't women generally curtsy?"

My eyes followed the voice to find another man leaning against the wall. He was tall and wore a long grey trench coat, his face partly hidden by a matching fedora. I recognized him all the same.

"Mr. E!" I breathed with relief to recognize the Mystery detective in this strange meeting. Jonathaniel Mystery was a difficult man to describe, since I knew so little about him, even after he helped me defeat a poltergeist and revealed his full name. I didn't know exactly how old he was, but guessed he was in his late forties, with his feather-greyed hair and weathered features.

My shout earned a surprised stare from the man in the horse cloak.

"Yes," he said. "Mr. John said you were acquainted."

The Mystery stepped forward from the shadows and gestured from me to the other man. "Ms. Finster, may I introduce you to Duke Konrad Fromm, the Horse, of Margen? Regarding his MIA status, his lordship has been in hiding, working behind the curtain to aid the rebellion against Lord Oswald's tyranny."

The duke spared me a small eyebrow raise, then he inhaled a long and deep breath, like he took in my very essence. After what felt like five minutes, he released it with a slow sigh, all the while, holding his gaze on me.

"Proclaim your name, title, and from whence you hail." He spoke in commands, as if I didn't have the option to remain silent. Otherwise, his voice was surprisingly similar to Theo's. He had a harsher, yet more proper accent, like if Theo never went to Contemporary, Romance, and instead spent his days debating politics and tea brands.

"Um, hello," I said in my attempt to be formal. I fumbled into a curtsy, trying my best for a half-decent impression to my future father-in-law. "My name's Pansy Finster. I was born and raised in Horror. I have a paramedical certification from Heartford University, and...I'm in love with your son, Theo."

"Yes, I heard as much," the duke said with a tone like he spoke to a lower business competitor. "What in your mind qualifies you to marry Lord Theodor of Margen?"

"Uh—what?" I stammered.

"I do not like to repeat myself," the duke snapped, "and you will do well to address me properly."

"Sorry, Duke Fromm," I said quickly, "but I don't understand your question."

He huffed. "You have no family, no land, and no dowry. Your education has been public and lacking. Your posture is dreary and manners are atrocious. Other than your first Adventure together, I fail to see what attracts my son to you. Any noble Fantastic would better suit Theodor and the position of Marchioness than a common Horror. So I repeat my question: what qualifies you to wed Theodor, the Trusted, Marquis and rightful heir to the Margen Duchy?"

I stood there, blinking, unsure how to respond. Supernaturals, this man made Mr. E's interrogations feel like jokes! He uncovered my secret insecurities, then put them in the spotlight. I wanted to crawl to him with feeble promises to do better.

"Duke Fromm," Mr. E interjected, "can I speak for Ms. Finster?"

Someday, the Mystery would say something that wouldn't surprise me. Today was not that day.

The duke nodded curtly and Mr. E continued. "I had the enlightening experience to work beside Ms. Finster during a Case that involved Horror's Supernaturals. I witnessed her skills to lead others, including the foolish and disbelieving, through dire circumstances. How many people do you know have sound minds even in distress? Many may be capable of making difficult decisions, but how many will act on them? Are you aware that Ms. Finster lives by a strict moral code? While it might be a little strange, it serves her well against dangers. In the least," he concluded, "how will you dissuade Lord Fromm's affections for her? You know that he persisted to pursue her despite my warnings? Perhaps he somehow knew he could trust her with his life as Ms. Finster went alone to sacrifice herself to rescue him."

I didn't know whether to gape or blush from Mr. E's recommendation. I probably did both.

Duke Fromm's jaw twitched before his eyes slid slowly to me. "A referral from Mr. John is not one to slight. I will take it into consideration."

"Thank you," I said, mostly to Mr. E.

The duke closed his eyes and rubbed the bridge of his nose. "As my second born, Theodor was allowed to live and marry for less political importance. Still, a foreign commoner is about as low as he can go. Now, he is Margen's best option for an honest heir. The young man has held true to his values and works hard for good purposes. As his father, I instilled what confidence I could in him. Unfortunately, his ability and combat skills were not tokens to boast."

I wanted to argue that his ability wasn't useless and explain his new wizardry magic. Besides that, his political knowledge and practice made him a perfect candidate. Couldn't he see how amazing Theo was?

"Furthermore," Duke Fromm continued, "Theodor can be hard on himself. By electing to marry a woman below his station, I feared he thought himself unworthy of noble blood. The only benefit of your union is that perhaps your peasantry status will boost the morale of Margen's working classes."

Um, ouch? Was I allowed to be offended by that? Since the duke hadn't asked a question, I remained silent.

The duke stepped around his minotaur guard until he came within reach. "I chose to speak to you alone simply to give you a warning. Listen closely and do not forget, because this is the only warning you will receive." He leaned forward, and his blue eyes bore into my brown, like an ocean beating on a rock. I couldn't help but recognize his power. Not the power of his ability, but his power and strength to rule and dictate. "If you do not serve your purpose properly as his wife and as

Marchioness, I will make you wish that you never stepped foot on this continent, little Horror."

I gulped down a heavy load of saliva and wondered why this man even had guards.

Chapter 14

FAIRIES

They are named for their fairness in beauty, not equality. Adventures often involve some element of magic, though fairies specifically are not required for Adventures in the land of Fairy.

-   Thesis of Adventures

THEO

My mind tickled with a thought that Pansy was in danger. Her aura had been light. Then why did I feel this sense of intense intimidation connected to her? I excused myself from my aunt's presence as gracefully as possible, then ran back to the foyer. Pansy was gone. I panicked.

"Pansy? Pansy!"

A shrill voice responded, "It's about time you returned to Margen." I turned upward towards the voice and winced at the bright torch-fire light.

"Careful, Theo," the voice said. "I've heard staring at a fire can blind you. Would you believe me if I said I'm naturally this bright?"

Hold on, I knew that squeaky voice and pompous attitude. "Lieutenant Greenblade!"

Shielding my eyes from the torch's light, I looked again for the speaker. Hovering above me was a little person with wings as large as his eight centimeter body. He wore green leaves for clothing that matched his bright dragonfly wings, and also wore a needle-thin sword at his belt. He fluttered down to my shoulder, then bowed to one knee.

"Lord Theo," the fairy said, "welcome back to Eimad."

"Thank you. It is good to see you again, though where is—"

"Aww." He fluttered up and posed, mocking innocence. "You missed me? I guess I'll forgive you for your absence as long as you reinstate my previous position as your personal guard."

I grinned. "Of course. I will have no one else."

"Yes!" The lieutenant flipped. "As fun as it was to boast about guarding the most helpless Fromm, it'll be far more impressive to say I guard the marquis."

"Greenblade," I said, staring him down, "I am hardly helpless."

He put his hands on his hips and bent perpendicular. "Are you sure? You were pretty helpless while you stumbled into the room like a lost butterfly."

"Speaking of which," I said, "where is Pansy?"

"By Pansy, I assume you mean the Horror girl, and not a little flower with black spots."

I blinked and waited for him to answer my question.

"I see you still have no sense of humor," the fairy pouted. "Your intended is meeting her future father-in-law."

"Pansy is with Father? The duke is here?"

"Do you have a father who isn't the duke?"

"What? No, I thought the duke was missing."

"Not missing, only hiding. He was cursed to forever keep his horse form, but, if you remember, The Rook has—"

"Magic negators," I finished for him. The Rook was originally built as an armory and command station for soldiers.

Then, rooms were created that negated magics or abilities to hold powerful prisoners.

Thus, my father hid in those rooms to avoid his curse.

Just as I considered searching The Rook one room at a time, the door opened. A royal middle-aged man stepped through the door. His curse instantly returned him to the form of a thorough-bred as he left the room that dispelled abilities.

"Father!"

He was followed by the minotaur guard, then Pansy and Mr. John—or Mr. E, as Pansy called him. I called to my betrothed and our Mystery friend, grinning to see familiar faces.

Pansy started to run to me. She hesitated and tensed with confusion as her eyes caught something to my side.

"By your expression," the fairy lieutenant squeaked, "I gather you've never seen a fairy before. Prepare to be disappointed if you meet another. I'm as good as it gets."

Pansy stepped closer, and I smirked. "Allow m

e to introduce you to Lieutenant Greenblade, my personal guard. As a fairy, the best way to communicate with them is with flattery. Regrettably, it goes straight to their heads."

"What was that, young lord?" the fairy squeaked.

"A mere comment to your intelligence," I said with my best politician's smile.

"Intelligence! At last, someone with enough brains to know who has the brains!"

I winked at Pansy, and she pressed her lips thin to suppress her smile.

Father shook his mane. "The longer you ignore me, the more you demonstrate how this woman is just a distraction from important matters."

"Father, I—"

"Save it," he said, then slowly approached me. "So, it has come to this. Dunstan was the first to fall, disowned as a renegade. Oswald sought after dark magics, then Greggory…"

I almost missed my father's pinched mouth—a subtle sign of a stressed horse.

Cautious, I asked, "What happened to Greggory? Di said he went searching for you, yet here you are. I assumed he was killed when his ring appeared; however, his ability storms above the city."

"I had hoped," the duke said, "the news of Greggory's death was false. As foreboding as those storm clouds are, they gave me hope that he still lived. I tried to send word to him about my situation, yet could not penetrate Oswald's security. If Greggory just waited a little longer…" He stomped his hoof. "Now, Margen must rely on my gutless son, or enter war from either Dunstan or Oswald's influence."

Pansy opened her mouth to defend me, though I sent her a pleading look to hold it. Arguing with the duke would disfavor her.

Still, he noticed the quarrel on the tip of her tongue, and his ears lowered back. A bad sign.

"A marriage," Father said, "to Princess Anwen will prove more beneficial."

I frowned. "Greggory's betrothed?"

"Indeed. Her position in Middle Novel will solidify yours here."

The cold logic was true. She was already trained and prepared for the title of marchioness. As an elven princess of Middle Novel, she had rightful authority and influence with diplomats throughout the northern kingdom. She was also skilled with the longbow and quarterstaff. Her name translated as "beautiful," and beauty had power and influence of its own.

Except, I also knew her to be obtuse. With an obsession to be known for more than her beauty, she flowered her language with complicated words, and at times used them incorrectly. I remembered a frustrating conversation of her discrediting everyone's opinions with her decorated diction. I told her, "Your floccinaucinihilipilification inspires hippopotomonstrosesquippedaliophobia." I counted it as one of my most successful sentences as she snapped her mouth shut and spoke with monosyllabic words for the rest of the evening.

However, the most important reason I could never marry Princess Anwen was the simple fact that she was not Pansy. I did not love her, and I doubted the possibility of ever loving anyone as much as I loved Pansy.

"Theo?" Pansy asked, her small voice melting any cold logic with tender humanity. "Are you actually considering it?"

"It" was such a vague word. What was I considering?

I hesitated, and Pansy's expression sank.

Before I could question her, Father spoke. "Any wedding ceremonies will need to be postponed until after Ruezdad is secured. Supposing the Royal Chapel has not been desecrated, tradition holds ceremonies of noble marriage and title promotions within that sacred building. I heard you restored Divinity, yet you have much to prove to me and our citizens before gaining the title. You must first stake your claim on Eimad's people, and cleanse Margen."

"Yes, Father," I said, still trying to deduce why Pansy was upset with me. The worst case scenario imagined Pansy realizing I was not worth the trials I put her through, then I would be doomed to wed the irritating Princess Anwen. Hold on, did Father say I needed to cleanse all of Margen before earning my right to become marquis and marry Pansy? How long would that take?

The duke stepped forward and dipped his long face towards the sword at my hip. "You and Godiva vanquished the giant, Magnanim? That is quite the feat, considering your fighting record."

I looked up, surprised. Was there a hint of pride in his words? He usually reserved that tone for Greggory.

He continued. "I suggest you use that reputation and every resource at your disposal to reclaim Ruezdad from Oswald. He and your stepmother have made a mess of our home."

Pansy muttered darkly, "We heard."

"What exactly have you heard?" Mr. John stepped forward, pulled out his favorite little notepad, and flipped through its pages. "Will your rumors match ours?"

I detailed what little we knew. The Mystery detective simply nodded while Father said, "Mr. John came at my request to help solve the riddle of the disappearing abilities. Mr. John believes that Duchess Abadda, The Lovely, has developed her ability to somehow extract people's abilities."

"Her ability?" I asked. "How does her beauty translate into extracting abilities?"

"Her ability was never as simple as that." Father harrumphed.

Mr. John asked, "Do you know how she received her beauty? Was it a naturally-born youthfulness? Then why did she sometimes look older? Why steal away young women?"

My mouth and eyes opened as the pieces fell into place.

"She steals her beauty from others," Father confirmed. "She absorbs it, then kills her prey. I could hardly believe it even when I caught her in the act. That was at the beginning of the new year. Since then, she has revealed her true wickedness."

I gaped, disgusted and horrified. She hid her true ability from us for all these years.

"So," Pansy slurred, "she's a witch. A bad one, like those in Horror."

"The worst," the duke said. "I was her unwilling test subject, and it backfired, cursing me to remain in horse form unless I stand in one of The Rook's rooms that negates abilities. We have reason to believe that her purpose in extracting abilities was to help Oswald abolish his."

"Wait a second," Pansy asked, raising a hand as if she was a student asking for permission to speak. "Stealing abilities, cursing you with yours—you say she did everything because Oswald asked her to *remove* his ability?"

Father gave her a flat stare. "I would not expect you to know of a mother's love for her son. Two years ago, Oswald showed interest in a lady and accidentally maimed her face with his fire breath. He despised his ability ever since and wished to learn magic instead."

"A mother's love," I scoffed. Oswald had her twisted around his greedy finger. "What form of magic has he sought?"

Father sighed. "We are unsure. Several magicians have been called into Ruezdad, never to return. We have struggled to gather our loyalists as our most capable warriors disappear in the night. After two months of recruiting, we hope to have enough strength to battle against Ruezdad within a week. However, before you plan to enter the castle, you must first see the new guards."

He gestured for us to follow him through the door to a training room. There were a few soldiers inside, sharpening and inspecting the tools. On the far side, a birdman sparred with a minotaur. As soon as we stepped through the door, all light disappeared.

Gasps, squeaks, and squeals echoed through the room. I blinked, though my eyes saw only the silhouettes of auras in blackness.

The scenario was strangely familiar.

"How do you have a power outage with torches?" Pansy muttered nearby.

The sun was past the zenith, though none of the windows illuminated us. A normal blackout would not leave us in such darkness. My father's horse aura stood to the side, ears flicking back and forth, speaking over the clamoring knights, and commanding everyone to remain calm.

I found Pansy's hand by the shortness of her aura. I clutched her fingers between mine, reassured by her closeness. "You know how I favor your brother's quote, 'It is never just a power-outage?'"

"Yeah?" she asked, her aura silhouette glancing around nervously.

"Other than our fond memories of a poltergeist chasing us in the dark, Dunstan is another reason why 'It is never just a power-outage.'"

"Your brother's here?" she gasped.

"Undoubtedly."

I wondered how my brother managed to extinguish even daylight, though abilities worked under different sciences than magic.

"Can you still see our auras?" Pansy asked.

"Yes, though—"

"Theodor," Father cut me off, "I hear light footsteps behind you. The Night Terror is here."

As if on cue, a cold, deep voice whispered a couple meters away, "As grand as it sounds, I never thought that title was appropriate for me."

Father stomped his hoof. "You killed dozens of citizens during your first raid in Vluz! Then you spread fear across Fantasy!"

"It's not my fault people are afraid of the dark."

I looked about the room, sure that he was inside. Our auras were dangerously dark. The only differences in shades I noticed were that Father's and my own were darker than the rest. I searched for one that was light, assuming Dunstan was safe. There were several auras from the soldiers in the room, and I was unable to determine if one was Dunstan.

What about length? I searched for him by determining the longest aura in the room. A long shadow moved within the darkness.

"Stuck as a horse, Father?" Dunstan chided. "Like a horse in a stable with nowhere to go. I honestly don't care to be marquis, but sheer common sense makes me a better heir."

"Theodor is older," the duke said. I cringed that Father saw my age as my best qualification.

Dunstan laughed. "Who will the people follow? A man with a useless ability, who spent the majority of these last six years outside the kingdom, filling his head with Romance and textbooks? How would he protect Margen? He can't fight to save his life—let alone the people's! These last three years, I traveled across Fantasy and beyond. Everyone knows my name and cowers before me. Under my rule, Margen won't be a duchy to someone else's kingdom."

"You would wage war," Father brayed, "to satisfy your pride? The people trust Theodor, and so must I."

"You're a blind fool!" Dunstan spat. "You fail to see the possibilities as you fail to see me now."

The long shadow stopped circling us, and Father's aura darkened.

"No!" I shouted, surprising even myself. I had not meant to burst out, though Father's plunge frightened me too much to stand in silence. The duke's aura remained dark. Could I dilute Dunstan's anger with confusion? "I can see you now."

In the stunned silence that followed, Dunstan shuffled uneasily. "I'll call your bluff."

It was my turn to chuckle, and I squeezed Pansy's hand for support. "Your aura is dark," I said. "No wonder you seemed invisible before. All this time, I thought your ability to darken your surroundings also negated my ability to see your aura. However, compared to the black spot of a poltergeist, you are still human."

"A polter—" My brother shuffled again. "Those rumors were *true*? You've strengthened your ability then."

"Not exactly," I said. "I understand it more. Although—"

I cut off as the light returned, bright as ever. The fires flickered as if they never died. The sudden brightness of the room momentarily blinded me. I blinked a couple times, hoping to quickly adjust my vision.

"I guess there's no use hiding if you can see me." Dunstan the Night Terror stood at the doorway. His aura was a lighter shade, though just as long as before.

If I thought Di had matured during my absence, Dunstan had antiquated. The last time I saw him was the summer before his fifteenth birthday, the last birthday he spent titled as The Night Shade. Now, I had to remind myself that he was only eighteen years old and titled The Night Terror. Life as a vagabond had been merciless. His face was that of a man with experiences beyond his age. Every feature was worn and haggard, though the faded stains and neatly trimmed beard testified of a conscious effort to clean himself before returning to Eimad.

He smirked. "Long time no see. And this is the bride? The one they say treads the paths Adventurers fear? She, I think, is the intruder here. Fantasy doesn't know her." He approached Pansy on silent feet, then loomed over her to whisper, "I know the paths you tread and I fear nothing."

Pansy straightened, then blurred. She became stationary again behind Dunstan, holding his hands behind his back in an arm lock and her Vulgur Knife to his neck.

"You want to bet on that?" she asked.

My eyes widened at her courage. Even Father was surprised, and Dunstan rocked off balance by her brazen confidence.

Yes, she would do quite well as a duchess.

Dunstan smiled. "Ohh, sexy. Theo, how did you catch a girl like this? Are you his dominatrix? What's your name again, babe?"

Pansy growled and pressed her knife into his skin until a thin line of blood appeared.

"Agh-ow!" Dunstan squirmed. "Girl, if you wanted to dance, you only had to say so!"

The room became pitch black again. My unadjusted eyes lost Dunstan's aura. Pansy yelped in a quick scuffle. The lights returned and we all blinked in the sudden light. Dunstan was gone.

"Where did he go?" I asked.

Father grumbled, "Probably to terrorize more people."

I sighed heavily. I had hoped to deal with Dunstan after securing Ruezdad and Eimad. Of course, my incommodious little brother never did anything according to my plans.

Pansy's face shifted into stern determination, as if she was at the height of a Haunting. "I'll check ahead," she said, then blurred with her ability.

I tapped into my speed ability, then ran around the room. I kicked open a closet door and poked my head in to make sure Theo's brother wasn't hiding inside. The duke wanted me to prove my worth as a Fantastic? Fine. I had an ability now, and using it to catch Dunstan would even my odds.

My heart tore a little to remember Theo's pause as he considered marriage to the princess. I couldn't even remember her name, but I wanted to spit it out. I hated how the idea of her made me feel—jealous, insecure, unworthy. Theo deserved a princess. He deserved someone who knew how to rule. He deserved a Fantastic.

With a thorough search of the room's perimeter, I concluded that Dunstan wasn't in the room. I walked back through the middle and felt a slight bend in the floor beneath me. I stood near the edge of a large rug and wondered if it was the fabric giving way, or something else. I tested the step behind myself, which seemed more firm, then stepped ahead. The rug sank through the floor. I rocked back, but the quick shift caused my back foot to snap through the floor's edge.

While experimenting with my ability, I discovered that people and objects could only move or be moved by my enhanced speed if I put direct force to them. My weight was direct gravitational force to the rug and the absence of floor beneath it. The rug slipped and crashed downward. I tried to reach up and grab something—anything—but the rug billowed around me and swallowed me whole.

My left ankle cracked on the basement floor. Weakened floorboards collapsed when my body hit. Splintering wood ripped through the rug, grazing my side and arms as I fell farther. My screams were muffled by a cacophony of crashing wood.

My cracked talus became fractured as it met stone. The rest of my body crumpled and the rug clamped shut around me. It served as a thick blanket covering as splintered wood rained on me. Eventually, the sprinkling of debris settled.

My left foot, shoulder, and hip screamed at me as I army crawled forward, feeling for the rug opening. I scrambled in the dark and rippling folds of the rug for a frustrating minute before breaking through.

A haze of dust and wood shavings lingered about the pile of wooden rubble like a halo. I had landed in a dark basement room. Anything else was difficult to describe between the dim light from above and the haze. I cautiously untapped my speed. People shouted from above.

Chapter 15

HAPPINESS IS EARNED:

From understanding another person
From loving another person
Not from magic.

- *Thesis of Adventures*

THEO

One second, Pansy was beside me, holding me back so she could scope the room. The next second she was gone…along with half of the room. A gaping hole replaced the rug in the middle, and the sounds came after like thunder. Actually, thunder was an apt description of the rumbling chaos that followed. A high pitched shout sent chills up my spine. I never heard Pansy scream for help before.

"Pansy!" I shouted back. "What happened? Where did she go?"

Even as I shouted, the floors below collapsed with creaks and crashes. After the final echo dissipated to smoke, a miserable cough replied from far below.

"I'm down here," Pansy moaned.

She fell more than one floor! Nearing the edge of the hole, I looked down into the darkness. I leaned forward, then retreated as the wood creaked beneath me.

"Pansy!" my voice echoed below. "Are you hurt? Can you see where you are?"

"I broke my ankle," she said. "Pain level seven. My left side feels like I jumped from a napper van, but as a whole is only a three. I can't see much around me. The dust and debris is still hazy and it's too dark. The walls and floor feel like stone… There's a small wooden door on this side."

"Are you in the dungeons?" I rocked back as the facts hit me. "Curses, are you alright? You fell over a dozen meters!"

A fearful delay worried my heart before she asked, "Do I have any cellmates down here?"

I paused. Good question. "I hope not."

"You hope not?" she shrieked. "What's that supposed to mean?"

It meant that we only kept the worst of our criminals in The Rook dungeons. When I visited Eimad last summer, there was only one convict still down there.

"Do you have any weapons on you?" I asked.

"I have my emergency pack," she shouted up to me. "Who else is down here?"

"Try to find your way out, and be careful! Last I heard, we kept a Berserker Orc down there. I am on my way."

"Theo?" she shrieked.

I wanted to say more, except my knowledge was outdated. Urzog could be dead and his cell taken by someone else with different skills and weaknesses. No information was better than wrong information. Knowing Pansy, now she would prepare for anything and everything.

"Father," I asked, "is Urzog still down there?"

The duke's ears flipped back and forth with worry. "No. Urzog completed his life sentence in the oubliette maze." Before I could breathe with relief, he continued. "However, a goblin stole the feet of Tom, the Swift, and sewed them to himself. With the feet of swiftness, he gathered a fearsome army within a matter of days. The only way we caught him was by challenging him to a race where the finish line was in a trap. We were unable to remove his feet, though."

My skin grew cold.

"Lieutenant Greenblade," I said, "use your dimming ability to fly down. Protect Pansy with your life."

"Yes, my lord." The fairy saluted me and zipped down the hole without a glow.

Father huffed. "Of all people, an accomplished Horror with enhanced speed is the only person I would wager against that goblin. Still, you did well to send Lieutenant Greenblade to her. He knows of our resident and his small stealth will assist her escape from that dark labyrinth. Come, the official entrance is this way. Let us hope that Dunstan has not set more traps."

I followed him and tried to quiet my internal screams for Pansy's welfare.

Prince Alun and Brooke barged into the room from a side door.

"Duke Konrad," the prince said, half out of breath. "We came as soon as we heard! Dunstan the Night Terror is here?"

"Father," I asked, "what exactly happened with Dunstan? All I know is that three years ago he and some soldiers destroyed a town near Vluz."

Father snorted. "You know as much as the rest of us. He fled without explanation when I sent a company to collect him. Either way, Dunstan has become what the rumors said—a renegade, stooping low enough to use hostages and threaten children to achieve his own goals. Whatever they may be."

We entered the hallway and stopped. Dunstan waited for us at the end.

"My trap only caught your woman?" He grunted and stretched as a waking man. "Ah, and the Sci-Fian prince is here. You know, I really don't get what you see in that place."

"You!"

We all turned towards Brooke, who stared wide-eyed and angry at Dunstan.

"Me?" Dunstan asked.

"Yeah, you!" she shouted. "You almost killed my dad!"

Dunstan raised a bored eyebrow. "You'll need to be more specific. I've almost killed lots of people."

"You *bet*, you steaming punk! You were supposed to be banished to space!"

"Obviously, I got away," Dunstan said with a shrug.

I growled, "Then get out of *our* way, and we can discuss this later. Margen has bigger problems right now, and Pansy needs help."

"Hey, wait." Brooke blinked and searched the room. "Where's Pansy?"

"Pansy?" Dunstan scoffed. "Seriously? Your woman's name is Pansy? I don't know if that's the most fitting or ironic thing I've ever heard. Maybe it's ironic, considering the way she grabbed me from behind and growled in my ear—"

"How *dare* you—"

"Ooh," Dunstan hooted. "Looks like I found a nerve. I didn't know you had one. That should make this interesting. I challenge your right to the duchy. Right here. Right now."

Curse him. This was a waste of time when I needed to reach Pansy.

I forced myself to take a couple calming breaths and analyzed his light aura. It was long, though only six centimeters. Still a little unsure about the meaning, I took a gamble. I drew Videliz from its scabbard, only to set it out of reach. "I do not want to fight you, Dunstan. Nor do I believe that you want to kill me."

He shrugged. "No, not really. But I doubt you're strong enough to go against Oswald even with your fascinating woman. I figured I'd take you out as a mercy."

I gulped heavily. I wanted to rescue Pansy. Instead, I was stuck staring down the hall at my younger brother.

I was four floors underground and completely alone. I sat in my stony prison, too shocked and bruised to move. My body ached, but my thoughts weighed heavier and offered no motivation to do more than breathe. Even that was difficult as the dust settled and stuck in the muggy air.

A soft fluttering descended from the hole. I caught the brief shadow of a small bug-like person flying down to me from the light above. As the dulled fairy descended, the hole in my ceiling shrank with a groan.

The hole was repairing itself!

"Curse The Rook and its security enchantments!" the fairy squeaked as he dove faster. The hole closed behind him, and the new ceiling engulfed my cell in darkness. Only a faint fire light filtered through the door's barred window to the hallway beyond.

"Miss, can you stand?" the fairy whispered.

"Greenblade? Why are we whispering?"

"Theo was misinformed, the silly boy. There's no brutish orc, but a feisty goblin down here," he said. "Use your ability and keep an eye out while I place us."

"What kind of goblin? And what do you mean, place us? How big is this dungeon?"

"Mr. Goblin's fast—possibly faster than you, if I dare say. We fairies sometimes come down here to play in the maze and tease Mr. Goblin. Serves him right for the armies of murderous goblins he used to plunder across Margen. Now, speed!"

At those words, I tapped into my ability and caught movement behind the door's barred window. The creature was fast even with my enhanced speed as it ducked out of sight. Watching its hiding place, I reached under my dress to my emergency pack tied around my thigh. As I did, the goblin behind the door made an impish snicker.

"Perverted crap," I muttered, searching for an appropriate weapon. If my opponent was faster than I was with my ability, I likely wouldn't hit it with my magical crossbow. The more time I spent in Fairy, the more I realized why they didn't use guns to fight and protect. I pulled out my knife from Professor Vieseth.

I grasped the magically-enhanced blade firmly in my hand. Oz taught me well enough how to fight with a blade, and Prince Alun showed me the basics of Vulgur's magical uses. Pressing a button on the handle sent either a bolt or beam of electricity from the blade.

In case the goblin tried to spy on me again, I hid to the side of the door. Greenblade slowly flew through the window to scope our surroundings. He was a fast flier, but still slow compared to my enhanced speed. The fairy dulled his natural fairy light to camouflage into the darkness of the dungeon.

As I waited for the lieutenant to return, I made myself a splint. I chose two sturdy pieces of the wood debris to sandwich my broken ankle all the way up to my knee. Using the first-aid kit in my emergency pack, I wrapped gauze around it like a mummy. It held my weight enough to let me limp across the room and back.

Then I worked on my dress. I prayed Di would forgive me as I cut off the puffy layers underneath. It pained me to mutilate the beautiful gown, but it was already a mess from the fall. The layers and length would only cause problems for my escape.

I undid my hair, snapping the band around my wrist and hooking it with the pins and barrettes. Next, I grabbed at the dirt and mold between the dungeon stones to smear it across my dress. A couple wood splinters scratched against my hands. At one point, I wasn't sure if I smeared grime or blood over myself.

I was in the dark, covered in blood and dirt, supported by rushed first-aid, and wearing a torn up dress. I was a Horror in her natural element.

Eventually, the fairy lieutenant returned to my cell, and I tapped out of my speed.

"Marchioness," he addressed me, and I couldn't help but laugh at the irony of my future title and current situation. He paused for a moment to look over my handiwork. "Well, someone knows how to set fashion statements."

I lifted an eyebrow. "What did you find?"

"Someone planned this," he said. "Probably Dunstan, that conniving little trickster. All the doors in the dungeons have been unlocked except the exiting hatches. I fear Mr. Goblin is waiting for us to lead him out of this maze. As soon as we leave this room, the nasty goblin will give chase on the stolen feet of Tom, the Swift. He is invisibly fast and the worst of his murderous kind."

"Okay," I said, "tell me everything you know about this creature." The more I knew, the better I could fight it.

The hallway lights vanished. I always wondered how my younger brother's ability worked scientifically. As if Dunstan flipped the switch of the sun itself, all window light evaporated. How? Science explained that darkness was not created—it was just the absence of light—yet Dunstan's ability seemingly created darkness.

"Dunstan," I called, hoping to locate him by his voice while my eyes adjusted, "why did you attack that town?"

He scoffed. "Does it matter? The truth didn't save me then, it won't save me now, after all these years. You can't change the past. You can't bring all those people back. I was tricked into doing what I thought was best."

I whispered "*Rodegad*" to project a shield before me. I kept my eyes forward, focused on the last place I saw Dunstan's aura. I leapt to the side as a dark aura punched at me. His fist waved past my face, emanating heat. Hold on—heat? Was that from Dunstan? How?

"Ah," he mused, "and here I hoped to make it quick and painless for you."

"Did you miss me, Dunstan?" I jeered, and stepped away. I knew he could still sense me from his blackout training.

To my unadjusted eyes, everything was black as a moonless night save for the safe auras of Prince Alun, Father, and Brooke. They huddled together against the wall, a safe distance from our duel.

I concentrated on my vision and whispered "*Lugz*." No light appeared. His ability negated all magic light, though not my ability to see auras. My own waved between dark and darker. With new understanding of the lengths, I noticed the slight decreases in Dunstan's aura as my own lightened.

"You do not want to do this," I said.

"What makes you say that?" Dunstan asked. His voice was closer than before. Distances were difficult to gauge in the dark.

"I learned the purpose for my auras," I said. "They warn me of danger, and I see your intent on killing me wavers."

"Congratulations!" Dunstan said with exaggerated praise. "Your ability isn't completely useless! Funny, it's still misleading. My intent on killing you is sure. I'm simply weighing my options on *how* to kill you. Tell me, Theodor, what does your aura say about my intent to kill you now?"

My aura blackened. I leapt to the side and landed hard on the ground. Another foray of fists jabbed at me. One grazed my shoulder, burning my left sleeve and bruising my arm. Unbidden shouts of pain escaped my lips as the heat burned my skin. How did Dunstan have fire? Had he obtained magic also?

His shadow ran around me to attack from another angle. Instinctively, I threw my wand hand out and cried, "*Rodegad!*" I could only imagine the translucent blue shield that formed before me in the darkness. The solid weight burdened my hand as multiple punches slammed into my new barrier. My shield sizzled as if struck by a hot iron.

"You learned magic!" Dunstan said. I smiled at the astonishment in his voice.

"As did you?" I asked.

"Hardly," Dunstan laughed. "The more powerful the ability, the harder it is to learn magic. You might have learned magic with your weak ability, but I learned how to turn my ability into an attack."

"You could have learned how to use it for good," I said, switching my shield to my other hand and freeing my wand hand.

Dunstan scoffed. "Now, there's an idea. Only you, Theo, would think there's a positive to absorbing light. That's like finding a silver lining in a mushroom cloud."

Before I could respond, Dunstan swung his fiery fists again.

Greenblade counted down to zero and I tapped into my speed ability. Standing was a balancing act on my left ankle splint, but I stepped to the door and opened it. The faint light glistened on my dress, reflecting a low shimmer into the hallway. Apparently, I missed a spot when camouflaging my dress with grime. If this dress killed me, I swore to haunt every fashion designer ever.

A small and starved creature jumped out and ran at me. Compared to the stagnant world around me, his speed startled me. At three feet tall, he had a slim build and sharp features. His eyes glinted yellow, and his dagger teeth snarled as he bore claw-like fingers. His legs were amputated below the calves. Instead of prosthetics, he ran on feet that were three sizes too large for his body. He was as hideous as the pillaging and ransacking stories Greenblade told me. I pictured all too easily the broken families, burnt houses, and torn towns that remained after a monster's terror. This goblin was a Mass Haunting all on his own.

He dove for my waist and scratched my arm, but his long nails couldn't cut through my corset.

Maybe there was a benefit to corsets after all.

The goblin launched a second attack, latching onto the frayed hem of my dress, tearing it as it whipped around.

"You're fast," he snarled, "but not fast enough!" He ran at me again, jumping for my dress and crawling up. My broken ankle made kicking difficult, so I swiped at him with my knife. He jumped back, narrowly dodging.

He grabbed a piece of broken flooring and chucked it at me. I ducked, but still heard a collision of wood and skin. Behind me, Lieutenant Greenblade was splayed, flying faster from the impact. One of his wings was crushed.

"No!" I grabbed for the fairy, careful not to cause extra gravitational forces on him as I slowed him to a stop.

The goblin giggled mischievously. "So we have a fool who slows herself to the thick levels of others. Methinks that makes herself thick."

I opened my mouth to retort, but the goblin charged me again. Releasing Greenblade, I swung myself around and smacked my fist into the goblin's face. As I struck, he clung on, biting into my hand and ripping my sleeve. Yelling from the pain, I jabbed my knife at him with a push of the electricity button.

He jumped back to dodge, but the zap of electricity tased the creature. He went limp and crumpled to the ground.

I turned around to rescue Greenblade two inches above the floor. When I turned back to behead the downed goblin, it was gone.

Crap, crap, crap! Where did it go?

I checked behind myself, above, and down the halls, but didn't dare peek into one of the nearby cells. That was a sure way to be surprised by a trap, and I needed to check on Greenblade. I couldn't escape this dungeon on my own.

Aching, bleeding, and badly limping, I ran down the hall and around the corner. I felt the grimy walls for a hiding place. Breaking hallways separated each prison room. I found an open door a couple halls away and closed myself in the cell.

I needed to be tapped into my speed to catch him sneaking up on us. But I couldn't feel the fairy's small breathing with my enhanced speed. I needed to make sure he was okay.

With my eye on the door, I untapped my speed.

I dove for the ground with my magic shield above as the Night Terror grabbed for me. I pushed my shield at him, and Dunstan grabbed it. The shield disappeared as he easily shoved it aside. A heated fist punched into my side. He burned into my doublet and bruised my right ribs.

I shouted out my pain with the incantation for a new shield. With the temporary defense, I managed to scramble away. Panting for breath, I backed up to the wall, keeping my shield before me.

Dunstan aimed another punch at my side. I swept him away with my shield, and he finally stepped back.

A small breather, a moment to think. Think! Dunstan would kill me in a battle of strength. I needed to find another angle. Maybe if I knew Dunstan's angle, I could work with that. "You say you were tricked?" I moved as I spoke to throw off his sense of sound.

"I thought the thirty-two people I killed were rebels."

Rebels? I involuntarily shivered at the thought of people who would dismantle my family's rule. If Dunstan had truly rid our kingdom of revolutionists, he would have been commended, not hunted.

What of the thirty-two? Had he read the reports, or did each person's death haunt him? Either way, he remembered the exact number.

I opened my mouth to ask more. My voice stuttered as Dunstan's aura disappeared in the middle of the wall. Where did he go?

Left in the dark, I stumbled to follow him. My shield made for a terrible walking stick as I felt for the wall on my right. I ran my hands along the wooden planks, feeling, searching for a draft or opening in the wall. I fumbled in the dark, tripping on my shield.

An echoing laugh bounced from above me. Shivers ran up my spine as I remembered running through darkened hallways in Romance as a poltergeist laughed. The laughter grew, enjoying my struggles.

At last, I felt a sliver of a cold draft. I pushed aside a loose board to open the gap and squeezed through. The wall's wood shavings scraped against me as I stumbled in. This new room was terribly narrow.

I was inside the wall! He used a hidden passage.

Dunstan's laughter filtered down to me. "Are we playing hide-and-go-seek? I'm ready! Come find me!"

I followed the echoes until my feet hit a wooden crate. I climbed on top and reached up, expecting to bump into the ceiling, except there was none. A hole led to an upper level. Pansy always warned against using staircases and elevators during Hauntings. This climb to a higher level could be just as hazardous. Sticking my hand to the side of the hole, I created a walled shield on the floor above. That allowed me to crawl up without being ambushed. Hefting myself through the hole, my shield cracked in the darkness as something hot struck it.

"Fine, be that way," Dunstan tsked from the end of the aisle. His aura scuffled to the left, followed by a swoosh of heavy fabric.

I pursued him down the upstairs hallway and felt the hole where Dunstan disappeared. The wooden panels opened behind a tapestry covering. I projected another handheld shield, then burst into the next blacked-out room. My shield vanished, and my aura darkened.

He led me to a room with magic negators!

Dunstan pummeled into me with his fists of fire. I narrowly dodged. His attacks forced me to retreat to the side until I bumped into the wall.

I was cornered!

He smashed and bashed his fists at me, snarling and growling like a beast. I helplessly felt for a door or another hole to retreat. Nothing. I was trapped, shielding my face with my arms, and my back with the corners of the walls. Strike after strike, my arms burned and bruised.

I needed a plan! We fought for Margen. I needed to defeat him, and I could not do that with only defensive maneuvers. I needed to attack…with what? I could not use my magic! I could punch back, except the very thought froze my limbs with nerves.

Dunstan laughed. "You're as hopeless as ever, Theo."

Weak. Useless.

With another punch, Dunstan slammed his fist into the side of my face, breaking my nose and burning my cheek in the process.

Dunstan threw another heated punch into my left arm. Something cracked. My pain came out as a yell as I lost balance and slipped to the floor. As luck would have it, my foot collided with Dunstan's shin on my way down.

His aura jumped back in surprise.

"Agh, get up," he chided. "It's no fun to hit you while you're down."

"Is it fun to hit me while I am cornered?" I panted. Dunstan also breathed heavily, and his aura shrank. Perhaps he needed the break too.

I allowed myself to rest on the floor for two more seconds before I forced myself to stand with shaking limbs.

"Did you honestly think you could beat me?" He laughed again. "Maybe not. Even if you had the ability to see me and the magic to attack, you don't have the nerve to kill me."

Blood leaked from my nose and into my mouth. I spat it out and analyzed the wavering length of his aura.

"I could say the same about you," I tried.

Dunstan growled, "Don't test me. I've killed before."

"On accident," I said. "You thought you were protecting Margen. I would wager that every death since then has been in self-defense against bounty hunters and assassins."

My aura darkened as Dunstan's grew. I had tickled the sleeping dragon.

With a mighty yell, he slammed his hand to my chest, branding me with his palm. I crumpled as pressure and heat burrowed into me.

Chapter 16

THE WICKED

Truly wicked hearts are beyond saving.
Their destiny is to receive the perils they would inflict on others.

- *Thesis of Adventures*

PANSY

"Lieutenant Greenblade!" I whispered as loudly as I dared. "I'm so sorry! Are you okay?"

The fairy raised one hand to his forehead as his other felt for his broken wing. He shook his head, groaning.

"What in Novel just happened?" He heaved forward and vomited over the edge of my hand. "I suppose that's what it feels like to be whiplashed. As much as I thrive on unique experiences, that was one I don't wish to happen again."

"I lost the goblin," I said, "but I don't know for how long. Can you fly?"

The lieutenant flapped his wings but slipped off balance as his broken wing puttered. "How about we stay down here until I heal?" Greenblade groaned. "Petal will have a fit if she hears I broke my wing again."

I humored the fairy with a half smile. "I might be a paramedic, but I've never worked on wings or a body as small as yours. All the same, I know it won't heal well without proper support. How do we get out of here?"

Greenblade looked around our cell. "All prison cells look the same to me. I hate to say it, but you've lost me."

"I went down the hall and turned right, continued straight, then left. We're in a cell on the right."

"Yes, I'm smart and amazingly talented, but not even I have the maze memorized enough to say where we are. There are too many break offs," he said with a sigh. "I need to fly out there to map it again."

"But you can't fly," I said.

"Right." His shoulders slumped.

"Greenblade," I said, "you're a fast flier, but I needed you to go faster out there with the goblin. What if you sat on my shoulder? Could you react fast enough to point the way out?"

The fairy stroked his chin thoughtfully. "My sparring companions say I have magnificent reaction speeds. Strap me to your shoulder and I will lead you true!"

Without a second thought, I ripped another shred from my dress. It didn't bother me this time, though Greenblade cringed. It was already ruined beyond repair. The lieutenant wrapped the strap around himself and tied it around my shoulder with, "Pardon me, Marchioness."

I shrugged, unconsciously bouncing the fairy up and down.

"Whoa," he said. "You want to warn me next time you test my ties?"

"You'll be thrown about much more than that if I fight the goblin again. Are you ready?"

Greenblade jabbed his finger forward. "Onward, then upward, till we see the lights!"

I tapped into my speed and opened the door with slow caution. Stepping into the hallway, I heard a scurrying to my left. Just my luck, that was the same direction Greenblade pointed.

Limping on my broken ankle, at least my blood didn't drip to leave a trail. I had cuts from the fall, but the goblin's claws left more sensitive wounds. Those around my wrist stung the most, while the slices on my leg were deep enough to require stitches. I shuffled down the hallway, keeping my back angled to the wall. The side doors made me wary. I didn't hear any more scuffling ahead, and I hoped the goblin took a different turn. My alert mode for Hauntings was on high, expecting it to jump from behind a door or from the ceiling.

What I didn't expect was to take a turn and see it running straight at me. I froze for a full speedy-enhanced second, unsure if I should run back the way I came, away from freedom, or try to lock myself in another cell.

He caught me off guard for that split second. Well, two could play that game.

I charged forward.

Emotions flashed through the goblin's eyes: first, surprise, like I planned, then hate and eagerness. I wanted to cry with every step on my ankle, but I kept running, playing chicken with a creature more hideous than a featherless bird. As the distance closed between us, the goblin's eyes flashed through each emotion again, adding a flicker of fear.

The goblin jumped to snatch at my chest. Before it could change direction, I leapt to the side and ran past it down the hall.

I laughed out loud. It worked!

Then his snarls came after me. I didn't have nightmares of demons chasing me down long dark hallways, but I suddenly knew exactly how they felt. I didn't like it.

Greenblade directed me to the right, and I skidded to change directions. As I turned, I checked back down the hall behind me. The space between the goblin and me was closing fast. Another quick turn to the left and another long hallway. I hoped the sudden turns were enough to throw off the goblin. My hopes were dashed as scuffling followed around the last corner. I had time for a quick glance behind myself as the creature launched at me.

The goblin latched onto my back and I scrambled about. He jeered in a nursery rhyme tune, jabbing sharp fingers at me with each word. "Slow poke, slow poke! Cries out 'don't poke!' That's what goblins do, is provoke!"

"Ow!" I cried out. "Stop!"

I jabbed my knife at the creature. I missed, then zapped the electricity. The goblin learned from the previous shock and jumped out of the way of an electric bullet. I had other plans. I angled my knife so its zapping light glistened off my bracelet gemstones, catching the goblin in the eyes. The creature screamed and covered his face. I used the distraction to snap off my hairband and barrettes. When the goblin turned toward me again, I snapped my barrettes at it, using my hairband as a sling-shot. One struck home in the goblin's eye before he retreated down the hall. The rest were barely nuisances and were lost in the darkness.

Greenblade still pointed the other way. I ran, limping on my ankle, checking over my shoulder frequently, hoping to put in some distance and possibly lose the goblin. After four turns, however, I ran into a dead end. Turning myself around, I waited in the intersection for a painful amount of time as Greenblade caught up with my perspective and changed his directions.

If Greenblade was this disoriented, I hoped the goblin was even more lost.

After three more lengthy hallways and five turns, I ran into another dead end.

No, Greenblade pointed upward. Twelve feet above me was a hatch! Was this the exit? I grabbed at the rock wall, which wasn't as moldy near the exit.

My foot kicked something from behind, and my broken ankle slipped. With no mossy or moldy cushion, the wall scratched my arm as I slid down. It took me a moment to realize why my legs felt even more scratched. The goblin dug its claws into my calves, crawling up my thighs to grab my face.

While the creature wasn't pretty from a distance, up close it set my heart in panic more than a massive poisonous spider on my arm. Skin stretched tight around its bared claws and sharp shoulders, but scrunched in wrinkles around his snarling lips and nose. I hadn't realized how sharp its teeth were. Their black decay camouflaged with the hollow emptiness of a starved mouth. Yellow and bloodshot eyes blazed into mine with deadly fury.

Either Dunstan left me alive, or death was the misery of never-ending pain. Despite the pain, I opened my eyes to check my faint aura in the darkness.

A haloed silhouette of a man crouched over me as a blur. My brother released his hand from my chest. He whimpered as his whole arm trembled.

The limited breathing space gave me an escape. I fell to the floor and slipped beyond his grasp. I felt along the wall until my hands found a door. Yanking it open, I collapsed into more darkness.

Pain surged across my broken ribs and bruised body. Breathing was laborious.

Desperate, I wiggled my wand arm. *"Rodegad."*

A shield formed before me. Thank Merlin, I could do magic again.

Careful footsteps and a long aura followed me to the new room. The change was imperceptible, subtle as it was, though I could pick out shapes of boxes around us.

Darkness was not created, it was only the absence of light. What had Dunstan said? His ability was not to create darkness. It was to absorb light.

My brother clenched his fists and flexed his arms, preparing for another foray of heated punches. Either his aura darkened, or the room around us grew lighter.

Or was it both?

Everything clicked together and I gasped. "Dunstan! It hurts you?"

The man of shadows paused and scoffed. "What?"

I struggled against my aching core to sit up. "Your ability. You absorb light, then convert it into heat. Doing so with your body is dangerous."

Dunstan growled and hurled another heated punch at me. His fist caught my shin and my boot singed.

"What would you know about endangering yourself, Theo?" he asked. He punched at me again, and I barely blocked with my shield projection. "You were the intellect," he snarled, "never pushing your body to the brink of exhaustion, never feeling the burning and shaking pain of muscle tension, realizing you're only halfway through the test! You never had to face your enemy from the floor, crawling in your own blood and sweat, forcing yourself to stand, even if it's no more than leaning on your sword, because you know if you don't, your enemy will hack. You. Down!" He finished each word with burning blows, making me roll, slide, and duck from danger. I failed to dodge half of them, and earned more burns across my body.

"I do know," I panted. "I know that you now push yourself to the very edge of your existence. My auras show me when a person is in danger, and with each surge of power you release, your aura darkens with death!" To my surprise, between the sweat and panting, tears streamed down my face.

Dunstan paused for a moment, also panting for breath, and perhaps recognizing my tears for him. Then he growled and lashed out another jab.

"What do you know?" he muttered between labored breaths.

He swung his fist at me, and I narrowly dodged. His arms sizzled and sparked, and Dunstan's aura dimmed farther.

"Dunstan!" I shouted. "Please stop—you will kill yourself!"

Desperate to end this fight, I considered a spell. Would water smother his heat, or would it just turn to steam? What other magic words did I know? Casting more fire was out of the question. Air would only fuel his heat. Perhaps I could pack enough soil to smother his arm, though that required more time than I had. What other words did Di teach me? Light.

"Lugz!"

I struck out with light, invisible in the darkness. Dunstan growled and raised his arm high, absorbing each flash, then stepped closer to me. His aura continued to blacken as the room fires flickered faintly back to life.

"Stop, Dunstan!" I cried. "Do not kill yourself to kill me!"

He reached me with a kick in my chest and my next light spell flew off course. My strength was exhausted. I ached too much to even scramble away or raise myself on my elbows. I lay there, hoping to have enough strength to escape in the next second. Maybe the next one. Or the next?

My mind screamed at my drained body. *Get up! Do something!*

The Night Terror stood over me, bending over with heavy breaths. Small sobs escaped with every exhale.

What if we both lost? Either way, I failed. Dunstan or Oswald would kill me and become the duchy's heir. Either way, Margen would remain in chaos. I failed Father. I failed Margen and all its people. I failed Pansy. She was deep in the dungeons, lost in a separate darkness.

Dunstan's aura wavered in and out. My burning chest lit with a glimmer of hope.

Then the plunges came. First, my aura dropped into black oblivion, darker than even Dunstan's.

Could I yield? Would it even stop him? If I managed to cry out, to what purpose? He would win and Margen would be lost. I would be exiled with Father, Pansy, probably even Di, and everyone who served us loyally. Or worse, we would be publicly humiliated and executed. That sounded more like Oswald. Dunstan would never want to see our faces again, though he probably would not hunt us down as Oswald would. Oswald would cut all ties of offenders, so none could oppose him. Even if I beat Dunstan now, I would need to face Oswald next. Yielding would not save me. Winning would only prolong the inevitable.

My heartbeats were numbered.

A strange realization hit me as Dunstan moaned closer. I had to trust him. Either to spare my life or to save Margen.

"Dunstan," I whispered, "will you save Margen?"

The second plunge was his burning fist towards my chest. There was no way to stop it, just prolong it. I closed my eyes.

"*Lugz.*" No light brightened the back of my eyelids.

Dunstan howled until my spell died.

I spent the last of my energy in that spell. I had nothing left in me. My brother and I struggled to cough.

Dunstan's ragged breath inched closer. He rested a heated fist over my heart.

At least this was a better death than the giant's stomach. I was not scorched by stomach acid, slowly digested until my bones were defecated somewhere in Divinity's mountains. No, I was in Eimad, my home, and dying a Hero's death, fighting for my land, my people, and for freedom against tyrants.

Light burst behind my eyelids. The room became bright around us.

"Save Margen yourself, you do-gooder Hero." Dunstan coughed blood onto my doublet. Then he collapsed. "I yield."

A light sparked off my shoulder and momentarily distracted the goblin's gaze. In the moment Greenblade flickered, I took my chance to swing my arm at the goblin. The creature grabbed onto my arm, breaking off my bracelet and slicing into my skin. I jabbed my knife at him, forcing him to jump away.

The hatch was right there! I could climb, but this thing would escape with me. That seemed like a bad idea.

Glancing at my shoulder, the fairy's strap dangled empty.

Where was Greenblade? I panicked, checking the goblin, but his angry eyes still snarled at me. The creature dove for my feet and dug in his claws before I swiped at him with my knife. I sliced his back, splattering my hand with its blood. He cried out, arching, and reaching higher to claw at my stomach. I sliced again, cutting deeply into his right arm. The creature howled and finally retreated a few feet back.

Momentarily secured, I searched for Greenblade again. I found him at the hatch, crawling up the stone wall to its metal lock.

Didn't he know the goblin was here? He was giving me an escape, but also releasing this monster!

Before I could turn back, the creature latched to my side and clung onto my dress. His clawed fingers dug into my corset, shredding at its thick barricade to my body. The goblin bled freely from his arm, bathing me with filth. I swiped at his neck. He dodged back. He scrambled to my backside, and I shoved him against the wall. I caught his left arm as he scurried around. He pushed his large feet into my right thigh, digging his massive toes in deep. He yanked his arm from the rocks, and I tumbled to the ground.

The echo of a slow click resounded through the hall. The goblin and I looked up to the hatch. Its lock turned. Greenblade flickered on the metal lock and waved his arms for my attention. A light glimmered in the goblin's eyes.

This was his chance for freedom, and he knew it. How long had he been down here? What dreams did he have of the outside world?

The glimmer in his eyes turned into a burn. A vengeful sneer crept up his lips, and I knew his dreams were not of joyfully returning to a family, quietly living out the rest of his days in peace. It was a Mass Haunting waiting for its release.

I had to stop it.

The goblin leapt onto the wall. I struggled onto my left knee and threw myself after him.

I didn't catch the creature as he climbed up, but I snatched my broken bracelet. I angled the largest gemstone and held down the trigger on my Vulgur Knife. A shot of electricity zapped from my knife's tip and struck the gemstone. Light and electricity scattered through the room like in a hall of mirrors. Two breakoffs came back and zapped my right arm, but five struck the goblin as he dashed up the wall. Straining to hold on, I angled my knife to direct more zaps at the goblin. He struggled upward as the currents narrowed on him. He slowed to agonizing twitches.

Then my knife flickered out. The goblin collapsed to the ground. I didn't have a second to lose. My right arm was numb and tingling from the electric shock. I crawled to the fallen creature with my elbows and knee, with a little help from my right hip. The pain was excruciating, and I cringed through my tears.

The goblin moaned and wiggled. I stretched out to grab his ankle. Half shouting, half screaming, I held my knife firmly as I dragged the creature back to me and through the blade.

Chapter 17

STATUS

Nobility may lose status from curses or disfigurement. However, a lower class Hero rarely receives nobility.

- *Thesis of Adventures*

THEO

Dunstan's aura shrank down to four centimeters. I closed my eyes to concentrate on my breathing, and only managed rasping heaves.

Voices rushed in from a side door. I opened my eyes to find a wizened face peering over me. Was she an angel, here to guide me to the home of the gods? Then I recognized her as Queen Alóvera, the Phoenix, of Fairy. My aunt knelt beside me and opened her medallion necklace. The glorious crown on her head remained steady as she leaned over to pour her healing tears over my wounds.

"Check Dunstan," I coughed.

She made some gestures to a group of people beyond my upturned line of sight.

"Thank you, Your Majesty."

My aunt's vial dripped empty as she squeezed a fresh tear from her eyes. She sighed with exhaustion, yet waved back two fussy attendees. Each tear was a labor, and I groaned to think how much my injuries cost her. She spared me a reassuring smile. The queen sat back on her heels and directed me through a breathing exercise.

"Dunstan?" I asked.

Queen Alóvera paused, a hint of doubt in her words. "He is unconscious. What did you do to him?"

A coughing fit delayed my answer. Then, "I reminded him of the man he is, and then trusted him."

"You—" She shook her head and laughed. "Regardless, you are the duel's victor. The guards have removed Dunstan to a cell. Congratulations, Marquis. The duchy is ensured in the hands of The Trusted."

Di joined my other side, adding an incantation to my wounds.

At last, I felt well enough to sit up. I did so, slowly and with help from Di and Queen Alóvera.

"I need to see him," I said.

Di argued, "Verily, you are not yet healed—"

"I need him to confirm his defeat with witnesses, or he may attack again."

"You were struck with an ability," Queen Alóvera said. "Only with my healing ability are you as well as you are."

Di nodded. "Your outside may feel whole, yet your insides remain broken. I began a prayer ascension from the tome Professor Vieseth gifted me. You shall return unblemished by the morrow, nevertheless, not before midnight."

Stubborn, I stood as straight as possible and braced myself. I stepped forward and nearly crumpled to the floor.

"Curses!" I shouted as pain shot through my body and immobilized me.

The queen and Di rushed to my side again.

Leaning on Di's arm, I took another step. Every movement left me limping and grinding my teeth, yet I eventually made it to the hallway. Father met me there as a magnificent white stallion. He was escorted by his usual guards and a couple other soldiers. They greeted me with a round of applause.

"Behold!" Father neighed. "Your rightful marquis! Spread the word of his victory over the Night Terror! Gather all who are loyal to our cause of justice, and we will storm Ruezdad to reclaim Eimad before the full moon!"

The cheers increased as two soldiers ran off to share the news.

From somewhere in the back of my mind, I remembered Pansy's words: "Don't celebrate too early."

"Pansy!" I panicked.

Father nodded and carried me to a room where Prince Alun, Brooke, and a small group of knights stood around the floor entrance to the oubliette.

Prince Alun reported, "We have heard echoes of a struggle. We unlocked the top latch and lowered the ladder, though this opening may be used by the goblin if he defeated the marquis's intended."

Before I could worry any further, the floor hatch slammed open to reveal a corpse bride. A couple of the soldiers cursed and jumped back in fright. Scratches and deep gashes bled down her legs and arms. Her dress was ripped free of its train and torn halfway up her leg in multiple places, revealing her bare feet and a scandalous amount of her scarred legs. What remained of the dress was smeared with blood and grime, masking any of its former blue shine. Her hair was a curly mess from her bun release. Her face makeup had become an artist's palette of animal innards. She held her knife in one hand and a broken jewelry chain in her other. Sitting on her shoulder was a limp green fairy.

With an insane little chuckle, she crawled from the dungeon entrance and collapsed to the ground.

I almost kissed the ground where my face landed.

Freedom! Fresh air, sweet light from above! I could write poetry about the simplicities of life!

Theo called my name and slid to the floor next to me. He grunted as he struggled to lift me to his lap.

Was I really that heavy? Sure, I was pretty close to dead weight, but I probably shed twenty pounds from my dress.

Theo turned me around to face him and I suddenly understood his struggles. There was a disturbing amount of blood and burn marks across his body, including a gaping hole near his heart.

I moaned and blinked back the moisture gathering in my eyes. As much as I worried what happened to him, my first words were an accusation. "Why didn't you tell me about the goblin? I thought you abandoned me."

"My knowledge was outdated," he said, cradling me. "Last I knew, we only had a slow-moving berserker orc down there. I hoped it was still locked in its cell. By the looks of it, I was wrong. Please, forgive me, my flower. If Dunstan had not challenged me, I would have come for you in a heartbeat."

My eyes roamed over him and I managed a weak smile. "Is that what happened to you? You're a disaster."

Theo's smile broke loose and he laughed, probably thinking the same about me. Our laughter choked and both of us coughed for a moment, catching our breath between our tired pain.

We stifled our coughing as a tall and beautiful woman approached. Balancing atop her head was the finest and most intricate piece of headwear I'd ever seen.

Theo shifted uncomfortably. "Your Majesty, please pardon our undignified manners and dress."

Majesty? Oh crap. This was Theo's aunt, Queen Alóvera, The Phoenix, of all Fairy. So much for first impressions.

Her Majesty smiled pleasantly and knelt beside us. "There is little I find more honorable than a recently victorious Hero and Heroine. Miss Finster, I would ask how you fare, though judging by your condition, I assume you need immediate medical attention."

I could only sigh, "Yes, please."

With my aunt's healing ability and Pansy's medical training, it was no surprise how quickly they became acquainted. As soon as Pansy started on her detailed and specific medical needs, they chatted like old friends.

Only understanding half of what they said, I left them to visit Dunstan's holding. The room was brightly lit by fairy dust. Two of the four guards standing outside the doorway were blind fighting masters. One of them and Father joined me in the room.

As soon as my heart crossed the threshold, everybody's auras disappeared. Father morphed back into a man in regal uniform. Ah, this was a room that negated abilities. How strange to see people without their usual glows. Even more strange was the realization that I had come to rely on them.

To my surprise, the duke remained by the door and silently gestured for me to speak with my brother. Father's confidence in me was both encouraging and boggling.

Dunstan sat limp on the floor with his hands chained above his head. He looked up at the sound of the closing door. I was struck by how much he resembled Mother. He had her bubbled nose, thin eyebrows, and even her emerald eyes. Since she had died while giving birth to him, I considered it a sweet condolence from the gods that he carried her features.

"It isn't over, Theodor," he coughed.

I stared at my younger brother sprawled on the floor. Did he deny defeat?

Instead, I asked, "Why are we fighting, Dunstan? We are brothers."

"It's *because* we're brothers." He coughed again, grimacing. "It's what we do. That's why defeating me only means that now you need to fight Oswald."

He accepted defeat then. I sighed in relief and knelt beside him. "How bad can the little weasel be?"

Dunstan tilted his head at me with an attitude. "He orchestrated my downfall. He was the one to tell me about the 'rebels' in the south. Of course our dear, sweet stepmother backed his story. When Greggy said he wouldn't do anything without confirmation, I decided to take matters into my own hands. So yeah, I was tricked. I made one mistake and was labeled a traitor, putting Oswald one step closer to taking the duchy."

"Will you not help us?" I asked. "Ruezdad was your home too. Help us fight Oswald and reclaim it."

My brother shook his head before I finished. "No, if you're not going to kill me, then you'll need to banish me. I can't let them take my ability. I've heard the rumors. Oswald's plotting something…terrible."

"What do you know of his plans?" I asked.

Dunstan stared up at me from tired eyes. "I know you can't defeat him," he grumbled. "He learned sorcery primarily for the hypnosis spell, but he knows more than that. Also, The Lovely Duchess isn't just stealing abilities. She's harvesting them."

My breath caught in my throat and the blood froze in my veins. "Is hypnosis not terrible enough? What do you mean, harvest? How do you know this?"

He scoffed. "When you become a rumor, rumors become your only source of information. You learn to piece the events together. Think about it: Greggy fell off a cliff, but we see his ability in those storm clouds above Eimad. Lord Freund lost his ability to see others' abilities. What's the point in taking that from someone unless you plan to use it to collect more? Then, Lord Greenwood lost his ability to locate rare herbs, and Lady Lehrer lost her ability for potion making. They're cooking something up, Theo. I don't know what, but it's probably rare and dangerous. It's the only explanation. That's why I hid and why I won't help you fight them. Can you imagine them with my ability? Or Prince Alun's? Go fight them if you must, but you'll have to go alone. They think your ability's useless. They have no reason to take it from you."

Time stilled as my heart raced and analyzed Dunstan's every word.

"One last thing…" He coughed. "Keep Di out of Ruezdad."

"Di? Why? She has no ability to steal."

"Yeah, but I heard Oswald's been asking for her. I don't know what he does to the young maids he kidnaps and never returns, but I don't want our sister anywhere near him. Besides, there's some prophecy that suggests Queen Alóvera will be the one to destroy them. If you need to take a healer with you, take her. Promise me you'll keep Di away from Ruezdad."

My smile warmed at the concern in his voice. My younger brother was a good man. Deep down. "I promise."

Dunstan nodded, satisfied. "Good. Oswald has no need for any of us, especially me. He probably has plans to knock me off too. I'll need to go far away, probably farther than I've ever been—which is saying something, because Sci-Fi was almost a blast."

I stood, unsure what else to say. Stringing together my thoughts, I said, "Take care of yourself, Dunstan. Even if you dishonored your title and you desire banishment, I hope you may return to Eimad under an oath of peace. You will be welcomed."

Dunstan smirked. "You always were the weird one, Theo. How about I work on leaving *good* rumors in my wake. Then we'll see."

I smiled. "We will see."

I clapped him on the knee, and stepped out of the room with Father. The duke transformed back into a horse, and my auras returned. We nearly bumped into Pansy in the next room. Di had fixed her dress and hair. My betrothed was impossibly more beautiful than before. I wanted to caress and kiss the partially healed scars across her skin.

In my stunned silence, Pansy spoke first. "Did you kill him?"

I blinked in surprise. "Sorry? No, for what purpose?"

"So he doesn't come after you again," she said, her tone synonymous with "of course."

I shook my head. "He admitted defeat and desires to leave Margen. I doubt he will cause us more trouble."

She opened her mouth to retort, then clamped it shut. She trusted me. That single expression swelled my heart with overwhelming love and gratitude for her.

Before I could engulf her in my passion, Father spoke.

"We should discuss how to reinstate Ruezdad," he said, heading towards The Rook's maps room. "Your victory over Dunstan will bolster the people's confidence in you. Also, with my sister and Alun in attendance, their support will encourage the people. This should increase our recruitment, that we may have enough support to battle against Ruezdad within a fortnight. Supposing you defeat Oswald and reclaim Margen, the people will be eager to celebrate with you during the traditional month-long marriage festivities. In that time, you would do well to reconsider Princess Anwen as marchioness."

My patience boiled by the time he finished. Interrupting him would not prove my maturity and responsibility.

"No," I said, drawing Pansy's discouraged stare away from the wall. "The one thing I know for certain about the future is that I want Pansy beside me for all of it. Starting today."

Father stomped his front hooves with irritation. "What do you mean?"

"If she will allow" —I fingered Pansy's hand and pleaded into her brown eyes— "please accept my proposal to marry me tonight."

Pansy's breath caught, and a smile grew on her bruised cheeks.

"Tonight?" Father pinned his ears back. "You will spit upon traditions and the sacred use of the Royal Chapel?"

"Those 'traditions,'" I scoffed, "have only been in place for two generations. Do not think me ignorant, Father, just because I lived the past six years in Romance. I studied our history better than any of my brothers. You speak of breaking tradition, yet your mockery of Pansy's station insults our heritage. Grandfather King Fromm, The Valiant, had been just a tailor who slew a giant. Pansy has fought a giant, a goblin, and even monstrous Hauntings. She has earned the right of marchioness on her own, and I can only hope to have earned the right to marry her."

I wanted Father to see my determination and strength of will. I wanted him to see my bravery and capability to solve problems with words, not fists.

Father's tail snapped up and down. Curses, he was furious. I swallowed and suppressed my trembling as much as possible. Father glared at me. "You love this woman enough to elope, even if it disowned you?"

My gut twisted. Did he disapprove of Pansy enough to disown me? What about the duchy? Who would be his heir? How would I support Pansy and a future family without honor?

Pansy silently fumed beside me.

Father nodded to her. "You have wisely kept your peace. Had you spoken out, I would have dismissed you immediately. For your acknowledgement of your place, I will allow you to say your part."

She drew in a quick breath, then burst, "Are you insane?"

"Pansy—"

"Don't you see what's happening to your people?" she continued. "Even if you disown Theo, do you really think we can walk away from them? We might not be able to solve all their problems, but condemn me to Horror if Theo won't try his hardest!" She huffed, then lowered her voice to properly end with, "Duke Fromm."

I just fell in love with her all over again. She cared not for my title or inheritance. She wanted to help my people anyway, and she believed in me.

Before my father could retaliate, I added, "Although your estrangement would cause me grief, yes, I am resolved."

Father stared at me, long and hard. Every inch of my insides squirmed. Pansy's hand slipped beside mine, and I found the strength to hold firm.

"Then it is decided," the duke said. "You have my permission to marry Pansy Finster, from Brimstone, Horror."

I blinked. "I have your permission?"

"Yes," he sighed. His muscles loosened and ears came forward. "Though you will not receive my blessing until after Oswald is defeated and Margen is allowed an official celebration of your union."

Grinning, I turned to my betrothed. "What do you think, my flower?"

"You're okay with a Horror wedding?" she asked.

"Yes. Anything for you."

Pansy's smile bloomed. She kissed my cheek, then called, "Where's Di? As a priestess, can she marry us?"

Father called the nearest soldier to summon my sister and Queen Alóvera. We met in a private room and explained our desires.

"Now?" My sister's eyes bulged with surprise and excitement. "You beseech me to aid your union? Gods forbid me not!"

I grinned. "Marry us now, and I promise to uphold any and all ridiculous traditions Father needs for an official ceremony and celebration."

Di tapped her finger to her chin in debate. "It is well enough. However, I cannot fathom how to perform the ceremony without the exchange of rings, candle light, and blessed drinks—"

"The words, Di," I said. "Just say the words. I care not for the flourishes and routines."

Di gaped at me, then turned to Pansy. "Verily, you agree with this madness?"

"Yeah," she said, beaming. "Most Horrors elope. The smaller, the better."

Di huffed and muttered of our lunacy as she thumbed through her book of rites. I held Pansy's hands as we began a starry-eyed staring contest. Our smiles widened until our cheeks hurt. Di's words could have been gibberish for all the attention I paid them. I listened for the one question that mattered, and answered, "I do."

My heart swelled when Pansy responded the same. We sealed our vows with a kiss that caused Queen Alóvera to swoon and my sister to gag. What better time to indulge our passion than the days before battle? Still holding hands, we ran out to the streets of Eimad. Between the delirious giggles of joy, I caught a glance at Ruezdad.

Lightning flickered above the castle as the storm gained new strength. Guards stood at every post in civilian clothes and armor. The Fromm flag that usually claimed the tallest tower had been replaced.

Chapter 18

CANNIBALS

Beware the quick wedding to a stranger.
Death by consumption is the most common threat among Adventurers.
Perhaps you are what you eat, and those monsters desire to be human.

-   Thesis of Adventures

PANSY

I had to remind myself that we didn't break Horror's number one rule. We weren't teenagers who lost control or secret lovers breaking vows. We were married. Sure, it was a little awkward at first, but it became…wonderful. Marital love was the dream of Romantics and Fairy Fantastics alike. We slept in and enjoyed the morning to ourselves with half the mind to never leave our little inn room.

At least until our stomachs complained. I pulled on a quick gown to grab some breakfast from the nearest diner.

"You like your eggs soft-boiled, right?" I asked.

Theo—my husband—followed me to the door to steal one more kiss. "I love how well you know me, though I should be the one to serve you breakfast in bed."

"Let me spoil you," I said, "but if you want to prepare a surprise for my return, I won't argue." I winked and made my way down the inn's hall. I wandered downstairs and considered where to find the kitchen. Rounding a corner, I nearly bumped into a young man with a massive basket over his shoulder.

"Sorry," I said. "Do you know where I could find some breakfast around here?"

The young man had burnt umber hair with red streaks, and blinked at me with matching eyes. He rested a hand on my shoulder and spoke clearly. "Yes. Jump into my wicker basket, and you can have enough food to satisfy a beef-witted flap-dragon."

What the Horror? That was a trap if I'd ever heard one. He couldn't have been more obvious if he tried, but…I wanted to jump in.

He set down his ginormous basket and removed the lid. I hefted my skirts to step in.

Supernaturals! What was I doing? Why couldn't I stop? My actions weren't my own! Like watching a horror film, my mind freaked over the stupidity of a character's actions, wondering why—why—*why?* Don't go into that house! Don't back up slowly into the darkness! Don't step into that basket for some stranger to steal me away!

I ducked below the lip and stared up at my captor. He slid the lid over me, but not before I caught his smile.

Theo?

The darkness of the basket enveloped me. I was lifted from the ground, then jostled back and forth. To the lucidity of my mind, it was the rocking of a cradle. I was so tired. I hadn't slept much that night and struggled to remember why. My eyes closed to the swaying tune of my captor. He sang about a rowboat on a calm stream. How happy and simple.

"Life…is…a dream."

I lounged on the bed for an extra lazy minute when Pansy left to grab breakfast. Pansy. My wife. She wanted to spoil me with breakfast in bed? Alright, then I would spoil her too. I drew out the tub and considered a spell to keep the water warm. What was the word for fire again?

I concentrated on an image of the water steaming, and not boiling, then said, "*Igniz*." Fire spurted from my wand as if from my wrist. Small flames landed in spots around the tub.

"Curses! Water—I mean—*Ajua!*"

I spent the next five minutes putting out the small fires and drying the excess water.

"Curses," I swore again. I still had no idea how to use magic. I wanted to transform all the dust in the air into flower petals for her return, though was clueless on what words to use. Where was Pansy?

I laced on some trousers and a tunic to go check on her. Maybe I could help bring the plates to our room. As soon as I opened the door, the innkeeper stood ready to knock. His face paled before me.

"L-Lord Fromm! Forgive me! I was unable to stop him! He came and went so fast! She ran right into him, and he would'a killed me for interfering!"

"Whoa," I said, raising my hands for him to slow down. "What are you saying? Who would have killed you?"

"Lord Fromm—I mean, the magician. The one who lives in Ruezdad."

"Oswald?"

The innkeeper nodded. "The youngest Lord of Margen has ensnared many a lass with his witchcraft. He poisons their minds to do his bidding, and he steals them away to the castle. I thought they were only rumors to explain the disappearances of the young maids of Eimad until I saw him cast a spell on your woman."

"Wait—he abducted Pansy? That bullbegging bullbeggar!" Even the harshest curse was insufficient for my half-brother. Neglecting all else, I stormed from the inn. Where was Pansy? Could I catch them if I ran? Did he take her to Ruezdad with the other abductees?

The streets were empty save for the morning workers and errand runners.

Curses. Curses!

I rubbed the back of my neck, then slid my tense hands around to grip my face. Pansy. Was she already behind the walls of Ruezdad?

One block further, I found a good angle to spy on the castle. Guards stood at every post. They wore no uniforms. Revolutionists? Just the sight of them clenched my heart with fear. If I was to break in, I needed help.

I ran to The Rook. Marching inside, I called, "How soon can we storm the castle?"

Dim light woke me as the basket lid was removed. The young man stood above me and beside a middle-aged woman. She was sickly pale with fiery red hair and black eyes. Her piercing gaze made me want to pull the basket lid over myself and hide. The young man stared at me with calculating eyes.

He asked the woman, "Is this the diamond in the rough you saw?"

"Yesss," the woman hissed. Her cat-like eyes roamed over me and widened with a sinister smile. "The mirror did not show her ability. It is mossst desirable. Keep thisss one alive."

"Yes, Your Highness," the young man said with a bow. The woman left, and the man reached for me. He looked like someone I knew very well, but I couldn't remember his name.

Either way, remaining in the confines of the basket sounded like a bad idea… though I couldn't say why. I took the young man's hand and stood.

"Welcome, Miss Finster," he said. "Today, you may be a common dirt-crawling woman, yet on the morrow, you may become my wife and the next Duchess of Margen."

Wife…Duchess of Margen…Yes, I was engaged to the heir of the Margen Duchy, a man with dark hair, creamy skin, and a beautiful smile…Yet…

"Your eyes are brown," I said.

"The better to match yours, my dear," he said.

I gestured to his red highlights. "Why is your hair red?"

"The better to present my passion, my dear."

"How are you so young?" Seriously, he couldn't have graduated from high school yet.

"The better to please you, my dear. Come, rise from your wicker confines."

I stepped from the basket to the stone floor. We were in a room as plain as a jail cell with a slit window. He led me to the side of the stone room where a small table beckoned me with all sorts of delicious fruits, breads, and cheeses.

I sat at the table and selected a three-course meal for myself. Some distant part of my mind warned me to wait for my host to eat first.

The young man bit into a roll and analyzed me with a small frown. "Despite your older age and foreign peasantry status, our queen esteems you worthy. We may wed after the ascensions; however, first I have a test."

"A test?" I asked, somewhat dazed. My mind was filled with dreams of another life. What was real?

The young man's hand brushed mine as he handed me a key of bone. I could feel him. I ate my own roll, savoring the crusty flavors of wheat and butter. I was awake. This was real.

"This key," he said, "is far more special than your impoverished brain can fathom. I need you to hold onto it until I return. Delicate as the finest wine, it will break if it drops. Do not allow it to leave your hand until I say."

"Okay," I said. "Why is it special?"

"This key belongs to a certain locked room. It is currently the only locked room in this castle. You may enter any room your heart desires, except I forbid you to enter the room that requires that key."

I frowned. "Then why are you giving me the key?"

"To test your capability to resist temptation," he said with his disarming smile. "I have duties to prepare today, but heed my warning; I will know if you enter that room."

"How?"

"The same way I knew many other young maids have failed me—you will drop the key, and it will break. The duchess's magic mirror claimed you to be the next duchess, but I have to know that I can trust you."

Trust. That word stirred a memory. Something about someone who was trusted…The memory faded, and I blinked to clear my mind. "You can trust me."

The young man gave me a sad smile. "The others said likewise. Farewell. I have a busy day. Explore Ruezdad as you wish, though you will only rule this kingdom with me if you leave that room alone."

With that, he turned away and bid me goodbye. How bizarre.

I watched him go and finished my meal. Obviously, the easiest way to keep the key safe and not be tempted to enter its room was to simply stay in my current room. Except this room was as pleasant as a jail cell.

Exiting the little cell, I found myself on the second floor of a beautiful courtyard. I leaned over the railing to marvel. The stone architecture was blue-grey and as magnificent as the Horror cathedrals of my dreams. Stone archways supported my pathway on the upper floor and opened to the outside within the walls. Mossy green grass surrounded a fiery red tree.

What was this place with stunning contrasts? Even the aged smell of wet stone and moss made me curious. This place had history. This place had secrets. And I wanted to explore every nook and cranny of it.

As far as my blurry memory could remember, I'd never been in a hallway grand enough to be called a corridor. This castle was filled with corridors. I wandered through, looking for a starting place. The castle was massive, built like a fortress, but furnished like a palace. Tapestries of wars clothed the walls, and every corner was stationed with a suit of armor. I took a path downstairs to explore the ground floor. I figured the best way to track my explorations was to begin at the bottom then make my way up. Entering a grand staircase, I measured five levels. I beamed at the prospect of so much to explore. Why bother with one locked room when there was so much more to see?

I discovered a grand library with books that stacked up its vaulted ceiling, a lounge with paintings across its walls, and a meeting chamber made entirely of marble. A whole section of the castle seemed designated for studies. One room was filled with maps and historical documents, another with an assortment of musical instruments, and the next with various amateur craftsmanship from glass window staining to blacksmithing.

All the study rooms seemed forgotten except the furthest, which glowed with candlelight and smoke. A table in the middle was covered with dead or barely alive caged animals. As much as I pitied the creatures, I shied away from their patched fur, foaming mouths, and red eyes. Along the walls were stacks of vials, labeled with every mineral, herb, and insect imaginable. A small shelf housed some ancient tomes larger than my...medical textbooks? My dreams said that I was a certified paramedic, but if so, why was I in this arcane place? What a random thought.

In the back corner, a large cauldron bubbled. I guessed that was the cause for the rancid smell. I turned around to leave when a light caught my eye. A mirror stood against the wall, cloudy and aged. I stepped up to it, surprised to see myself in a simple gown. Odd. Or was it? I wore the dress all day. Why was it strange to see myself wearing a gown?

My dreams said that it was because I was a Contemporary Horror, who only wore clothes good for running. Except I wore this dress now, so that couldn't be right.

The mirror's image moved. I stepped back in surprise as the clouds on the mirror swirled, as if they were inside the mirror. I squinted and leaned forward to examine it closer. Some deep instinct screamed at me for making such a stupid action.

Sure enough, a face that wasn't mine emerged in the upper corner. I shrieked and jumped back.

An older woman stood behind me. It was the same woman who greeted me from the basket. Her red hair was tied back in a bun so tight that it performed a facelift. She wore a dress of deep purples that swirled into black points. She stroked a ferret on her shoulder as she stared at me with a blank expression.

"I sssee the little wench has found my magic mirror," she rasped. "It shall be of no ussse to thee, as it will not answer another question until sunsssset."

"It answers questions?" I asked.

"Onccce a day it proclaims a name," the woman explained. "Yesternight I asssked who is most eligible to become Margen's next duchessss. Thou, little wench, cannot begin to comprehend my sssurprise when it announced the name of a foreign commoner. Yet the mirror doesss not lie. Consider thy dim stars blessssed to be duchess when I become queen."

She turned sharply away, closing her cold conversation. She squeezed the ferret from her shoulder and slammed it down to a table. My eyes froze on her brutality. The terrible woman breathed in deeply, as if inhaling the creature's soul. Her hair softened and shined, and the moles on her face disappeared. At the same time, the ferret's fur withered with grease, then shrank and fell off. I thought to cry out and help the squirming creature, but she pressed hard against its vertebrae. A small crack silenced the ferret's struggles, and the witch sighed with pleasure. Her disgusting smile dampened back to her perpetual frown as she jerked toward me. I stumbled back, scared and repulsed. Her irises were black and her whites were blood red.

"Have you nothing better to do than gawk?" she snapped. I turned and fled to the corridor. I tried to shake the morbid death from my mind, but it stuck like blood on my hands. Why did the gruesome scene bring back so many memories from my dreams?

Eager to distract myself from the woman's conversation, I continued to explore. Despite all my explorations, I was still on the main floor. I opened doors to a long dance room with mirrors on one side and windows on the other, a dining room with a sixteen seat table, and…a room that didn't open.

I didn't expect to find the locked room on the ground floor. My instinct told me to leave it alone. I didn't need to see what was inside. Except, after so many open doors, this one locked door irritated me. Frustration boiled within me as I realized a castle with fifty locked doors wouldn't have bothered me so much as this one.

Why this one? What did the young man not want me to see? What was he trying to hide?

One hand still held the locked knob. My other hand clenched the bone key.

My dream life argued, shouted, and screamed for me to leave it alone. Stupid curiosity got the better of me.

I unlocked the door and peeked inside.

It was the kitchen. Stone countertops, wooden cupboards, a brick fireplace, oven, and metal icebox. They were all covered with blood. Parts of humanoid beings piled across every surface. Pelts of leather, fur, scales, or feathers had their own piles. On the wall were seven profile drawings: human, mermaid, cat-like, and even bird-like. They only had one commonality—they were all women who could have won beauty contests.

My grasp on the key loosened. Shock and horror weakened my capability to hold strong. Shock...and Horror...I recognized a scene like this from my dream when I snuck into the secret shed of one of my orphanages.

I tightened my grip on the bone key. The young man was a murderer. And I was a survivor from Horror. Everything else from my past was a blur, but this one fact became solid. I'd faced monsters both human and inhuman, cursed and undead. A butchering serial killer was no more than another Haunting to outwit and destroy.

I locked the door and set out to explore the castle with a new focus. This was his turf. I was in the Haunting's lair. That meant that he had the home field advantage until I could scout it completely. A person's home also revealed a lot about him, and I was determined to learn and exploit all I could. I examined the castle with sharpened eyes. The gory tapestries, gothic architecture, and suits of armor challenged my fears. For each suit of armor that I passed, I removed the swords and helmets. Now they couldn't be used as weapons or hiding places.

I finished stashing the swords and helmets in a closet when a shadow approached from behind. I turned to come face to face with a poltergeist. I stumbled back to the wall.

Wait a second, why did I assume it was a poltergeist? The ghost didn't hold any physical items or stare down at me with death. In fact, his expression was bored. His glazed eyes stared off to some distant daydream as he spoke to me.

"The young lord has returned and he desires to see you in his drawing room. I will escort you."

"His withdrawing room?" I clarified, then said in a rush, "No thanks, I think I know where it is."

"Very well." He bowed and left.

I sighed with relief. My muscles eased with each second the ghost drifted away. Despite the specter's tame expression, everything about his presence threatened me. He reminded me of dreams spent in heart-pounding terror and heart-wrenching agony. He made me feel the utter despair of loneliness.

I stared after him until he disappeared around a corner. Then, I went back toward the study rooms. The duchess's room was obvious enough, and I was fairly certain that my fiancé's study room was next to hers.

I knocked on the door. "Can I come in?"

He laughed from somewhere within. "Not by the hair of my chinny-chin-chin."

Then why did he ask me to come? Confused, I said, "Oh."

He laughed again, his voice coming closer. "I tease, my dear. No need to huff and puff and blow your way in."

He opened the door and stood before me. This was my fiancé? Something was off. I analyzed his red highlights, youthful face, and brown eyes again. It was like my best friend wore a disguise. I recognized him and didn't at the same time.

He reached his hand to me. "Did you enter the locked room?"

Rather than lie, I handed him the bone key. "Whole and in one piece." Unlike the female bodies behind that door.

He stared at the little white key, surprised. "You passed the test. Well, well, well. You shall be my princess after all."

"Maybe," I said, "but I don't even know your name."

He grinned and stepped lightly back for a bow. I imagined a gallant cloak sweeping over his shoulder and a smile to weaken my knees.

"You have earned the right to call me by my first name. My name is Oswald."

"Oswald," I tested his name in my mouth. "Are you sure it's not Oz? Or, I don't know, for some reason I can't get the name Theo out of my head."

Oswald narrowed his eyes. "I suppose you can shorten my name to Oz if you prefer it, dearest. I haven't the slightest idea where you concocted Theo. I forbid you to use it. It reminds me of my detested half-sibling."

"Oz it is then," I said. Yes, there was familiarity and fondness for someone with that name. I cared about Oz. But I couldn't shake the feeling that I loved Theo…whoever he was.

Chapter 19

THE IMPOSSIBLE

No wish, spell, or potion can grant:
unlimited wishes,
fabricated true love,
or immortality.

- *Thesis of Adventures*

THEO

Curses of Merlin's beard and bullbeggars. I finally married the love of my life, and she was stolen away from me within twelve hours. To my utter frustration, the morning and afternoon passed without Pansy in my arms.

The Fairy Kingdom was particularly good at spontaneous celebrations such as our wedding announcement. However, gathering an army for an ambush was the opposite of a spontaneous celebration. The warriors of Eimad were already stretched thin between the disappearances to Ruezdad and emigrations to Divinity. Our best recruitment tagline was "The rightful heir has returned! Join us to avenge the tyrants and restore Margen!" Fantastic. How high should we set those expectations?

Prince Alun and Brooke recruited while I brainstormed how to ambush Ruezdad with Queen Alóvera, Father, and Di.

Father chose the form of a warhorse for this discussion. An empty portrait sat on an easel in the corner of our war room.

"From Mr. John's analysis," Father explained, "we know a spell has been cast on the Ruezdad guards to make them appear as our greatest fears."

Di nodded. "Verily, it is a complicated spell that takes a minimum of a couple hours to prepare. It is wondrous that our little brother can cast such a spell over so many."

"If he is truly the caster, Oswald has achieved a great and terrible status," Father said. "Mr. John also determined that the spell has been used in reverse, making us appear as the guard's worst fear."

"Hold your horses," Queen Alóvera said, "the guards fear us as much as we fear them?"

"Yes," the duke said, pointedly ignoring his sister's horse jest. "They see us as enemies and vermin attempting to invade the home they've sworn to protect."

"Fantastic," I groaned. The Guards of Fear that I saw as revolutionists were some of our most loyal subjects. I saw them with unkempt and unprofessional clothes that spoke of loathing for my family's nobility. They guarded Ruezdad as if they owned it, as if my home was only a shell, hollowed out of all beloved memories…as if they killed or enslaved every member and employee of my family. I doubted that their long auras were part of the illusion. They would kill me if given the chance.

Eager to move to another subject, I asked, "What do we know of Ruezdad's inner mechanisms? Have they changed the layout, added traps, or created forbidden paths?"

My father stomped his hoof. "I had suspicions of Oswald's activities and desires while I was still in residence. All I knew for sure was that he kept secrets. I took a risk when I fled Ruezdad. I abandoned the stronghold in order to support the people. However" —he knocked on the frame of the empty portrait— "we recently acquired an inside man for that information." The picture came to life as a disgruntled man wearing traveling gear stepped into the frame. I gasped to recognize Lord Doran. He had been painted for the purpose to travel between several scenic landscape pictures which hung throughout Ruezdad. He acted as a messenger and scryer within the castle walls. He snapped to attention as soon as he identified us.

"Honorable Fromms! Your Majesty! How glad Lord Doran is to see you! You have stolen away my portrait from Ruezdad! How splendid! Where are you? How may Lord Doran assist you?"

"Lord Doran," Father commanded, "locate Oswald and the Duchess in Ruezdad. We need you to scry on them."

The man in the portrait saluted. "Lord Doran will do his best to serve his Duke and Majesty," he said, then disappeared into the side of his frame.

In another minute, the empty portrait rippled. The plain background changed to a stone room. Father leaned forward to study the picture. "They are in the library."

Truly? The room was a far cry from any room that resembled Ruezdad from my memory. The stone walls had black mold growing in the cracks. Despite the afternoon sun, the curtains blocked any sunlight, and the room was smoky from torches. I missed the days when my mother had decorated the library as a lounge, lit with fairy dust and glowing orbs, alive with various herbs and flowers. Now, it was a cave of disorganization and weapons on every surface.

The frame featured the current actions of Lord Oswald and Duchess Abadda. Though my stepmother was as horrendously beautiful as ever, I hardly recognized my half-brother. The young man of sixteen had managed to embody the image of a pompous weasel. He was unnaturally skinny under his heavy leathers, which were dyed purple and embroidered in black and gold. Red streaks burned like snakes of fire through his dark brown hair. I gaped at his aura of eight centimeters long. Were they talking about me, or did he hate me passively?

My stepmother's low voice graveled more than the streets of Contemporary roads.

"—and dessserve to rule this kingdom. Thou shalt keep this kingdom from falling during our exxxpansion. My ssson, it is for thy sssake that we perform the spell tonight."

Queen Alóvera frowned. "Traitors confirmed straight from the horse's mouth."

"Tonight?" Oswald asked. That was Oswald? His voice was much deeper than I remembered.

The duchess continued to growl to her son. "The potion ssshall ripen with the new moon tonight. Rebels ssscheme against us, but they shall be no match for usss if we act now."

Dunstan had been right. They were concocting a potion.

Oswald sighed, though I could not tell whether of relief or submission. "Prepare the dagger, my loyal mother. You said the potion only needs one more ingredient?"

"Yesss," Duchess Abadda hissed. "Blood. If your new wench dissspleases you, she may ssstill be of use."

My insides tightened. "Pansy?"

Duchess Abadda inclined her head as Oswald departed. Her eyes slid near the portrait, and she grinned something sinister.

The picture rippled away. I was the first to break the silence. "What will they do to Pansy? What spell were they talking about? With a potion and a dagger?"

Di's face became ashen. "Pray tell, do they have the iron cauldron?"

Queen Alóvera's lips pinched thin. "It was reported missing last month."

"By the heavens," Di swore and leaned against the table for support.

"Di," I asked, "what is it?"

My sister swallowed. "While I was still stationed in the Eimad Abbey, I was assigned to care and watch over the forbidden scrolls. I could only decipher certain words, though one caught my attention as it involved a spell, a sacrifice on the new moon, and a potion brewed in the iron cauldron. It was—" she swallowed again "—for immortality."

We all stared. Immortality? Was it possible? Unlimited wishes, fabricated true love, and immortality were supposed to be the three impossible dreams. No wish, spell, or potion could grant them, though the deepest of black magics rumored possibilities.

"Can we stop it?" I asked.

Di shrugged. "I know not all the intricacies; verily, there are many. Among its various ingredients, I only deciphered firethorn root and a disturbing amount of blood."

I cringed. Firethorn root was the most dangerous herb grown in Fairy. One touch was enough to kill someone, and only phoenix tears could cure it.

Then there was the matter of blood. How many people did they kill for their potion? They threatened to add Pansy to their list. Over my dead body. What did they hope to accomplish with their longevity? They already made a mess of Margen.

Father's ears pinned back to his neck. "Then Abadda and Oswald have become abominations. They will lose their souls for immortality."

Lost in thought, my eyes drifted to the map of Novel on the wall. Pieces fell into place. "If only that was the worst of their plans."

My aunt tilted her head. "What dark horse is worse than seeking immortality?"

Father glowered at his sister, though I spoke over his retorts. "Abadda assured Oswald that he will rule this kingdom. Margen is a duchy, not a kingdom."

Queen Alóvera puffed her chest. "You think they mean to overthrow my family?"

"Look at you," Father scoffed, "proud as a peacock."

"I think," I said, "that their plans aim higher than the Fairy Kingdom. Oswald learned magic, though Abadda has collected abilities that work *outside* of Fantasy. If they become immortal, they could wage war across all of Novel."

No one spoke for several seconds as they considered my words.

"So it shall be written," Di muttered. "How do you propose we prevent their wickedness?"

Alóvera spread a map of Ruezdad's grounds across the table. "That is a horse of another color. My last recruitment report announced that seventy-six people have volunteered to storm Ruezdad."

Father huffed. "We employ fifty guards for the wall and turrets alone. Ruezdad has tactical advantage with the high ground and murder holes."

I analyzed the map for strategies. "An ambush will only distract the Guards of Fear. Oswald and Abadda can easily hide and accomplish their wicked plans before we reach them."

"What do you propose?" Alóvera asked, and Di leaned in.

We needed to end Oswald's hypnosis spell on the Guards of Fear as fast as possible to keep casualties low. A crowded ambush would take too long to reach Oswald and Abadda. An idea sprouted, and I gestured at the map.

"The army can attack, though remain outside the portcullis to avoid the barbican murder holes. They will bait the enemy by feigning offense while playing defense. If I can vault the east wall, I can sneak into the side of Ruezdad via the servant's entries to confront Oswald."

Father nodded. "If Oswald is controlling the Guards of Fear, perhaps we can kill two birds with one stone by apprehending him."

My aunt frowned. "You assume the outpost guards will not stop you. How do you plan to vault the wall?"

I rubbed the back of my neck. "Magic?"

Di piped up her hand. "Verily, let me aid you! My connection with soil shall take you over or under the wall according to your desires."

"No," I said. "You will stay here."

Her face dropped with dismay. I explained, "Dunstan said that Oswald wants you to come to Ruezdad. He thinks Oswald set a trap for you."

"Nay, Oswald is our brother!"

"Half-brother," I sneered. "A monster deep in black magics." My sister pouted at my terseness. I forced a quick calming breath, then pleaded, "Stay here. Our forces will need your magic and healing powers."

"Verily, what of your need for healing?"

Queen Alóvera stepped forward. "I will go. The reason I came to Eimad was to fulfill a prophecy that stated, 'Only the royal bridge between life and death can destroy the root of Ruezdad's evil.' I am The Phoenix Queen, after all."

"Alóvera—" her brother began. He cut off as she met his gaze.

"This is not debatable," she said. "Do you know another royal who fits the description of 'the bridge between life and death?'" Her voice softened as she continued, "Konrad, we cannot back the wrong horse and send someone else. You and Alun will lead our forces here. Theodor and I will confront Oswald and Abadda."

"Fantastic," I said, already regretting my own plan. "May the gods bless your safety."

Chapter 20

PROPHECIES

They ought to be studied thoroughly.
Never discount or underestimate a prophecy.
Do not expect to exactly understand them.

- *Thesis of Adventures*

THEO

An hour later, I was fitted with our most advanced armor and Videliz the Giant Slayer at my hip. Queen Alóvera and I snuck into an abandoned theater house near the walls of Ruezdad. As soon as people were recruited, they were instructed to gear themselves then casually approach the walls. The buildings along the wall were crowded with an army, waiting for our signal. The signal came as Di sent a great spark into the sky from her position outside the North-West wall of Ruezdad. Light burst in the air like a firework and shouts exploded below. Every building spewed with citizens as they charged the gate.

An alarm sounded from the castle. Men and magic quickly fortified the gate, and every element and weapon imaginable was hurled from the walls.

The battle for Ruezdad had begun.

Spells of every sort flew in both directions. Our army below sent spells for hives or other non-lethal distractions.

Citizens transformed into beasts or elemental creatures, then commanded other animals of their kind to attack in their own ways. The air became spotted with shields.

I recognized the lightning speed of an archer on Ruezdad's left turret. Lord Fischer wore the unknown face and clothes of a revolutionist, though his skill was undeniable. These were our friends, teachers, or family members. These were my people, and I had to protect them even as they attacked the army below. It was Oswald's fault that they saw each other as our greatest fears.

I tapped my foot, anxious to do my part. My aunt rested her hand on my shoulder, remarkably calm for the havoc before us. We waited for the guards to gather at the front.

The queen shimmered beside me, morphing with her ability. The clawed foot of a hawk-sized bird replaced her hand on my shoulder. My aunt had transformed into a beautiful red and gold phoenix.

"Make haste to our position," she said, her voice still human, yet more melodic. With a single nod, I obeyed my queen and ran eastward around the wall. Alóvera took to the air to scout from above. I ran, suddenly grateful for all the morning jogs I took with Pansy in Heartford. I dodged between buildings and skirted the castle fortress that I once called home. I knew Ruezdad's layout, its strengths and weaknesses. I knew the security flaw of the royal chapel. Its separation from all other buildings offered it a sense of holiness, though it also presented a narrow gap between buildings for sneaking.

I gauged our position based on the roof of the chapel. I ran to an alleyway just to the north of the chapel, between Ruezdad's two widely-spaced turrets. Normally, each turret was assigned two guards. With the front gate under attack, only one hateful revolutionist remained in each post.

"Their attention should be towards the gate," Alóvera said. "Shall I lift you by your armor?"

I turned to the bird. "Are you sure you can carry me, Your Majesty?"

The queen tsked. "I carried the iron cauldron to drop it on my stepmother's head. You are hardly a heavyweight such as my half-dwarf sons."

"Neither am I a lightweight," I said. "I am a fair bit taller than the princes."

"Is that a comment on their girth?" my queen asked.

I fumbled with my words until the bird chuckled.

"They would take that as a compliment. Skyward now."

Claws grabbed the top of my back plate. The fabric of my tunic underneath crunched as the spindly claws tightened and lifted.

I knew not whether to spread my arms out or squeeze in as wings pounded the air. I quickly said goodbye to the safety of the ground, the thatched rooftops, then even the wobbly treetops.

Curses of Merlin's beard—Oh, curses!

A paradoxically sweet voice spoke above me. "Are you afraid of flying? We will only go fifty feet to crest the cliffs and wall."

"I—" I gasped, failing to form the words about my first flight. "How high now?" How was my aura still light?

We hovered, weightless in the air for a blissful second. Then that second ended. Alóvera pumped her wings to shoot us back down. A small shout may have escaped my lips as we dropped fifteen feet to the cobblestone paths within Ruezdad. With another flap of her wings, the phoenix backed us into the narrow alleyway between the royal chapel and bake house.

My aunt released me, and I disguised my flustered breath by flustering with my abused tunic. I considered drawing

Videliz from its scabbard now that we were on enemy territory. Strange to think that about my childhood home. I decided to keep my hands free. Besides, if I met any hypnotized Guards of Fear, I did not want to kill them. I only wanted to keep them from attacking me while I went for Oswald and Abadda. My magic was sufficient for that purpose.

The queen tilted her little bird head sideways, and I held out my arm for her to perch there.

I asked, "Are you remaining a phoenix?"

"For this particular Adventure, I think I shall," she said. "Shall we divide and conquer?"

"'Never split up,'" I quoted Pansy, then added, "Your Highness."

"Very well. Lead the way, rightful Marquis."

I lingered in the shadows to spy on the visible turrets. Two were within sight, plus the back side of the barbican. Could I sneak to the gate and open it from the inside? That thought was quickly dashed by the probability of death before I even reached the gate. No, we were on our own to save Pansy and confront Oswald.

Hugging the walls, I dashed into the closest door and into the bake house. There was no one inside. The smells of spoiled loaves testified that no one had been there for a while. The room was occupied mostly by a massive island counter with storage cupboards underneath. Large jars and measuring spoons littered the top. I strode across the room towards the wine house. We paused at our first obstacle: a locked door.

I grunted at my wand arm. "How do you say 'unlock' in Latin?"

"Unlock?" the queen pondered. "I believe it is *reserare*."

"*Rezerare*," I translated.

The door opened with a solid click and we snuck inside. I pushed the door open as slowly as possible. I winced as it screeched like a witch. We hurried through the door into the winery. Large barrels lined the east wall, and the place smelled of rotten fruit. Flies buzzed about the open tubs, which also seemed abandoned in the middle of the job.

"Where is everyone?" I asked.

"Good question," the queen bird said, "and I fear the answer."

Across the room and up a few steps, we made our way into the kitchens of Ruezdad. At least, what was formerly known as the kitchens. The layout was familiar, and that was all. Someone had taken my home and turned it into a nightmare. I stood speechless in the cannibalistic butcher house, unable to breathe for fear of the rancid smell poisoning me. My mind was forever poisoned by the image.

The bird murmured beside me, "I was afraid of this. Come, let us find a portrait of Lord Doran to locate your marchioness and bring justice to these treacherous monsters."

I stared at the bloody carnage before me.

"Marquis?"

Arms in the sink. Feet on the counter.

"Lord Fromm?"

Marred and shriveled faces of women far too young.

"Theodor!"

I jumped. "Yes?"

"Locate Lord Doran."

"Of course, sorry, your Majesty."

Alóvera chirped and flew to the other door. I stepped through the room, careful not to touch anything. This door was locked from our side, and we quickly escaped. The lanterns remained unlit in the early twilight. Sounds of laughter and roars echoed from distant hallways. A shadow moved across the courtyard. I slid into the great hall two doors away.

As a room for common dining and gathering, it was the closest room with a portrait connected to Lord Doran. Dust frosted every surface, and the windows and mirrors needed washing. I stepped to Lord Doran's portrait and whispered for him.

A minute later, he came. "Your Highness! Lord Theodor! You—"

"Shh-shh!"

"Oh." He crouched and spoke with a strained whisper, "Are you sneaking through the castle? Never you worry, Lord Doran helped Lord Greggory sneak by the duchess and youngest lord many a time."

"Fantastic. Do you know where they are?"

"Yes, the duchess just had me call Lord Oswald to her drawing room."

"Her drawing room." I mentally mapped my home. "Is that still on the far side of the west wing?"

"Yes, though she did some frightful redecorating."

"Can you scry on them?"

Lord Doran frowned. "The wicked woman did not appreciate my comments on her new hobbies and has covered my portrait in the room. Nevertheless, Lord Doran can transfer sound."

"That will be enough. Go."

The painted man saluted me, then disappeared behind the frame. Within seconds, I heard animals scuffling and a distant bubbling. Someone knocked on a door.

"Come," Duchess Abadda's voice rasped.

The door squeaked, and light footfalls entered.

"Your Highness summoned me?" Oswald asked.

"Yesss," she hissed. "I was told that you wed and bed the wench without my permissssion!"

"I beg your pardon?" Oswald voiced my own question. "Miss Finster was the first to pass my test, but I planned to marry her only after our ascension."

Hold on—what? My blood boiled at my half-brother's audacity. He kidnapped Pansy and assumed to marry her? That cannibalistic monster did not deserve her magnificence! Curses, would he treat her like the women in the kitchen? If I was disgusted with Oswald before, now I was livid.

"Then why," the duchess spat, "did the mirror proclaim Pansy *Fromm* isss with *child*? The mirror named her Pansy Finssster only last sunsssset!"

Hold on! *What?*

Queen Alóvera tilted her head at me. "It seems you will have an heir. Congratulations."

I gaped at the blank portrait. Pansy was pregnant? Sure, we consummated our wedding last night, though how would my stepmother know that? Merlin's beard, I would be a father!

Meanwhile, Oswald argued, "What do you mean? You asked yesterday who was most suited to become the next Duchess of Margen, and it said Pansy Finster. What did you ask today to make it name my intended a Fromm?"

Abadda sniffed. "I sssaid, 'Mirror, give me an army of death. Tell me who can give thisss breath?' Quoth the mirror, 'In the womb of Pansssy Fromm, he is dead when he isss calm.'"

Curses, what did that mean? The thought of fathering a son elated me, yet I trembled to think how he would be "dead when he is calm."

The phoenix said nothing, though her narrow eyes suggested a foray of thoughts.

Oswald scoffed. "Your mirror speaks in riddles. How would I know why the mirror said that? It should have known better than to suggest such an old maid! She must be five years my senior!"

"She isss," Abadda hissed, "the right age for your elder brothersss. If the mirror claimed her to be a Fromm, she mussst have wed one of them between last sunset and thisss morning."

"Theo." Oswald gasped, then cursed, "Fairy feces! She wanted to call me Theo! That vexing, common-loving scut! How did the useless Theodor break through my hypnosis spell? I hate him! I will drink his blood tonight!"

"Patienccce," the duchess said. "If we have his wench, sssurely he will come for her. Prepare to meet him and harvessst your final ingredient. You shall drink more than hisss blood tonight."

Oswald's anger morphed into a wicked venom. "I know exactly what to do. If you need me, I shall be in my chambers with the wench."

My stomach churned to think of what he would do with Pansy there. Without another word from Lord Doran's portrait, I turned to leave.

"Where are you going?" Queen Alóvera demanded.

"To help Pansy."

"Remember our goal," she said, flying before my face, forcing me to stop and meet her eyes. "We must stop them from perfecting the immortality spell."

"Pansy is my goal. Always has been, always will be."

"Theodor, you were the intellect of the family. Do not let your emotions cloud your judgement."

"My judgement is focused," I said. "Oswald is likely casting the spell over the Guards of Fear. Aiding Pansy will also serve those fighting at the barbican."

The phoenix fluttered to perch on my arm. "I see. Then we subdue Oswald and hope that Abadda cannot perform the spell correctly."

I grimaced. "We divide and conquer. Only you can stop the root of Ruezdad's evil, and that immortality spell cannot be good." Pansy would argue to stay together, except there was no other way to stop them both.

"I have new doubts," my aunt said, "whether the prophecy referred to me. However, if not I, then it will likely be years before the prophecy is fulfilled and this evil vanquished."

I shared a solemn nod with my aunt. Her aura was a foreboding shade. "Long live Queen Alóvera."

"Long live Marquis Theodor," she returned.

I opened the door to exit the great hall and boosted the phoenix from my arm perch. She flew with a trail of gold through the courtyard and over the turrets of Ruezdad. I watched her disappear, then faced my own path down the courtyard.

Several headless suits of armor creaked into motion.

Chapter 21

TO BREAK A CURSE:

Accept normalcy
Let courage conquer
Dismiss fortunes
Love the unlovable

-    *Thesis of Adventures*

THEO

"Rodegad!"

A shield glistened around my darkened aura just as the nearest suit of armor leapt for me. I jumped away in time for it to crash to the floor. Metallic hands reached centimeters from my ankles. Every suit of armor creaked and clanged towards me.

So much for the element of surprise.

I ran down the middle of the long courtyard, right to the center of their circle. I vowed to never again grumble about a morning jog. I considered adding wrestling to my regular exercise as bodies of armor lunged for me. I ducked, jumped, and side-stepped to dodge their assaults. Most of all, I watched my wavering aura. These animated suits had no auras to show me which one was the most threatening. I had to rely on the lightness of my own aura to discern which step to take.

Two suits jumped at me from opposite sides. I dodged only to narrowly evade a bear hug from another.

Where were their heads? I counted my blessings that they were weaponless.

I crouched down from a sweeping arm and rolled from a side grapple. I was only halfway through the courtyard and already strained. The armor was relentless.

My own sword bounced against my leg. I considered drawing it, though for what purpose? Videliz would not intimidate or stop them.

Could I use magic against them? My vocabulary was limited to the four basic elements, "light," and "shield." How could I use those against metallic, soulless bodies?

I considered a fire spell, raking my memory of basic black-smithing for what extreme temperatures would melt the armor. As if that information was easy to remember during a test.

My leg caught on a protruding limb, and I fell to the ground. Two suits jumped onto my legs. Another couple pinned my arms and shoulders. I lost count as they piled on and began beating whatever surface they could reach. They punched me with gauntlets, kneed me with poleyns, and kicked me with spurs. I wiggled in vain to escape. Solid sheets smacked across my bones. Tips of metal bit through my own armor and into my skin.

I was stuck in place. I needed space. I needed air.

Punching my wand arm, I shouted, "*Aura!*"

A burst of air sent all dozen suits of armor exploding away from me. Some were thrown back to the grass as others crashed into corridor pillars. I had to be more careful with that spell. At the moment, I was just happy to be free.

Their daze wore off as I gained my feet. I prayed to the gods that their hesitation was enough for me to escape the corridor. I said a prayer of thanks as I neared the archway to exit the courtyard. The suits of armor ran at me again. I needed to stop them from following. I could not fight them all the way to the royal chambers on the second floor of the west wing.

Leaping through the archway to the intersection of Ruezdad, I twisted back towards the opening. Pieces of armor jumbled together as they crowded at the bottleneck. I pointed my wand arm at the center of their mass.

"Aura!"

My air spell slammed into the front row of suits and sent them back across the corridor. I did not wait to see if they stood again. I ran through the small intersection to the courtyard of the west wing.

I expected to find more headless armory lining the corridors to the royal drawing rooms. The second courtyard was empty, though crowded with sounds. Shouts and clatters echoed behind a door on the far end—the Duchess's drawing room. As much as I yearned to help the queen fight the armored suits and my wicked stepmother, my heart pounded to find Pansy.

I passed through the archway on my left to come face to face with a revolutionist.

Curses.

This foe had a head and a cheap sword. My heart clenched and my muscles froze.

Curses! I thought that I overcame my inability to fight! I had acted and moved against the enchanted armor, though this foe was different. This was no animated hunk of metal. This was a Fantastic being with a vendetta for blood—the blood of my family. The spell on it was specific to appear as my greatest fear. I was perhaps one of the few to see the Guards of Fear for who they were: everyday citizens.

Unfortunately, I remembered a second too late that the Guards of Fear also saw me as their greatest fears. The moment

I froze was consumed by the guard's surprise at my sudden appearance around the corner. He snapped out first. His eyes of intense fear shifted into burning hatred. The aura around him spiked outward. He raised his sword with a battle cry and charged at me.

Move move *move!*

My trembling fueled my motion. Shaking legs took me to the stairwell. The revolutionist's sword swiped behind me as I took the steps two at a time. I considered casting "aura" again. A small wind burst would send him tumbling down the stairs, and hopefully keep him down there.

His aura blackened with my plan. No. He had every intention to kill me, though he was also confused. Somewhere in the back of my mind, I knew this man was only a citizen protecting my home from the monsters of his own mind. My attacks needed to stun only…or trap.

My longer legs took me faster to the second floor. I slipped through the archway to the upstairs of the west wing courtyard and cast a shield over the opening.

The guard slammed into the shield, then growled in frustration as it held strong. I took the reprieve to pant for breath with my hands to my knees.

"Ho, there!"

My attention snapped across the corridor. Three more revolutionists shouted at me. One of them loaded a crossbow. Of course, why make it easy for me?

I cast a shield over myself, then spurred myself forward. Oswald's bedchamber was behind the Guards of Fear. Thoughts of Pansy energized my blood. My wife was behind that door. I vowed to stay by her side. If I failed her after one day of marriage, what hope could I have as Margen's duke?

My muscles cried in rebellion. They wanted to hold still and wait for the revolutionists to come to me. They wanted to curl into a ball and rest. I forced them to sprint.

The crossbowman held back as a swordsman met my charge. The third revolutionist stepped to the side of the bowman and began to weave her hands. A magician! The shorter aura of the swordsman said that he was just a distraction from the real dangers of the bowman and magician.

The swordsman was a very good distraction as he readied his longsword for a thrust. His aura lengthened.

"*Rodegad!*" I shouted at the swordsman. A blue translucent shield boxed around him. He jabbed his sword at the barrier. A splintering crack spiderwebbed around his sword's tip, though the shield held.

"No!" he screamed, and slammed his fist against the translucent wall.

I stepped behind the shield box to barricade myself from the crossbowman just as a click released an arrow. The arrow chipped off a corner of the shield box as it raced past. Curses, that would have killed me!

"*Igniz!*" the woman shouted. A ball of fire shot from her palm and detonated the wall behind me. I stepped back around the swordsman's box shield to avoid most of the fire blast. Bits of flaming rock smacked and heated my armor, and one piece flared across my cheek. Sweating from my run up the stairs and from her magical heat, I loosened my armor.

Alright, the magician was next.

I threw my arm around my barricade and shouted, "*Lugz!*" Bright white light burst from my wand. The Guards of Fear flinched away and shielded their eyes. I ran at my blinded foes. Three meters away, I cast "*Rodegad!*" twice more to encase the long-distance fighters in separate shield boxes.

Oswald's room was the smallest on the left. I reached for the door and hesitated. I had hoped for the element of surprise. If I still had it during the fight with the armored suits, I lost it while fighting the Guards of Fear.

Grunting, I barged into Oswald's bedchamber.

The worst of my thoughts feared finding Oswald turning Pansy into a corpse like those in the kitchen. None of my fears predicted to find five living young maids. They squealed at my rude entrance, then quickly rushed at me.

"What are you doing here?" I demanded. "Where is Pansy? And Oswald?"

"You know Oswald?" one girl asked. She looked to be the youngest, no more than twelve years old. My insides squirmed to imagine their worried families. At least they were alive and whole, unlike the women in the kitchen.

In a rush, they surrounded me, asking a hundred questions at once.

"Where's Ozzy?"

"Did Oswald send you?"

"When will Oz come back?"

"How do you know Wald?"

"Did you know you kind of look like Oswald?"

"Would you tell Ozzy I love him?"

"Will you bring Oz to me?"

They pressed into me, their fingers reaching, clinging, grasping.

"Whoa!" I tried to back up and ended up stepping on one of their toes.

The oldest woman of about twenty years squeezed through the others to put her face right up to mine.

"Please, where is Ozzy?"

What had my half-brother done to these poor women? Their desperation pulled my emotional strings. I wanted to rescue them. I wanted to free them from Oswald and take them away.

"Come," I said, "we should leave this place."

"No, Oswald doesn't want us to leave."

"He gets very mad if we leave."

"I'm Oz's most faithful, because I've never tried to leave."

I frowned. Apparently, stealing away these girls wasn't going to be that easy. I had to trick them into leaving. "How do you expect to find Oswald if you stay in here?"

"Yes, we need to find Oz!"

"Wald told us to wait for him here!"

"Oh, good sir" —the oldest one batted long lashes at me— "could you find Ozzy and bring him back?"

"Of course," I said, backing towards the door. "Anything."

"You'll come back for us, won't you?"

"Promise?"

"I—" Something about making promises sounded like a bad idea, though I could not remember why or who told me. I struggled with the doorknob as the girls continued to press against me.

"Won't you promise to come back with Oz?"

"Why won't you promise to return?"

The older woman drew her face up to mine as she worked to remove my armor. "If you don't plan to return with Ozzy, then you should stay with us."

"Yes, stay and wait for Oswald!"

"Stay with us!"

"I-I need to go," I said. Their nimble fingers picked at my armor. Why was I wearing them again? They were an embarrassment of wrinkles, dirt stains, and scorch marks from…some events? Their presence tugged at my mind as the women begged me to stay with them. They needed me. Or—no, they wanted Oswald. The more these women fawned over me, the more I hated him. He did not deserve their affections. He did not deserve these girls.

Jerking myself from their wanting eyes, I forced my way through them to the door.

"Wait!"

"Don't leave us!"

"Where are you going?"

I yanked the door open and shed my last piece of armor to gain release from their hands. Outside, two people climbed from translucent boxes. Memories of recent events trickled back into my brain.

Curses! What?

A crossbowman readied a bolt. A magician formed a ball of fire. Five women reached for me from behind.

Which fate was worse?

"Attack! Attack!"

Every face turned upwards as two little white doves flew towards us. Alto and Soprano?

Di's birds dived for the magician and crossbowman, who immediately shifted their focus. The women squealed and scattered back into the room while the Guards of Fear swatted at the doves. I saluted the birds in thanks.

Using their distraction, I continued my search for Pansy. She had to be here somewhere. I opened the next door, which was formerly Dunstan's room. His black room was covered in furniture sheets. Next was Greggory's room. As much as I wanted to pass through memory lane, I peered into the rooms only long enough to confirm their emptiness. Father's room was supposed to smell like hay. Its dark abyss smelled rancid instead. Abadda's room—finally!

Oswald had taken over the second largest room in the castle. He sat in the middle of the room, cross-legged, with his eyes closed, his hands empty and resting on his knees. He was eight years younger than I, and his dark hair had stripes of red. He was alone.

The room was stately, with bookshelves, a magnificent red bed, a grand fireplace, and a divider to hide the tub and toilet. It was also gruesome, with an assortment of torture chains, incision tools, and large knives. There was a significant amount of dried blood around the bed. I could smell the rancid potion of abomination brewing from the duchess's drawing room below.

"Hello." Oswald's red-brown eyes slid open and remained cold as he smiled. "I think I have something of yours."

"Where is Pansy?" I demanded.

"You found quite an interesting woman, Brother."

I glared at my half-sibling as he continued to chatter like an overconfident villain. "Tell me, did she bully her way into your life so she could become a Lady of Margen? It wouldn't surprise me one bit if the only reason you have this foolish idea for the duchy is because she urged you into it. Greggory might have made a decent marquis, but he was no future duke. I cannot even imagine you in command. I, on the other hand, will be respected and obeyed."

Feared and hated was more accurate. Even if I still doubted my skills to save the duchy from this monster, I had to believe that my willingness to fight for it made me worthy. "It is my obligation after Greggory's death. Did you truly think you could usurp the rights and authority of your older siblings?"

Oswald laughed. "Of course. Everything is going according to plan. Did you bring Queen Alóvera?"

"Why?" I asked, knowing better than to confirm his suspicions.

"Her blood is necessary for our ascension. As is yours."

Chapter 22

POISON

As a favorite weapon of the wicked, be wary of:
Fruit
Needles
Combs
Any gift from a stranger

- *Thesis of Adventures*

PANSY

I hid behind a divider, listening to Oz talk with the new masculine voice in the room. My vision blurred around the edges. Memories and dreams collided. What was real? Who was Oz? Was he my fiancé or my brother? It seemed like a terrible relationship to mix. Between memories and dreams, all I knew was that I cared about him enough to fight to the death for him.

He sat in the middle of the room, subtly waving his fingers at me and laughing at jokes I didn't understand.

"Oswald," the new man muttered, "what happened to you?"

A memory flashed and I saw myself kneeling beside my brother, Oz. He'd barricaded himself in our bedroom, using both beds and the dresser to block the door. The door was open anyway. Oz had a ring of salt around him, candles and flashlights, and an emptied revolver. Silver bullet shells littered the floor. For all the good they did him.

His body was ripped to shreds, his face half torn off.

"Oz!" I had cried aloud, though I hoped no was around to hear. "What happened to you?"

He was alone when he died. All alone because I was gone at school.

That left me all alone.

No! No, Oz was always there for me. It had to be a fake, a setup. He faked his death…and left me behind?

Nothing made sense. Oz couldn't be dead. He was my older brother, my strength, my teacher to survive, my *reason* to survive.

I blinked and the memory faded. Oz's spirit grinned from the middle of the room. I left my hiding spot to step toward him. Across the bedroom was the werewolf who killed my brother.

I growled and gripped the knife in my hand.

I would avenge Oz!

Pansy stepped into view. My heart leapt for joy before I registered her massive aura. Her blue-green glow was amazing and terrifying.

My wife stared at me with murder in her eyes. Oswald just laughed.

I sneered. "What did you do to her?"

"It is a similar spell as those on the guards," he said between bouts of laughter. "Is it not amazing? Even those with the strongest constitution cannot deny me. In fact, it works to my advantage, as the headstrong are usually more determined to fight."

Pansy brandished her knife and ran at me. She swept in for a slice at my stomach.

"*Aura!*" I pushed her back with a light gust of wind.

"You learned magic too?" Oswald gasped. His surprise lasted a full second before he returned to laughter. "Hah! I knew you were bluffing about having an ability! You claimed to see auras, did you not? But they were meaningless! I cannot blame you for wanting to learn magic. I gave up my ability to the duchess so I could learn sorcery. One spell enchants a woman, then I can take all the time I want to dissect them before her Highness absorbs their beauty."

Bile rose in my throat. I would have vocalized my disgust if not for Pansy's next charge. Instead, my mouth was distracted with another wind spell. Pansy was prepared this time and held her ground until I aimed a boxed shield spell at her. This was worse than fighting the Guards of Fear. I could not attack her even if she was determined to kill me. The thought of hurting her repulsed me. Though she moved too fast to put in a shield box. The most I could do was fortify my own shield and send a light wind spell to push her back.

Pansy swept back up to her feet. She whispered with a side glance to Oswald, "If you fall down, get back up. You taught me that, Oz."

Pansy threw her knife at me and it smacked into my shin. Something cracked. I buckled over in pain, then sucked back the pain to—

"*Rodegad!*"

I leveled out my shield projection in time to catch Oswald's fireball. The fire splattered across the room. Oswald's lavish decorations and wooden bedchamber was a recipe for disaster if he cast many more of those.

He laughed. "Is this not fantastic? I say it is an improvement over breathing fire!"

My half-brother was certifiably insane. Was there any way to stop this without ending his life?

The werewolf kept pushing me back with strange wind gusts like he didn't want to fight me himself.

Coward.

I rolled to retrieve my knife and regained my footing. Flecks of fire caught hold of various spots in the room. This fight would need to be quick. The feral man-dog roared at me. It was disgusting and unnatural. No good thing could come from such a monster.

It had to die.

I stayed in motion as the werewolf raised instant cages in places where I recently stood. I charged it with my knife, zig-zagging and unpredictable. I reached for his heart with my blade. He swept his arm down and barked. A gust of wind erupted from around him and slammed me across the room. My back was bruised in several places, but I could stand. Werewolves had no mercy. He killed my brother. He would kill me if I didn't kill him.

Oz fought with me, sending some Supernatural fire projectile at the werewolf. The Haunting swept it back with more air, spreading the fire spots across the room. I took the moment to search through my emergency pack for something silver. Where was my stake? My hand grazed a cold arrowhead. My crossbow.

Why didn't I have this out earlier?

I needed to load it. I rummaged through my pack for my silver-tipped arrows.

The werewolf whined and rubbed the back of its neck at the sight of my crossbow.

He was scared. Good. Some deep memory of a dream recognized the nervous tick, but I pushed the notion away.

Air blindsided me and sent me sprawling across the room. I rolled an extra time to pat out the fire that caught on my dress. My emergency pack flew from my hands and I was left with only my crossbow and two silver arrows. The room would collapse any minute now and I needed a weapon to pass the werewolf by the door.

The werewolf looked terrified now. I grinned.

I crouched in a solid position, ready to dodge from a counterattack. Oz threw a ball of fire at the werewolf, and he blocked with some water spurt.

That was odd. I assumed the wind was like some version of the wolf huffing and puffing to blow a house down, but werewolves didn't fight with water. My mind fuzzed around the edges as I loaded the crossbow with my two silver arrows. Didn't I already avenge Oz? I spared a quick glance back at my brother's spirit. He smiled with confidence.

I turned back and took aim with my crossbow. The werewolf made some translucent shield to cover his center.

Idiot. I didn't need to shoot his vitals to poison him with a silver arrow.

I fired into his thigh.

The werewolf fell with a cry and doubled over to grip his leg. I shot him again, this time in the bicep. I was out of arrows, but the silver in the two arrowheads was enough to cripple the monster. This was my chance to shove a stake through its heart. I grabbed my knife and rushed over to the monster. The blade wasn't made of silver, but a stab through the shield and heart would likely cripple the werewolf until I found something officially lethal.

The werewolf crumpled to the ground, weaker than I expected for a Haunting. He looked up at me, pleading. His eyes—were they blue or green? A tender thought crept into me, but I pushed it away.

"Pathetic," I spat. "Did you give Oz mercy?"

Oz's spirit laughed from behind.

That wasn't right. Oz didn't treat Hauntings like games. Even the smallest of threats was a life and death situation to him.

"Pansy," Oz's voice whispered through my memories. "I couldn't trust my own mind. That's what really killed me in the end."

I knew the eyes of the werewolf, and that trembling smile.

I held my knife over the werewolf's heart, where I needed to stab him…where Sean linked me to Theo. I slammed my hand to his chest—my empty hand.

My vision and mind burst with a familiar white light.

Three and a half years ago, I huddled by Oz's mangled body until the Brimstone police arrived. Our apartment reeked of something awful, but I couldn't leave my brother. I distracted myself by reading a book I'd found in his dismembered desk. It was his life's work, left to me in case something happened to him.

The police led me away as exorcists walked in with gallons of gasoline. The next thing I remembered was sipping soup at an orphanage. I'd turn eighteen next year, but until then, the law required that I had a home and education.

A boy about my age sat next to me. He had dirty blond hair, pale skin, and muscles that claimed a friendly relationship with the gym.

"Hey," he said, "I heard you avoided this place by living with your brother."

I made no motion that I'd heard him.

"Um," the boy continued awkwardly, "I'm sorry for your loss. I just wanted to say that I respect your bravery. You must know a lot about how to survive out there."

Survive…That word made me turn. I needed to survive. That meant I couldn't be alone.

"My name's Pansy," I said.

The boy smiled and reached to shake my hand. He had a nice smile.

"I'm Sean."

I gasped as my memories and consciousness returned.

"Pansy?" Theo asked, a trembling terror in his voice.

"Theo! Condemnation! What did I do?" My hands trembled, and my knife tumbled harmlessly to the floor.

"You gave me the scare of my life," Theo said through quick and heavy breathing.

Someone clapped from behind. I turned to glare at the young man I now recognized as Oswald.

"She is a tough one, Theodor. I thought it was impossible to overcome the hypnosis spell."

"Was it our link from Sean?" Theo wondered.

Probably. Now wasn't the time to theorize though. I snarled, "Let's shut down this circus. I'm done playing with this clown."

"No matter." Oswald grinned. "She spilled your blood. That was all I needed."

Oswald reached for something in his coat pocket. I didn't want to find out the hard way what his next plan was. I hated this man for playing with my mind. I tapped into my speed, grateful I hadn't known to use my ability while mindless. I snatched my knife and rushed over to pull out his hand.

He held something in a gloved fist. I struggled to remove it from his grasp. It was small and gnarled like a root. I threw the sticky herb across the room where Theo could grab it in case it was important.

I put my knife to his throat as Oswald's hand moved beneath mine. He moved faster than usual. Or was I moving slower? How? I untapped my speed.

"Well," Oswald smirked, "that was too easy."

"You're telling me," I said.

Then the pain struck. I gasped and looked at my hands. My palms blistered with boils and burned like charred paper.

"Pansy!" Theo shouted, waving his wand arm at Oswald and me. A force of wind threw us apart.

Oswald sneered at me as I crumpled. The burning spread to my fingertips and wrists. The pain seared into my nerves so I couldn't feel my fingers. My skin blistered before my eyes. They grew to great bubbles and burst with a scorching pain. Was that a distal bone underneath?

"What did you do to her?" Theo demanded.

Oswald laughed. "Firethorn."

Theo's already pale face went ashen.

"What is this?" I cried. My vision blurred with shameless tears. After everything I survived, from poltergeists to a hypnotic cannibal, I was going to die from a root!

"Of course," Oswald said, "she does not know the dangers of firethorn root since she does not belong here." He stepped away, confident and uninjured while Theo and I lay on the floor. My whole body writhed with pain, refusing to obey me. I watched, helpless, as Oswald stooped over Theo.

"Is this where your wench shot you?" Oswald gripped Theo's leg and squeezed.

My husband's pain became audible and tangible as his shout pierced me. I was the one who shot him. His pain was my fault.

Oswald spat at his brother. "Consider this your reward for tripping over a foreign commoner. Disgusting. I could end both of your miseries now, but I gain so much more pleasure to make you watch as she slowly disintegrates and you bleed to death. Time to make a drop on the duchess."

Weaving both hands, he gathered all the fire in the room into a massive ball. He squeezed the fire until it shrunk and disappeared with a little *pop*. Then he turned to the wood floor. He slid his palm across several panels and whispered a slow poem. With a snap of his fingers, the wood beneath us disappeared. Oswald fell gracefully while Theo and I collapsed to the floor below.

"Oswald!" the duchess yelled. "Ssstop vaporizing roomsss!"

Oswald shrugged and waved his hands again to make the wood and furniture float back into place above us. "The stairs take too long. I have Theodor's blood."

What little of my mind wasn't consumed with the scalding pain wanted to run to Theo and tend his wounds. Instead, my body twisted out of my control as Theo coughed and struggled to crawl to me. He slid across the filthy room on his good arm and leg while his other limbs dragged blood.

"We need Queen Alóvera," Theo whispered. "She can cure firethorn root with her ability."

A glimmer of hope lit my heart. Whatever fragment of hope I had then disappeared into the darkness of the wicked duchess standing behind Theo. She wore black and purple, and a sinister smile. My consciousness faded into the pain of my body boiling.

The last words I heard were from her rasping voice, "The queen is dead. I took her ability and have her blood as the final ingredient."

Chapter 23

BARGAINS

Never strike a bargain with a wicked heart.
If caught unawares, consider the histories of
Rumpelstiltskin, The Frog King, and The Yellow Dwarf.

-    *Thesis of Adventures*

THEO

My aunt, Queen Alóvera, was dead?

I turned around to face the speaker for confirmation, and flinched back. My wicked stepmother's aura was as dark as Dunstan's and as long as Pansy's when she had murder in her eyes. I almost misplaced her from the black fuzz around her body. She was even worse than I remembered. No longer did she feign love for my family. No longer did she hide her wickedness. She presented herself in her true hideousness. Her fair skin seemed bleached to my eyes. Her thick and fiery hair was twisted and ready to ensnare.

I shuffled away from her and pulled my wife to my lap. Pansy's fingers were mostly bone, her skin decayed up her wrists, and her veins bled black up her arms. I trembled with the thought of losing her, half hoping my shaking would wake her. I wondered if CPR would bring her back. Could I perform chest compressions with only one arm? Perhaps electric shock? Was there a Latin word for electricity? Maybe lightning? Could I combine the words for fire and light?

Every thought was foolish. I had no idea what I was doing. Pansy was the paramedic, not me. Surely, she would know what to do. Even still, this was magic poisoning, and no spell or prayer could stop it except Queen Alóvera's ability. Now, Queen Alóvera was dead, and so was Pansy's hope to survive.

"Thou fool," the wicked duchess said to Oswald. "The girl could have been ussseful to us."

"But you said I could kill them," my half-brother whined.

"I sssaid," she snarled, "you could kill *him*. Ssshe carries a vessel with godly powersss. He was the key to global dominanccce. I cannot asssk my mirror for another name since it was dessstroyed while fighting the former queen."

Their conversation befuddled me, yet their tone was clear enough.

"You regret Pansy's poisoning?" I asked. "Then save her! You have the Phoenix Queen's ability! You have the power!"

"I have her ability," the duchess hissed, "and the ability to sssee abilities. 'In the womb of Pansy Fromm. He is dead when he isss calm,'" she quoted her broken mirror. She snapped her attention to me. "The abilitiesss your little wench carries are… desssirable." She stared at Pansy with a hunger only known to the envious.

Pansy's tremors of pain lessened. She stopped breathing.

"Pansy! No!" My good arm tightened around my wife as a new anguish tightened around my heart. She could not be gone. Not Pansy—not my flower! I never loved someone so deeply. To lose her would be to lose a part of myself. She was my flower that never wilted with fear, never dried of ideas, never shrank in the darkness. Her already short and black aura dimmed, then disappeared.

"Save her!" I cried.

Abadda grinned. "You want me to sssave your precious peasant? I demand the possssession of your firstborn ssson. That is my priccce."

"My—" My mind stuttered at the thought. Right, Pansy and I would have a son…and my wicked stepmother wanted him. "Curses, no!"

Oswald laughed, somehow still calm in the chaos. "Are you a dunce, Theodor? You refuse to give up your unborn son to save your pathetic wife? They will *both* die for your pride!"

I ground my teeth, hating that he was right. Pansy would die. I would be loveless without her. I would have no sons or daughters at all. Yet I could not give up my child to this monster. What did she want with him?

Maybe I promised her my firstborn son, and what would it matter if I never had a son? What would it matter if we destroyed Abadda and her wickedness tonight? If I saved Pansy now, then there would be time to save the child later. There were several histories of Heroes swindling out of unfavorable curses or bargains.

I bent over and kissed Pansy, tears rolling from my cheeks to hers. Her skin was cold and stiff.

With one more tear, I pulled her chest closer to mine, yearning to feel her heartbeat. Regardless of the terrors, the curses, and taboos, I was tempted by the witch's bargain. Anything to have Pansy back. Still, the words scratched from my throat and tasted like bile.

"I accept. Now, save Pansy."

"Excccellent," she hissed. "As insssurance, I also want your ability."

Oswald looked back and forth between his mother and me. "He has no ability, your Highness. He learned magic, like I did."

"The useless Fromm has magic alssso?" The wicked duchess stared at me, confused. "How can he have magic when his ability is so ssstrong? I cannot sssee what his auras mean, though I can senssse that they are reliable and unfailing."

There was no time to debate. Pansy needed to be saved. I needed to use their confusion about my ability and magic to my advantage.

"My ability is useless," I lied, then gestured to my arm brace. "The Wand of Gandiduz is my real power, as it gives me magic, despite my ability."

"The Wand of Gandiduz?" Oswald gasped. "Oh, your Majesty, please let me have that! I already know sorcery, and wizardry should come easily!"

"Yesss, take the wand," Abadda said, "and we ssshall have a bargain."

My exhausted strength and wounded limbs made it difficult to struggle against Oswald as he yanked my wand brace off of my good arm. The abilities thief sneered as she poured the last teardrop from a vial onto Pansy's forehead. The tear glowed as it seeped into her skin.

A feral hunger grew behind Abadda's expression. Just as I prepared to swindle her out of taking my ability and unborn son, I knew she planned to swindle me out of everything I ever loved. She would beat me until she could extract my ability, then have no other use than to kill me. She would save Pansy now, only to lock her in a prison cell until our son was born. Who knew how she planned to use him, though I doubted her global domination would be out of the goodness of her heart.

Pansy's lungs swelled with air. I pulled her close to make sure.

She was breathing!

Her short aura returned as the blackness in her veins lightened and ebbed away. Pansy's eyes fluttered open.

"Hi." Her tired eyebrows tensed briefly with curiosity. "What happened? Did I fall asleep? I can't move."

"You were poisoned," I said. "I gave up my wand to save you."

Pansy drew in a slow gasp. "Your wand—"

"Worth it."

Honestly, I cared not how, I was just glad she was alive. Her boils receded and skin reknit. Muscles stretched around her bony fingers. I hugged my wife to my chest and kissed her again.

Meanwhile, Oswald laughed like a birthday kid, playing with my wand as if it was some new toy. The duchess took his vial of my blood over to the boiling cauldron. She poured it in, then retrieved a wicked knife. She dipped it into the potion, stirred it a couple times one way, then once again the opposite way. She lifted the knife, drenched with a thick liquid that morphed between putrid green, muddy brown, and blood red.

Sore and exhausted, I had no energy to stop them. Pansy breathed in my arms, though she was limp and heavy from her recent resurrection. The blisters appeared no worse than red bruises. All I could do was hold onto Pansy with my good arm and pray that the potion went awry.

"The blade isss prepared, my son," she said. "Tessst it on thy queen. We must ssspare thy life in cassse it is wrong. Perform thy duty, and prove me now thy loyalty and love."

Abadda handed Oswald the knife and he grasped it firmly. To my surprise, she spread her arms out, as if offering herself as a sacrifice.

"I…" My half-brother stepped forward, though hung back. His focus switched between the knife and his mother. "This spell is twisted. It requires someone who loves us to pierce our hearts? What if it fails? I do not want to hurt you."

A wicked smile curled her lips. "Do you love me, boy?"

"Yes."

"Then it will work. Trussst me."

Oswald clenched his jaw and tightened his grip. Then he stabbed his mother straight in the heart.

She jolted from the impact. A great howling roared through the room as wind surged into my wicked stepmother like a vortex. Her long aura blackened until she was as dark as the poltergeist. The duchess screamed a wretched sound and Oswald fell to the ground. He clung to a table as the wind continued to surge into the woman. Tendrils of black smoke emanated from the duchess as she exhaled and the air currents pushed back out. She slowly lowered her arms as the air returned to normal. Was that the effect of the spell or had she used Greggory's Wind Mastery?

"Fassscinating," she said. Her raspy voice had taken on the hushed tones of a Horror. "I feel ssstrong and weightlessss. I am neither living nor dead."

Pansy shivered in my arms. "That makes her undead. Theo—"

"I know." Though I had no idea what to do about it.

My half-brother beamed, seeming quite pleased with himself.

"Long live Queen Abadda," Oswald said, and bowed reverently.

She sneered. "Yes, I ssshall be Queen Abadda of all Fantasy! I ssshall rule from the Urban cities to Mountains of Myssstery! Then, we shall exxxpand our horizons to the heathenssss who look down on usss! We shall take our powers and claim these lands! The Mysssteries shall know true justice! The weak people of Romanccce and Childrens will ssserve us! Western, Thriller, and Horror will cower in fear! I will rule every land in Novel, and all ssshall bow to me as Empresssss!"

Oswald jumped with excitement. "Then you will name me King of all Fantasy!"

Abadda's sickly bones straightened to the posture of a proud queen, and her voice grew stronger to reverberate through the room and beyond. She took the knife and dipped it in the cauldron again. Then she loomed over Oswald.

"You have ssserved me well. Now, it is your turn to reap your reward."

Oswald's aura pitched black.

"Oswald!" I shouted.

Duchess Abadda lunged at him with a horrific screech and a powerful force. My wicked stepmother plunged the knife into her son's heart. The wind returned, darker than before. Oswald screamed his agony without shame.

"Mother!"

His skin ripped off and molded onto hers. Blood seeped from him and filled the immortal woman. His bones withered and dried as Abadda grew more flawless. Oswald's was the gruesome ending of every violent fairy tale I had ever known.

The ritual was meant to be performed by someone who loved them. Oswald loved his mother, so Abadda became immortal. The horrifying reality before us revealed my stepmother as a heartless monster who did not love even her own son.

Oswald had no chance.

I panicked. Just like that, Oswald died. My mind grappled for solutions, possible advantages, or even crazy ideas to beat the immortal creature. We could not beat this monstrosity before us. She revealed her goals to take over Fantasy and the whole world. Forget my desires to secure Eimad. This monster would set Fantasy into another dark age of war for as long as she lived.

And she was immortal.

Curses, how were we supposed to defeat her? Was it even possible? My body ached with arrows, burns, and bruises. The Wand of Gandiduz was somewhere across the room where Oswald had died. Pansy's aura was a shade lighter than obsidian. Mine was closer to onyx. I was done.

I clung onto Pansy, thinking of how to spend these last moments of life. I always thought that I wanted to die holding the love of my life. She quivered in my arms. It was not enough.

I wanted to die fighting. My physical body was spent, yet my mind and will were still strong. Trembling and aching, I lifted myself and Pansy to stand. We both leaned heavily against the wall.

I palmed Pansy's heart, reaching for her strength, her will to fight…our link. I had no idea what to do. I just knew that I had to do something. If anything, we had to escape to survive.

The last of Oswald wisped through the whirlwind to become absorbed by the wicked assumed-Queen Abadda. The wind lessened and stilled as she took a deep, strong breath. Then she turned her attention on us.

"Bow before thy queen," she rasped, "and relinquisssh thy abilities."

As she spoke, sparks of fire flickered off her tongue from Oswald's ability. She swept her hands around, causing wind to gather around her. Her hair and skin glowed with health, strength, and beauty.

She was a monstrosity. I would never bow to such a being.

"Your wickedness will not prevail," I said, lifting my hand from Pansy's heart to stand straight. Pansy leaned on me for support, though she stood beside me. "As long as there are beating hearts in Margen, the people will fight you."

I drew Videliz from its scabbard, then charged at my stepmother.

Perhaps it was the sheer stupidity of my actions that caught her off guard. She hesitated and blocked too slowly. I rammed the giant-slaying sword at her gut. The weapon sliced through her bodice…then slipped along her stomach.

I stumbled. All eyes gaped at the cut clothing and whole flesh beneath it. Videliz had cut through the thick neck and bones of a giant, yet it could not pierce Abadda's skin.

Abadda's vicious smile grew like a fungus across her face. She laughed, pushing me back to the wall beside Pansy with a force of Greggory's wind ability.

"Thou cannot kill me!" she laughed. "I am invincccible!"

Did I recognize that phrase from somewhere? A history? No, a little book written by Pansy's brother.

"Perfect," Pansy grunted. "Famous last words. Now we can beat you."

"Thou fool!" she hissed. "Only the royal bridge between life and death can kill me!"

I slowly stood and made eye contact with my wife. "Then your doom is sealed between Pansy and me. I was returned to life by Horror's Supernaturals, and you just restored the marchioness."

Fear flashed through Abadda's eyes for the briefest second. Then she snarled with hate. With a terrifying scream, the wicked duchess unleashed her power. Wind knocked us to the side. Fiery breath followed. I ducked and rolled behind one of the tables. Pansy blurred as she tapped into her speed and slid Videliz from my hand. Cages filled with abused animals rattled off the top and onto me. A couple rats and lizards came loose to add to the chaos. I climbed forward on my good arm and leg, my eyes combing the laboratory for something useful.

More cages slammed open across the room as Pansy released every animal.

"Avenge your brothers and sisters!" she cried to the animals. She blurred again to toss the insects at Abadda.

A stick slid across the filthy floor and rolled to my knees. The wand! Pansy must have thrown it to me. I snatched it as flames licked my back.

"*Ajua!*"

A spout of water burst from the wand. Abadda yelled in surprise. It was hardly an attack, though I was happy to have any sort of defense.

My eyes locked with Pansy's for a brief second. I wanted to say thanks for retrieving my wand. Instead, so much more transpired between us: a memory of a Supernatural bonding us, an expression of love, and a plan to survive. My part in the plan was unfavorable, though I trusted Pansy.

Our gazes broke though our connection strengthened. Pansy went to work at the tables to alter Videliz while I turned back to Abadda.

I cast spell after spell, wave after wave, slash after slash. I spoke words of magic without translation, yet I knew what they would do. I was a flurry of motion, speed, and grace. I tried to remember when I learned to move with such determined attacks. I had several years of teachers with swords and modes of combat, though I never attacked…like Pansy did.

These were her motions! This was her energy and knowledge of Latin! I moved with the finesse of my dancing combined with Pansy's self-defense training. My magical capabilities were enhanced by her practice of Latin.

The room was a whirlwind of fire and lashing water. The duchess blocked and dodged most of my attacks. What she failed to dodge was easily healed from Queen Alóvera's ability. No matter. I only needed to protect Pansy.

A light glinted off Pansy's project and into Abadda's eyes. Curses, I lost her attention! Abadda blew wind and fire at my wife. I caused lightning to reflect off the walls and strike at the wicked woman from different angles. Abadda screeched as she twitched unnaturally.

Pansy finished her material collecting and placements. I knew she needed a spell. Without a word, we switched focuses. I released my lightning on Abadda as Pansy ran at her with blurring speed. Latin words filled my mind and translated into magic. I cast a spell of specific heat over the craft, then we switched back. Pansy poured her holy water onto the material to cool it, and steam filled the room.

Even with our combined strength and will to survive, I quickly lost my energy. Abadda was relentless. Like the suits of armor, she had no soul to tire. I had to hope that Pansy's plan worked.

Abadda's irritation grew into a fury the longer we fought. She inhaled, and the air dragged me towards her. Then she exhaled to slam me against the wall. The Wand of Gandiduz flipped out of my hand.

My aura blackened.

Pansy blurred at my side. She carried Videliz, though I hardly recognized it. The sword was now wrapped with silver, laced with gold, and grafted with the wood of a white oak. I had no idea that those were the three elements best known to kill Hauntings. Pansy did. Likewise, Pansy knew little of blacksmithing basics. I did.

Together, Pansy and I grabbed the hand-and-a-half weapon.

Abadda had a brief moment to realize the threat. Her eyes widened with surprise and a hint of amusement, though no whites brightened her black pupils. No light reflected our determination to rid the world of her evil. With all the strength we could muster, we rammed the killing sword into her neck. This time, the sword punctured her skin. We stabbed her, then swiped outward. Another slice with Pansy's speed severed what little remained attached between the duchess's head and body.

She screamed something wretched. Curses, she continued to scream even after her beheading!

A blur ran by me, then solidified in front of the duchess as her screams muffled. Pansy knelt in front of the head with a needle and thread. Her hands blurred as she sewed Abadda's mouth closed.

With a final tug, she collapsed back to normal time, and gasped, "Enjoy the garlic. Keep your stitches dry for the next twenty-four hours, and resist the urge to scratch. You can set a return appointment to have them removed…never."

Chapter 24

HAPPILY EVER AFTER

This does not mean the characters never have another
Adventure.
This is just a phrase used by storytellers to say they are
done
and the listeners ought to be satisfied.

- Thesis of Adventures

PANSY

Theo laughed with delirium. "You stuffed her with garlic before sewing her shut?"

He shoved the nose-screaming head into a bag as I tied the hands and feet together with twine. The body was mostly immobile, but I wouldn't chance it coming after us when we collapsed together. Who knew a stone laboratory floor could be so comfortable?

I didn't have the energy to shrug. I struggled to even catch my breath. While Theo fought for ten minutes, I ran around crazy for a whole hour with my ability. I felt so weak and tired that I could have had mononucleosis. Having been recently brought back to life though, I didn't complain.

"Pansy?" Theo propped himself up with his right arm.

Right, he expected a response. "I didn't peel the garlic, so she'll get some flavor when the outer layers dissolve.

Eventually. She might be immortal, but the next foreseeable years are going to be a living horror."

My husband collapsed again with exhausted laughter. "You can be truly malicious at times. Gods forbid me from ever receiving your ire…again."

"Supernaturals, I shot you, didn't I?"

"Twice."

"Condemnation, I'd kill Oswald if he wasn't already dead."

Despite my desire to sleep, I grabbed various first aid items from around the lab, then sat beside Theo. I couldn't apologize enough as I carefully removed the arrow from his leg.

"By the way," he said with a wince from my cleaning, "can we discuss what just happened? I had your knowledge of Latin, and we worked together without speaking."

I nodded. "I know what makes a good dagger or knife, but I've never made one before—much less a sword. Suddenly, I knew about swords and what made them different. You're a novice blacksmith, and that was a rush job. But all we needed was a grafting that held together and was sharp enough to behead her."

We spared a glance at Videliz's strange new elements that decapitated the duchess. Theo's stepmom continued to scream from the bag and between her muffle. I finished off the stitches on Theo's leg and shuffled upward to begin on his arm. Theo's eyes met mine.

"Was it our bond from Sean?"

I shrugged. "Probably. I wonder if we can do it again on purpose."

"Perhaps. We should test—" He cut off to tense up and suck air through his teeth.

"I'm really so sorry about this," I apologized again, tightening his skin back together with stitches.

"At least you shot my non-wand arm."

I finished his stitches and ignored his concerns over my own health. I was mostly uninjured, thanks to Abadda's revival, but I was physically, mentally, and emotionally exhausted.

Our return to Ruezdad's gate was slow and painful, but we heard the cheers before exiting the castle. Ruezdad was reclaimed by its rightful owners. The Guards of Fear were released from their hypnosis spells, and Theo directed a healing crew to attend five women upstairs. The stolen abilities were still lost, but Eimad city was cleansed from its curses. The Margen Duchy was secured in the hands of The Trusted Marquis.

When the citizens caught sight of us, emotions stirred. They had several reasons to celebrate. Many within the army were wounded, but Prince Alun reported a historical low number of casualties. The possessed guards were released. Families were reunited. Their Heroes walked a long path between them, asking after their health and circumstances.

It was a happily ever after…except we lost Queen Alóvera.

My father-in-law met us to retrieve and carry his sister's body from the castle. His curse remained, but he transformed as a magnificent stallion to deliver Alóvera in a state coach back to Faenor for The Phoenix Queen's final resting place. The whole town mourned and celebrated through the night.

Between spontaneous festivities, Theo, Mr. E, and I snuck out to dispose of Duchess Abadda. My usual exorcism tools did little to subdue her. Apparently, even holy water and fire couldn't cleanse her. We carted her head and body bags outside of Eimad.

"If she can't be killed," I said, "we should bury her pieces separately outside the city."

Theo nodded. "There is an abandoned mine deep within the Thornwood Forest. It is already marked on our maps as dangerous."

"Good," I agreed. "We can secure her body in a concrete coffin, throw it in a cave, then seal it. In a separate coffin, her head can take a trip out to sea so she can't sweet talk anyone even if she rips open her stitches."

"Davy Jones' Locker is just the place for her." Theo smirked. "We can arrange guards to do routine checks to ensure that she stays buried."

"Why so many precautions?" Mr. E asked. "Do you think the Duchess might escape?"

"As long as she lives," I said, "there's a chance."

The Mystery detective muttered under his breath, "Knowing your luck?"

Supernaturals help us if that ever happened.

Three hours later, the sun poked its head over the valley. Theo and I joined the healers' tent with Di, Prince Alun, and Brooke. We shared battle stories and jokes when a messenger bird dropped off a letter for Theo. He read it and groaned.

"What is it?" Prince Alun asked.

Theo grimaced. "My capstone professor wonders how my Master's thesis is coming along. Relentless. May he forgive me for being otherwise preoccupied with fighting for my life."

Di laughed. "Verily, you tried your best to avoid your fate. You nearly had yourself digested by a giant, then murdered by your brother, half-brother, and stepmother. Alas, education beckons us higher."

"I may need to update my thesis regarding recent events." Theo frowned. "The royal family has been wounded. We lost our queen, duchess, eldest marquis, and youngest Lord of Margen. I trust High Prince Aneirin to be a fair king, and regardless of my father's curse, he will lead Margen with the stubbornness of a mule. All the same, I think my second act as Margen's Marquis will invite Dunstan back to Eimad as a priest."

"Second?" Di asked. "What will be your first?"

"To abolish all discrimination against non-humans and half-kinds," he said. I took his hand and gave him a supporting squeeze. "Prejudice can hurt people more than mere politics. Margen will need time to heal."

Prince Alun stroked his beard thoughtfully. "You want to make Dunstan a priest? Magic would be nearly impossible for him to learn with his ability."

Theo shrugged. "Divine magic can only be used through devotion to the gods. If Dunstan sees something to gain through repentance, he will be more likely to change. Also, the abbey has a code to allow sanctuary to all. By the codes, he is safe from our laws and we are safe from his vagabond attitude as long as he stays there."

Di laughed again. "Verily, it is a brilliant idea inasmuch as our now-youngest brother accepts the offer."

Theo smiled at me. "Maybe this can be a 'happily ever after' after all."

Within the week, I was given the grand tour of Theo's childhood home. Our home.

I asked Di to do Fantasy's version of an exorcism, but it was the influence of the duke and Theo that transformed Ruezdad into a palace of light. The graphic war tapestries were replaced by colorful rugs and shimmering drapery. Even at night, the castle glowed with life. The stained glass windows shone, fireplaces danced, and the corridors sparkled with fairy dust.

They let me remodel the duchess's study room to my own liking. I had it scrubbed spotless and lit with the whitest and brightest glow orbs. Then, I replaced the witch's occultist tomes with my medical textbooks. Theo helped me organize the herbs and fungi on the wall.

"I think this will be a nice setup for you," Theo said, labeling a vial of purple mushrooms.

"Me too," I said. "I won't be a paramedic like I planned, but maybe I can explore a connection between modern medicine and healing magic. I also want to draw up some security updates for Ruezdad."

Theo smiled and chuckled. "Of course you do."

That had to wait, though, since our official Fantasy ceremonial wedding absorbed all our time for the next month. Di took over as my maid of honor and planned everything. Brooke and Heather helped as my perfect bridesmaids. A royal Fantasy wedding was already a lot to handle, but all of Margen wanted to celebrate the restoration of Eimad and Divinity. The cities of Aven and Vluz were also happy to relieve their refugees. Theo took the advantage to emphasize friendship and comradery between mankind, half-kind, and cursed beings during the festivities.

Di's birds magically crafted the perfect wedding dress. She gave me a queen's high collar and sweetheart neckline. Laces on my back pulled in my waist tight before it A-lined to the floor. It was bright white with a shimmer of light blue at the right angles. The sheer sleeves draped from my shoulders, made of some slippery magic material that didn't catch on anything. I especially appreciated the dexterity option to remove the ten foot train.

At first, I was more than a little nervous about marrying on the site of the curses. But after the cleansing by Di and the maids' decorations, I hardly recognized Ruezdad. The great hall and joining courtyard were transformed into a crystal palace with clear stones framing the walls and archways. Ice sculptures center-pieced each banquet table, and everything was frosted with glass and diamonds. I had no idea where Di gathered so many white flower petals. They coated the floor of the small royal chapel and magically floated from the ceiling.

My favorite decoration was the man at the altar: Marquis Theodor Fromm, The Trusted, of Margen.

Supernaturals, my heart stopped at the sight of him. He looked like a prince. He wore a crisp blue-gray tunic with red trimming and gold embroidery. The cape on his shoulders was thick and designed enough to be a lavish rug. Medals and ribbons pinned to his chest, and some honorary rope sashed across to the sword of gold, silver, and white oak at his hip.

The wedding was more perfect than I could have imagined. The guests congratulated us with waves and quick remarks, wishing us well and saying we were the most Heroic couple they'd ever met.

Our guests preferred to mingle and dance, which was fine with me. The music was both elegant and exhilarating, while the dancing held no standard forms. With dignitaries from all across Novel, not even the waltz was common to every guest. The fairies definitely had their own style. Regardless of what music played, they twisted, turned, and spun around the other dancers, spreading their twinkling laughter.

Theo and I spent most of the celebrations at an elevated table. Every time our feet touched the dance floor, the crowds circled around to watch. The attention unnerved me until I became lost in Theo's arms. After a couple blissful minutes, the piece would end and I would remember how dangerous it was to lose track of my surroundings.

I never expected living in Fantasy to be easy, and I proved myself right. Still, as long as Theo was at my side, I felt safe and confident of our future. I considered marriage to be a security, but with Theo it was so much more than that. It was daily Adventures of learning, working together, loving, and trusting. Was this how Romantics always felt? Funny how it took me some time to live in Fantasy to finally understand. I trusted Theo with not only my life, but my heart and future.

Speaking of The Trusted, since I married into a royal Fantasy family, the people of Eimad gave me a title too: The Unsettled. Yeah, I wasn't sure how to respond. Duke Fromm said it matched the way I "blurred" when I used my speed ability, and also my paranoia of Hauntings.

Concerning Hauntings, I wrote out a new copy of *Oz's Haunting Survival Book*, and Theo helped me sort out the pros and cons of publishing it. He gave his support for whichever I decided, though Di and Duke Fromm pushed me toward publishing. I worried that others would abuse my brother's book, but there were many more reasons to share its wisdom. I planned for a large distribution in Horror so Oz's legacy could save more lives than my own.

One month after our wedding festival, I learned that I was pregnant! For some reason, Theo wasn't all that surprised. He hoped it would be a girl, but I loved imagining a mini version of Theo. While thoughts of little feet running around excited me, they also terrified me. Seriously, I wrote Heather a dozen desperate letters for help. I had no idea what we were getting into. If I thought ruling a duchy was intimidating, I sweat buckets for this next stage! Being heirs to a duchy wasn't as hard as I thought; we had the duke and dozens of lords to help. Kids though? I was glad to have seven more months to prepare. Seven months…like the reprieve before another Adventure.

This was only the beginning of my Happily Ever After as Marchioness Pansy Fromm, the Unsettled, of Margen.

THE STORY CONTINUES...

Finish Pansy and Theo's haunted romance in this intense rescue within the Inferno of Dante's *Divine Comedy*. Fans of Seth Graham-Smith and Neil Gaiman will find "Don't Dance with Death" hard to put down.

Don't Dance with Death
A Dark Romantic Comedy
C. Rae D'Arc

ACKNOWLEDGEMENTS

This. Book. I started to write "Haunted Fantasy" Oct. 18, 2016. One year and ten days later, I had three-hundred-fifty pages of D&D/Tolkien fantasy. Oops. Over the following years, it slowly became what it is now.

If Frankenstein wrote a book while doing the hokey pokey, it would have been like this. I wrote the "first draft" of this book four times. Between the second and third revisions, I drafted book 3 of this series and finally figured out why this one didn't feel right. A big thank you to "The Story Grid," by Shawn Coyne, for helping me to sort out my genres, then to the Grimm brothers for inspiring my tone and satire. I didn't plan to use my university capstone class on fairy tales this way.

Thanks again to my editors from Salt and Sage Editing for helping me to buff this book to the same quality as the first one. Yeah, I'm talking about Mrs. Awesome and Jeigh Meredith!

This book needs a big acknowledgement to Robyn Cheatham for Alpha reading my frankensteined 4th revision and for pointing out the holes I missed; poor Theo has more problems because of you. Thanks for your encouraging words and writing sprints! NaNoWriMo and CampNaNoWriMo for the win!

Big thanks to the comments and support from my beta readers, Abby Smith, Lisa Gartner, and Colleen Dowda.

A huge thank you goes to Michael, who deserves this book's dedication. You put up with my "storm braining" and read the word vomit of revision 2.5. This book had no hope without you (particularly in the resolutions against Dunstan and Abadda).

As always, my greatest "thank you" goes to God, my Heavenly Father. He is my inspiration and muse, the one who gives me ideas, and the one who makes it possible for me to write them.

ABOUT THE AUTHOR

C. Rae D'Arc has been involved in every stage of a book's life. As a writer, editor, retailer, reader, and reviewer she has worked four part-time jobs at once. Thankfully, one of them actually paid her. She received her bachelors in English from Brigham Young University, and now lives in the Tri-Cities of Washington with her husband and Aussie dog.

PS. D'Arc is pronounced with one syllable.

You can check out more from C. Rae D'Arc at
her blog: www.craedarc.com
Facebook: www.facebook.com/c.rae.darc
and Instagram: www.instagram.com/craedarc